BISON LEAP

When Man and Nature Co-operate
Our Near Future on the Central Plains and Western Mountain Foothills of North America.

Hevan Herth

Bison Leap

tellwell

Tellwell Talent
www.tellwell.ca

ISBN
978-1-77302-874-3 (Paperback)
978-1-77302-875-0 (eBook)

A caution. Be forewarned: some views expressed by characters or scenes in this novel may appear offensive to certain readers. If so, you may be assured that may not be the author's intention.

Know this is a work of fiction, somewhat disguised as fact, or if your imagination is actively vivid, fact disguised as fiction. Either way, the intention is to activate, stimulate, and instigate positive interaction.

A warm Thank You to:

David Antrobus – editor
Stefanie St. Denis – illustrator
Tellwell – publisher
The many who've helped along the way.
And to all those who have, do, and will
make Earth an enjoyable place.

Table of Contents

Bison Leap

Preface

A conscious wish,
a dream,
starts
with a subtle awakening
of perception.

Then, with consistent effort,
perception transforms the Great Plains
and western mountain foothills
from its present
into a time when humans begin to comprehend
the possibilities.
Human's, as organism's,
begins to appreciate, to interact, to co-operate.

Bison Leap, the novel, is a condensed recording of this transformation.
One of many possible futures, for earth and humanity.

1. Born of Earth

Our parents have more than most people; they have everything they need, everything they want. They have the best of each other, plus my sister Sarah and I, and a small farm in the creek bottom with a half section of natural bunchgrass grazing land up on the dry, open flats. With a little help from Dad, Mom grows most of our own food in a big garden, and Dad has a small hayfield he puts up to overwinter our few range cattle. In the fall Dad hunts a bit, and once or twice a year we catch a supper of energized tasty-sweet trout at Big Crooked Creek, ten miles yonder. Dad teaches me how to sneak up on them.

I remember the first time Dad took me to the creek when I was almost five. He gets out of the old farm truck, comes around to my side, puts his finger upright across his lips, and shushes me. Helps me down and carefully, quietly, pushes closed the door. He lifts a long bamboo pole from the back of the truck. It has just enough line tied on the small end to reach the handle. On the dangling end of the almost invisible line, a tiny wee hook is tied, no sinker and no bobber.

He points all this out to me as he squats down and then whispers in my ear, reminding me of the things he told me on our truck ride over. "Son, we can't make any noise, we can't even talk or ask questions. We got to move real slow and put our feet down gentle or they'll hear us. If we touch the ground hard they'll feel the vibration through the earth and it'll scare them. We can't move our arms fast or shake the willow bushes. They're smart, wild trout, and if they feel or see anything different they'll go hide, and we'll catch nothing all day but mosquito bites."

Then he reaches in the back of the truck and lifts out the small plastic bottle with a whittled stick plugging its small top hole.

We spent a while early this morning in the lean-to woodshed, poking tiny air holes all over the bottle with a sharp nail. With our hands we captured a baker's dozen of middle-sized grasshoppers, no wings yet, before the sun came up to warm them. Dad said, "Twelve... plus one more for luck."

Even I know once the sun warms them you can't get close. Just as you put your hand out, they jump and you have to try again. In the cool of the morning they're sluggish and just sit, waiting, like they have no control over their lives.

Dad asks me, "Get a cool, wet cloth from Mom to wrap the bottle in so the hoppers won't overheat."

When I get the wetted cloth, Mom gives me a paper bag with two roast beef sandwiches on fresh homemade buttered bread. She says, "The big one's for Dad and the little one's for you."

Dad's sandwich has a smear of horseradish on it, and I don't want a bite of that, but I peek in the bag and see two fat dill pickles wrapped in stretchy plastic. Mom smiles, because she knows they're my favorites.

She holds up her long fingers on one hand with her thumb folded, tells me, "Catch four fish: a really big one for Dad, a nice one for Mom, and two more a bit smaller. One for you and one for your sleepy sister, Sarah." Then she wiggles her thumb. "And one for luck."

She kneels down and gives me a soft squeeze, then scoots me out the door.

I mind what Dad whispers in the pullout beside the creek bridge, because his voice is deep, kind, and I admire him lots. Dad puts the wet cloth in a plastic bag and tucks it into my backpack. He winks, saying, "We'll need that later."

He puts the bottle of hoppers in his pants pocket and hoists me up onto his wide shoulders. He holds the sharp little hook between his thumb and one finger on his left hand, then with his right hand he spins the pole slow, so the line wraps around it. He carefully pokes the point of the little hook into a leather-wrap on the handle. I watch him closely because I want to be a good fisherman someday too.

We set off, up the old cow trail, following along outside the thick willows growing on the creek bank. I keep my hands on Dad's forehead just below his hat brim, being extra careful not to let them slip down over his eyes. I have our sandwiches and pickles in the small backpack Mom sewed for me.

Sometimes I get funny and hold onto Dad's ears when I'm riding, pretending I'm steering a horse, but today I don't do none of that. We walk a long ways up the trail away from the road.

He sets me down once and, tickling my ear with his breath, he whispers, "We want to go far enough away from the noisy road because that's where the best fish live."

With his folding pocket knife, he cuts a forked green willow branch that overhangs our trail, rubs his hand down it till all its leaves come off, and we carry it along with us.

When he sets me down again, we're under the shade of a big cottonwood tree. He takes my little pack and hangs it high as he can reach, and that's a long ways up, on a small branch. We sit still as the leaves for a few minutes, side by side with our backs against the tree. He puts his finger across his lips again to remind me to keep quiet, then eases the stopper out of the hopper bottle and hands the little stick to me. When a hopper crawls up and pokes his head out, Dad gently holds him between his fingers. He tilts the bottle toward me, and I slip the stick back in to replug the hole. He hooks the hopper near its shoulder, just behind its head, and lets it dangle there with its kicking legs and wiggling body.

Again, he lifts me to his shoulders, squeezes my hands a little to let me know to hang on, lifts the pole and, ever so slowly, we step toward the creek. He parts the thick willow bushes with one hand and takes a few more slow easy steps to the grassy creek bank.

This whole time I never hear a sound except for a song-bird, sweetly singing, telling today of its love, the breeze gently tickling the leaves, and the murmur of moving water. We stand, quiet as a tree for a few more minutes; he slowly checks my hands to make sure I'm hanging on good, then eases the pole out and lowers the hooked hopper down. As soon as the hopper touches the water's surface it gives big kicks and wiggles. I almost start to laugh, but Dad squeezes my leg with his free hand to remind me again. He reaches way out, lowering the tip of the pole down closer to the water. The hopper floats, kicking ripples downstream. An old bark-less log lays with one end on the willow bank, its other end angled down into the cool, shaded water. This kicking hopper almost makes it to the big log when the water whirlpools into a terrific splash.

I come close to falling off Dad's shoulders, but he's hanging on to my leg. After all the quiet, the whirlpool and the big, fast splash scared me jumping. Dad has him hooked, and I can see he's a big one. He's bending the bamboo pole trying to get back under his shading log. Dad eases him out, holding the pole angled upstream. This pretty trout darts back and forth, fighting under the water, trying to get away. Dad steps into the stream and lets him fight, darting this way and that way, jumping once, clear out of the water, then Dad eases him over toward the grassy bank. With a flick of the pole, the trout lands up on the bank and we follow quick.

The pole lays stretched in the grass, I'm standing on my own two feet, and Dad is reaching with both hands to capture this flopping fish before he gets back to the water. With a big wide grin on his face, Dad holds him up for me to see. His eyes are smiling at me and at this vibrant-colored fish.

He's a beauty, a big one, all speckled and spotted, sleek and strong. I'm smiling so much my face hurts; I tickle, like I have butterflies fluttering inside under my belly skin.

The fish is doing a real dancey wiggle trying to get away, but Dad has his fingers pinched in a little, behind the fish's head where his gills are. He whispers, "Go get the forked willow stick." I get it quick without a sound. Dad puts one end up through the space in the fish's gills and out his mouth. Then he eases the little hook out of the fish's lip and hands the willow stick to me. This is one lively fish, longer than my forearm and heavy. His swooshing tail touches the ground and his head is up to my knee.

Dad pulls a long, strong string out of his pocket, ties one end on the fish's forked willow and the other onto a live willow bush rooted on the creek bank, and he lowers this still-lively fish back into the cool water.

We leave the pole and the hopper bottle by the shady creek and eat our sandwiches under the big cottonwood. Them pickles are tongue-tangy good. Dad makes me eat all my sandwich first; then after I crunch up my pickle he gives me half of his. I sure like my dad for catching this fish, for giving me half his pickle, and I like my mom too. She put the pickles in our lunch special for me.

After we rest a bit, Dad shushes me again and we walk over and look at the nice fish still swimming with the willow through his mouth. He can't go anywhere, just moves side to side. Dad picks up the pole and the hoppers, lifts me up, and we walk slow again a little ways upstream on the dirt cow trail. Riding up high on Dad's shoulders I can see good, and I think I spy it first: another big fallen-down tree, half in the water.

Dad sets me down, puts a hopper on the hook, holds my little hand in his big warm hand, and we part the willows to the creek. He does the same thing as he did last time, except now I stand close against his leg. Scares me jumping when another fish makes a rush and grabs the hooked hopper. In hardly no time at all, Dad has him up on the bank, through the willows, and holds him between two fingers. Dad takes the hook out, motions me to follow. He carries this fish, fast, back to where the other one is tied and puts them together on the willow. He lowers them back into the water, and I can see this one is a bit longer than the first one.

Dad spies my big eyes and my even bigger smile, sits down with me in his lap and whispers in my ear, "You can talk now, but real quiet."

I don't want to talk; I just want to look at these nice fish, with my dad's strong arms holding me.

We sit for a bit, looking, listening, and feeling each other breathe.

He asks me to go get the cloth out of my backpack. He soaks it in the creek, unties the string from the willow bush, lifts up both fish, and wraps them in the wet cloth. He carries these fish, walking slowly, and I follow close behind, back to where we left the pole and the hoppers. He unwraps our fish, eases them back into the water, and ties the string good. He lifts me back up on his shoulders, picks up the pole, hoppers, and wet cloth, and we walk quiet farther up the trail.

Soon, we come to a big, almost open water. The creek has sticks piled all the way across; the water is wider and higher on the top side of these sticks. We step halfway across the packed sticks on a narrow, flat, smoothed-out trail. He squats down on one knee, stands me down on the sticks in front of him, hooks a hopper, and helps me hold the long pole. With his big hands over top of mine we flick the pole, and the hopper lands way out on the still water. Not still for long: a ripple and a tug, and we have another one. Dad leaves me holding the pole with the handle under my armpit and both hands squeezed tight on the pole.

I look at Dad and I look at the pole and the fish is tugging, so I hang on tight while he goes and cuts another forked willow stick. My arms are tired when he gets back, but I still have the fish. He helps me lift it out of the water, then he puts the willow through its mouth and, after sticking one end of the bendy willow deep in the dirt, he lowers my little fish back into the water. He helps me catch three more from this very same spot, each time giving me his big smile and shiny eyes.

When we have the fourth one on the willow, he says, "We can talk now."

I'm so happy for our fish, for Dad's smiles and shiny eyes, for my sore arms, and for Mom and my sister because I know they'll be proud of us and we'll have a special supper. I can't tell him all of that, but I think and feel it inside of me. Just now we hear a loud splash really close, and after I regain my balance from the noisy fright I see a shiny, wet, brown animal swimming away.

"Dad, what's that?"

"Mister beaver. See all these sticks and hard, dry mud you're standing on. Him and his family built all this to make the water deep so they can swim without the coyotes getting them." Then he points way across the pond. "See that high round pile of sticks. That's their house and some day we'll go see it, but today we should get these beautiful fish home to Mom before it gets too hot. Dad's got some other work needs doing this afternoon."

As he shakes all the extra hoppers out of the bottle and we watch them float, drifting over the water, he says, "These are for the fish. It's our thank-you to them for the ones we'll eat tonight."

After cutting the hook and line off the pole and putting it into the empty bottle, he stuffs it into his pocket and hangs the bamboo pole high in a dead tree. He winks. "We'll come back again soon, maybe bring your mom and sister and a picnic lunch. The beavers won't bother this pole up in an old dead tree; they only like sweet, green trees with fresh, juicy bark."

We get my four small fish and, after wrapping them in the wet cloth, he lifts me and we walk fast back to the two bigger fish. Dad is a big, strong man with long legs, and I feel like a bird sometimes, way up on his shoulders.

We soak the cloth again, wrap all the fish together, and he tells me, "This will keep 'em fresh and cool till we get home."

He helps me put my backpack on and we head for the truck. He ducks every time we come to a low-hanging branch. I feel safe, warm, and happy riding on Dad's shoulders. He dunks the fish and cloth one more time before we get in the truck. I curl up on the seat with my head resting on Dad's leg. He nudges me awake when we drive in the yard.

"Jim, we're home. How about I lift you up in the back and you get the fish?"

Sleepy, I say, "My fish are so little."

"Those are the sweetest ones, Jim. I'm proud of you, and your mom will be proud of you too."

She sure is.

Dad tells us, "I got some fence to fix on the back line. I'll be back before supper." He takes the old green Jeep, a shovel, and some hand tools and heads out the back gate.

Mom, Sarah, and I carry the fish down to our little creek. It's too small to have its own fish, but it's nice cold springwater. Sarah carries a scraping spoon and a flat pan, I carry a sharp knife wrapped in leather, and Mom carries our spotted fish. With her free hand she keeps rubbing my hair, teasing and smiling at me.

Even Sarah says, "You're a good fisherman, Jim," and "We're gonna have yummy-yummy tonight."

Mom cleans all six fish on a flat board by the creek, rinses them off in the cold water, and places them side by side in the pan Sarah brought. Mom puts all the heads and innards in a plastic bag.

"I'll bury these later beside the rosebush to make the flowers grow. Thank you, Jim. Because of you we're gonna have a special supper tonight."

I'm proud of myself now, and we do have a special supper. Tender oven-baked trout with a real lemon squeezed on top; fresh-picked, buttered corn on the cob from our garden; a big slice each of juicy red tomato; and some little smooth-skinned potatoes that Mom carefully dug.

She says, "They ain't finished growing yet, but tonight is special so two little potatoes each, plus one extra for Dad, to go with them beautiful trout."

I'm so happy I'm almost crying, but I'm glad I don't 'cause just then Dad walks in. He carries his hat in his hand, and it's half full of sweet ripe blackberries, and in his other hand is tender, tangy young watercress he picked in the spring on his way home. I want to be strong in front of my dad, so I'm glad I never cried.

After supper, we're all cozy, resting our full bellies, and sitting close together on the couch—Sarah and I tucked in between Dad and Mom.

Dad says, "You kids want to know a secret story about your mom?"

Both me and Sarah sit up straight because we know Dad tells good stories. I look at him and he has dreamy eyes, and I look at Mom and she is smiling a little bit shy.

Dad gives both Sarah and me a squeeze with his long arm, and then he squeezes Mom's shoulder a little with his big strong hand. He says, "When your mom and I first met, we carried a tiny picnic basket to that same old grandma cottonwood where you and I ate our lunch today, Jim. We have one small sandwich each, and we share a big juicy-sweet Florida orange and a bottle of cold spring-water. The mosquitoes are biting hungry; even though it's sunny and warm they know it will be rainy and cold next day, so they need our nutritious blood.

"I really want some quiet, peaceful time with your mom. I'm not going to tell you what else I want, but I will tell you I don't want to leave yet, so after we eat our sweet, juicy orange I get some dry sticks and make a little fire. After it's going good I add the orange peels and a few green leaves for smoke, to keep the mosquitoes away."

He winks at mom. Then he says, "Maybe I just wanted to show your mom this big city boy knows how to make a fire in the woods. I want your mom to like me. The smoky leaves and the citrus smell from the orange peel keeps the mosquitoes from biting us. Your mom and I sit by the fire talking, teasing, and getting to know each other a little. Soon your mom says—"

Dad is an entertaining storyteller, and his voice rises up a little, almost sounding like Mom's voice.

"'I'm just going to wash my sticky hands in the creek. Sit here quiet and don't you go anywhere. I'll be back in a few minutes.'

"So I do exactly what your mom told me. I sit quiet by the little fire and think about how beautiful and graceful your mom is. I'm thinking I want to be a friend of hers. I'm thinking some other things too, but they're all good. I even think a little about you, Jim and Sarah, too, but I don't know you yet.

"I'm thinking all these things, sitting there dreaming with my eyes closed when I feels a shadow on me. I open my eyes and there's your mom, standing prettier than a picture with a trout dangling from her outstretched hand. I says to your mom, 'Where'd you get that fish?' She just smiles this beautiful smile of hers and asks if she can borrow my pocketknife. She goes back near the creek with the wiggling trout and my pocketknife. She cleans the fish, rinses both it and my knife off in the cool water, cuts a green willow stick, pokes the sharpened stick through this nice fresh fish, comes back near the fire, hands me back my clean folded knife, and starts cooking the fish over the fire, all this time smiling at me and

I'm smiling back at her. We eat this beautiful tasty fish with our fingers because we don't have any forks or plates with us. This fish, I think, was just about the tenderest, juiciest, sweetest fish I ever ate. I'd say it was almost as good as the ones Jim caught today."

I squirm a little bit, but Dad keeps talking so I listen close. He says, "This fish was so good and juicy, but I'm still a little hungry and I want some more. Then I notice your mom's long fingers still have some oily fish juice on them, so I grabs her hands with mine and starts licking the tasty juice off them. She's laughing and telling me to quit it, but I won't quit till she tells me where she got that fish from. So after I have the juice licked off all eight of her fingers and both of her thumbs she finally gives in and says, 'Okay, I'll show you. But you gotta be quiet and stand real still, and you can't be smiling at me neither.'

"She takes one of my hands in hers and shushes me, just like I shushed you today, Jim. Then she leads me up the creek trail a bit and makes me stand quiet on the grassy bank. She takes off her shoes and socks, rolls up her pants legs, and I'm thinking maybe I'd like to tickle them toes of hers, but I promised not to smile, so I just stand still as a tree and watch her ease into the water. She stands quiet as a great blue heron in the water, not moving a bit, and now I'm not thinking about tickling her toes anymore, but I am thinking how beautiful she is and how much I want to be by her side with my arms wrapped around her, giving her a warm, close hug...

"But I don't move or even smile, because I've already promised her I wouldn't. Soon, she starts moving slow with her feet sliding across the smooth rocks on the creek bottom, and then she bends forward with one long, graceful arm hanging down into the water with the palm of her hand up and the back of that same beautiful hand resting on the smooth rocks at the bottom of the creek. I can see her hand and her feet 'cause the water is clear and not much above her knees. She moves slow over toward the same big log where we caught that second fish today, Jim. Real slow, she reaches her submerged hand under that old log. I can see the dark shadow of a trout resting there and I guess somehow she knew it was there all along. She moves her hand slow under the fish, tickles his soft belly with them long, graceful fingers of hers, those same ones I just cleaned with my lips and tongue, keeps moving her hand along his belly till she gets up near his head, and easy like, she squeezes two fingers, one on each side of him, into the hollow space of his gills.

"She lifts him up high out of the water for me to see, and she smiles like the sun and moon and stars all inside my head and heart. We clean and cook and eat this fish, together by our little fire, and we've been the best of friends ever since."

He smiles at Mom, and then he smiles at Sarah and at me.

"Your mom tells me, 'When you bring your hand under a fish and tickle his soft belly with your fingers, he thinks it's just the plants growing on the bottom of the water and he's not scared a bit, but if you try and come down from on top of him he'll be gone in less than a half blink of a chipmunk's eye.'

"Maybe one day she'll show you how to catch a fish with just your hands."

When I go to bed this night, my belly is so full it almost hurts from all the good food, my heart almost hurts from all the love I have from Mom, Dad, and Sarah, and I'm so happy for them fish and the garden and the water. I sleep with stardust-sprinkled happy dreams all night.

When Sarah and I go to school our first day, the teacher asks us to think of a good story that happened to us over the summer. She says, "Think of a really good one, and we'll share it with the whole class tomorrow."

That night I think of catching fish with Dad and my mom catching fish with no pole or hook, just her hands, so next day I tells the story. Everybody likes my story, except one boy wrinkles up his nose and snorts, like he don't believe me. At lunch hour when we're playing outside, this same boy comes up to me and loud says, "You're a terrible liar and your mom ain't nothin' but a dirty old nigger-squaw."

Sarah is there beside me and she starts crying and, without thinking at all, I punches him hard, right on the end of his ugly, wrinkled-up nose. He's bigger than me but I'm too mad to be scared, and when I punch his nose he almost falls over. His eyes are watering and bright red blood starts pouring out of his nose all down the front of his pretty new school shirt. He puts both his hands over his face and goes bawling into the school for the teacher.

Now I'm scared, and I feel bad 'cause I'd never done nothin' like this before, but I think he sure enough deserved it.

I follow him into school to punch him again because of what he said and how Sarah is crying, but I know better. I'm real sorry and I start crying too, because I feel so bad about everything.

The teacher leads the boy quick into the washroom, so he won't get blood all over the clean school floor. She holds a cold, wet cloth on his face and nose. I sit on a chair just wet-eyed and shaking a little with my head down.

Soon, I feels the teacher's hand on my shoulder, and she says in a soft, almost motherly voice, "Jim, tell me what happened, son."

Well, right then I know I like this teacher 'cause she's not mad at me, or even at the bleeding boy for getting blood all over the school floor. I don't want to say those words 'cause they is making me mad all over again, but finally I tells Miss Shelly what the boy said. Miss Shelly says she is awful sorry for what Derin said and asks me to go back outside till she rings the bell again. I wipe the tears off my face with my shirtsleeve and then I think of my sister.

I find Sarah still sobbing at the side of the school and I try to wipe her tears away too, but she pushes my arm away and says she can do it herself. We just sit side by side till we hear the bell ring, then we goes back inside to our desks.

Miss Shelly stands beside her desk up near the big blackboard and Derin, the one I punched, is at his own desk holding the wet, blood-stained cloth over his nose. I feel bad all over again and wish I'd never have to come to school ever again.

Miss Shelly says, "Class, I want you all to listen well today because we've got a very special lesson. Now, I want you all to know how important today is, and I want you all to remember that what we are going to talk about today will help make the whole rest of your lives very much better. I want you to know you have to listen with both your ears wide open and all of your smart young minds open, and I especially want to talk to each of your big, beautiful hearts."

Everybody sits quiet and looks at her, even Derin with the wet pink cloth on his face.

Miss Shelly talks for a long time about all kinds of people and how we are all born the same inside our hearts, even when we look different outside on our skin. She says things like I've heard my mom and dad say sometimes when they really love us or when we're confused, angry, and hurt. Sometimes I look over at Sarah and she is smiling like her and my mom does most every day, and I look over at Derin and he is sitting up straight without the wet cloth over his face. He isn't smiling, but he's listening to Miss Shelly and I'm thinking I should say I'm sorry for hitting him so hard, and then Miss Shelly says we should all go out and play for recess and we'll talk more later.

Before I go out, I tell Miss Shelly I'm sorry for causing trouble.

She says, "You're a good boy, Jim. You know, I've met your mom and I think she is a wonderful person. I am so sorry for what Derin said, and it was not proper for him to have spoken that way, but you must forgive him, Jim, for that is just the way he was taught. It is not his fault he speaks this way. He doesn't know better, but perhaps if you speak to him with your heart the way that I know you can, he will see you are a kind, strong person that he would be proud to call his friend, and then he will change his words and open up his heart. You must remember, Jim, even when it is very difficult for you—you must use your mind and your heart properly to make your words come out so this world will be a better place. If you use your fists to try to make things better, it only hurts your fists and makes all things far worse, not better. It does not help to use your fists. Will you try to use your words, Jim, to make things better?"

"Yes, Miss Shelly... I'll try my best."

And then she asks me if I would please check on Derin to make sure his nose doesn't start bleeding again.

I say, "I will," and I do too.

I tell Derin I'm sure sorry for hittin' him so hard, and he says, "It ain't nothin', my nose starts bleedin' every time I bumps it a little." And then he tells me he ain't never gonna say words like that again 'cause he don't ever want to see Sarah cry ever again, and he asks if maybe we can be friends and I tell him sure thing, Derin, and then Miss Shelly rings the handle-bell and we all go up the steps, back into class.

Miss Shelly smiles her warm smile at us all, and I see in her eyes a special understanding and a kindness. As I listen to Miss Shelly, I think and I feel that I will really like this school and all the kids to play with, and I know I will especially like Miss Shelly because she is so warm and smart, just like my mother.

At the supper table this night, Mom and Dad asks us how school was today. After Sarah and I tell almost everything we can remember, Mom says she will snip her favorite rose tomorrow morning and Sarah can give it to Miss Shelly, and Dad asks me if I would want to give my little pocketknife to Derin. I had my little folding knife since I was three. It isn't big or sharp enough to clean a fish, and mostly I just use it to clean garden dirt from under my fingernails. Dad says if I want to give it to Derin for a friendship present I can, but I don't have to. It's all up to me. Sarah brings Mom's pretty red rose to school next morning in a little colored-glass jar with water. Miss Shelly smiles big when Sarah hands her Mom's rose. At recess I give Derin my little folding knife, and we shake hands just like we see some big dads do.

When Sarah and I get home from school, laying on the table in the same place where I always eat is a brand new shiny knife with two folding blades. In Sarah's place is a small pole with line and tiny, real sharp hooks. I opens up this knife, and both blades are sharp enough to clean a fish or even a rabbit. Dad says he was saving it for my next birthday, but because we are going fishing this Saturday he figures I can use it now. He makes me promise to never take it to school, but I can keep it in my pocket any days I'm not in school. It's a swell knife, and I do believe I still have it somewhere, and that was oh, such a very long time ago.

2. Encompassing Awakening

Positive change—we longed for it, and beckoned its coming—was a while manifesting, but it did slowly start, where the Great Plains and western mountains meet. The foothills... *It became contagious, then, like wildfire, it spread!*

Two green-eyed, permanently tanned twins—a brother and a sister—are born and raised in the middle of nowhere. Least it is *nowhere* to most earth folks of this time. The planet's population seen an exponential increase in growth these recent years, but the west-central North American grassy flats and in some places, rough and windblown rolling hills, with their vast spaces, winter blizzards, and hot summer droughts, are mostly known as "a place to be avoided." The thawing chinooks are an interesting phenomena, but nobody really wants to live through a cold, howling whiteout just to have the pleasure of one.

"Nothing familiar enough going on there," they say, when they think of it at all and, except for resource extraction, mostly leave it be. This suits Sarah and me almost fine, as we've occasionally been to the built-up population centers, with their hard steel, concrete, and glass, and their noise, crime, confusion, and pollution. There are surely some inviting things in the city to see and do, but generally it just makes us two lonesome for our familiar wildlands of home.

Of course, most human social structures are making an attempt to change their ways a little, but we prefer the beckoning, life-stirring sounds, the wind on the ridges and birdsong in the creek bottoms. We learn to love this wildland and wonder what it must have been like before the asphalt byways carved it all up. It's sure a pretty country, if your brain manages to let your eyes see.

What was it like before thousands of miles of train tracks and barbed wire fences were built? Before fast and heavy, ear-hurting air-horned freight trucks squished curious-but-naive free-spirited antelope like they are annoying bugs? Before the fish and game department of the state government is forced by the auto insurance companies to declare an extended open season on all the undomesticated, independent wild critters that stray near these many roads. After all, people—whole families, *even little kids and babies*—are too often mangled or killed at a very costly rate, from high-speed critter collisions.

These accidents mostly occur in the darkness of the night hours. The grass grows better along the road edges because of the extra water that runs off the paved asphalt surface. This runoff gives the ditch plants many times the moisture the surrounding dry land receives. These plants are also mowed twice a year, so they are usually young and fresh.

These succulent plants attract the appetites of the wild grazers, but the worst happens in the dark hours of night. When a fast-traveling car's lights shine on a critter, it causes a shadow. This shadow moves quick, just as the car gets close. Every fast-moving shadow appears to the grazer as an attacking predator. Their instant reaction is to jump away from it, so they jump toward *the only place left visible.* This often lands them—*smack! crunch!*—into the brightly lit path of a car; hence the bad wrecks.

Some critters learn to ignore these jumping shadows, but most that are attracted to the sweet roadside plants don't live long enough to comprehend this modern spook. Most predators shy away from the constant noisy activity of these roadways, and that makes it even more inviting for the ungulates. Too frequently, these heartbreaking wrecks also occur in daylight. It's a shockingly repulsive, bent, and bloody mess.

These large free-roaming wild critters are of no real monetary value to anyone in office, so 'they have to go'.

"They didn't kill 'em all, lucky us." We two sparkling-eyed and tanned children talk of what the past must have been like, and as we get a little older we begin to discuss what is possible for our future.

Our mom, Samantha, is a Cherokee-West African true beauty, an exceptionally strong, graceful, and big-hearted woman. She mostly stays near home tending our family garden, cooking, cleaning, and looking after our few domestic animals.

Some of her not-so-distant ancestors had their spirits broken when their flesh and blood children were forcibly ripped from nurturing arms and auctioned off to distant strangers, while others left their unburied bones along the Trail of Tears. She knows a little of the harsh, possessive ways of industrious man, but, thankfully, has not let that diminish her ever-present love of life.

Our dad, Jake, is a tall, athletic, and determined descendant of central Europeans, who left his home in New York at an adventurous age. There are more than a few ghosts in his family's background. He never met any of his grandparents, but in his childhood he occasionally heard pieces of family conversations about the explosively destructive turmoil that tore Europe asunder and other snippets about a mysterious ancestor who jumped ship when a Chinese freighter docked on the north coast of the Mediterranean.

Dad started his youthful work career as a New York high-rise rigger. An unexpected storm blew in from the north Atlantic and hit the eastern seaboard when he was precariously perched thirty stories above the unforgiving concrete street. He clung for hours to a swaying steel girder, and that convinced him to keep his feet, head, and heart closer to the pliable and forgiving softness of dirt, so he headed out west, for the elbow room, and peaceful quiet of the touchable earth.

Dad and Mom met at a funky little run-down diner, in the middle of back-roads Wyoming. They fell in love, not exactly at first sight, but they strived to build a deep love, an extraordinary honor. They developed a true commitment to each other, to this land, and to us children.

"Two's enough," they agreed, "so we can give them the things they need to have a fulfilling healthy life."

Sarah and I are gifted decent horses that take us many animal-trail miles through wildlands on wondrous adventures few dare dream of.

Dad provides for us as best he can. He sometimes says, "I don't like it much," but every summer, from spring thaw till winter freeze-up, he takes a job on the state road building crew. It pays well with lots of bonuses and perks and our family needs the money to continue living on this land that we love. It's a conflict of interest for him, but what else can he do? There doesn't seem to be a way he can give our family the material things we need by working at what he truly loves and believes in.

Sarah and I see all this, and we wonder, in between adventures, if we can make it better somehow. We are smart, observant kids, and we love this land too.

We talk of 'someday,' 'when we will be adults,' with families of our own. Could we live on this land and do something good for this, our land, for the fluid wildness we love, and for our very own souls. Would we have to someday do things we feel with our hearts is wrong, just to feed and shelter our families? To keep the wolf from our door, so to speak?

We seldom want for anything, except to never forget about our adventurous youthful hearts, and to learn how to not have to spend our future working confined in a repetitious cage, our artistic wildness trapped in a noisy, harsh-edged, concrete jungle.

Dad and Mom tell us both, many a time and right from an early young age, that we have to learn in school so we will know this world well.

Mom says, "Not just the world you learn in the garden or on horseback, but also the world and its ways, the past history and ever-changing present, of life-giving planet Earth and wondrous, but sometimes energetically-confused, man."

So we do; we ride the bus many miles to school, we pay attention in class and on the playground, and we study our books (when we need to). We both get good grades and learn how to interact well with our classmates and teachers. Our teachers often praise us, telling us we are excellent students. They direct us to many opportunities that are to stand us well in future years.

Modern communication machines are a fun easy-breeze. Learning interpersonal skills is a lot more—sometimes agonizingly stormy—challenging. Our teachers, recognizing our potential, encourage us to attend special emotional intelligence and conflict resolution classes. Occasionally, we are even sent to the big cities for a week or two at a time to partake of special conferences, put on by the world's best traveling social communicators.

At one of these conferences, a guest speaker flies in from Japan to inspire the attendant audience and stimulate our pliable young imaginations. His talk is particularly memorable and it sticks with us. He calls it "Water, Magic, and Miracles."

As we grow, we often talk of this special story about water and how it is affected, how it records all the things in its environment that present themselves. It is interesting to us how his story relates to humans, as we are mostly water.

This speaker has made a lifelong commitment of attempting to prove how not only dissolved minerals, chemicals, and such affect water, but also how energies like thoughts and feelings do, and have a long time recorded effect. In our youth, we speak of this man as an explainer of creation. As we mature, we come to understand that he spoke somewhat like a quantum physicist. He was a man of deep knowledge, a true artist.

Years later, we hear he's been discounted, even ostracized by some of his contemporaries, but we think there may be some misdirected jealousy involved, perhaps partially because he is not credentialed. He is somewhat different from respectable, regimented normal. We really don't know for sure because we never took the time to investigate this ourselves, but the point is, he was personable and inspiring, and he resonates with us. We admire his concern and his insights.

Being different is often threatening, as it sometimes shakes our habitual ingrained beliefs and leaves us shivering in our exposed nakedness. Quaking in our boots. That is never pleasant, so we project walls, resistant to change. It takes more than a little inner strength and self-confidence to make room within our own beliefs in order to feel the depths of another's beliefs, which may well be alien to our own.

If we feel the depth of another, once in a while, we could sure enough resolve a lot of conflict without resorting to walls and wars. That doesn't mean we'd be vulnerable and obligated to take on another's ways or beliefs, but it'd sure help our understanding and our ability to acknowledge for others their right to exist.

Come with us now, for a quick peek into our youthful memories, and we'll try to recapture the essence of this man's presentation. For it was indeed a stimulating and uplifting experience for us to absorb his words.

This man and his mentor spend many long years learning how to capture, present, and demonstrate their insights. In a nutshell, what they do is subject a container of pure water to a thought, feeling, or even just a photo of an object or animal. They then freeze this water, observe its crystalline structure under a powerful microscope, and observe that the water has recorded an image of its environment.

The image is too subtle to see in liquid water, but, once frozen, the crystal pattern is obvious. The difficulty is that the liquid water is very susceptible to influence and, as you may imagine, it's more than a little difficult to hold any one projection in your thoughts or feelings for the length of time it takes for a droplet of water to go from liquid to frozen. Perhaps that is why no one seems to be able to duplicate their results. You see, invisible to the eye, subtle energy within an elemental particle changes when you think about it, just because of the energy you project when you are thinking about or feeling it. Your thoughts and feelings influence the structure, and that is one very simplified explanation that falls within the realm of quantum physics.

They print these images for public presentation. Liquid water inundated with appreciative feelings forms lovely crystalline patterns when frozen. Water shown pictures will crystallize into the shape of the presented picture. Water subjected to negative feelings forms chaotic crystal patterns.

This is repeated thousands of times, so there is no room for doubt. Then they take it further to realize and record that water also retains DNA images of presented organisms. It is transformationally amazing.

Now we get to the miracle part. Hearing the word *miracle* makes us listeners wonder if the words *mirage*, *mirror*, and *miracle* have a similar root source.

But back to the miracle part of this man's presentation. When he is done talking, he invites the audience to ask questions.

The first question is, "If a water molecule retains the DNA patterns of an organism, would it be possible to bring back, into solid existence, a long-extinct species?"

The man thinks for a moment, then replies, "It would be unlikely, because when the water molecule evaporates, the DNA pattern that was suspended there would also disperse, the same as its H_2O retainer."

That prompts a second question: "If the DNA is dispersed and mixes with other dispersed patterns, then a new water molecule forms from many other water vapors, would it then be possible that a totally new DNA organism might have a chance of manifesting into being?"

Again, before replying, he thinks for a moment. "Yes, that may be possible."

So when Sarah and I talk all of this through, and remember stories we've heard about people being able to transfer themselves through—or manifest objects out of—thin air, we wonder, is this the basic mechanics of how it's done?

And we also wonder if, when a human organism dies and its soul or energetic body is released to the vast sea of energy, perhaps its energy, its individual energetic awareness, also disperses and mixes with that vast sea, no longer able to retain, or maintain, its individuality. Then, when a human baby is born, they could be a conglomerate of pieces of many, who at one time were separate individuals. This might explain so-called past life memories.

We think of a simplified example. We talk of a hundred glasses full of water. These glasses full of water represent separate individuals, and cannot mix because their containers hold them apart. Now, if we take these individual containers and spill them all into the same lake, the waves and currents mix them with the lake water. When we refill these same glasses from the same lake, do we not have some bits of water from all the other previous cups contained within each now present cup? We wonder, are we really that energetically connected?

Magic is not just 'imagination in the air,' for us kids. We have it all, the best of many worlds. We have never been told that things are impossible, so we still have what all of us are naturally born with—perceptive smarts and big open hearts fully capable of taking advantage of every nuance of life. We know who we are. Our parents solidified in us a purpose, a connection, and a respect for all living things.

We even talk, as best we can, of our understanding of the many ways of man we ourselves do not approve of. We know mankind disappears many living things around us. Not because of hate, but mostly because 'they've learned no other way'. So, as we grow in age and knowledge, we share amazing talks at our home dinner table, near our favorite fishing hole, on our long horse rides, and, yes, very much so at these special conferences.

We talk about the world we love: "Can we somehow show the rest of Earth's people, mostly city folks, a glimpse of this world?" We speak of the wild world that we have been blessed with. Perhaps it's possible. But how?

How can one show another something that the other has no comprehension of, no understanding of, no love for, possibly only just fear of, because the disconnect is so vast? Ahh, quite a task. But *remember*... we are special kids. We're strong, athletic inside and out, both of us energetic, and we know we're handsome. But we've been well told and shown what happens to people who let their heads—their egos—swell up, and we were also intentionally taught what happens to people who take advantage of other people just because they can.

We are surrounded and driven by committed, yet unpossessive, love. We are fully capable of understanding, and we have the unrestrained support of all the many mentors who have come into our lives, not the least of whom have been our parents. They started us on life's path by making sure we knew we could do anything our hearts desired. We just had to work at it, put our hearts and minds behind it, and most important of all, never forget to love.

Our two special parents teach us, repetitively, that no matter how smart, talented, handsome, or dedicated we are, if we forget to truly love, all else will be for naught. We keep all this in mind, and we get good at it. Soon most all those we come across can feel a presence that baffles some, although most admire it, and, from there, a mutual, fluid respect develops.

3. Big Cities and School

Soon it's time to leave our protected cocoon, our supportive childhood home, for big cities and advanced education. We are now in the world of money and enormously concentrated human power. A world where the right or wrong words and a simple signature, or a stamped seal on a document, can get whole landscapes rearranged and whole cultures annihilated. A world sometimes blinded by its own needs, its possessive insecurities, and its lack of empathetic understanding. Maybe it happens to be this way not because of its cold, obstinate heart, but because its heart is shielded, callused, and jaded from previous lacks of warmth.

How do you warm a cold heart? For only a warm heart has the strength and the flexibility to feel enough to understand and appreciate. But the important question was and remains: How do you warm a cold heart? *Remember...* we grew up watching the wild-world we loved, slowly but surely shrinking because of the lack of understanding and the lack of love from our fellow humans.

We are now young adults. We learned from experience that it's not from lack of ability that our modern human race does not appreciate the natural flow of the wildlands. This lack of understanding is simply because people do not know the effects of their actions. How could they? Most are so busy just trying to survive that they don't have time. Some have never even touched real dirt before, never listened to the sweetness of a wild bird singing, never gotten anywhere near an undomesticated animal. This will all have to change if anything natural is to continue living for the next generation, or for their and our kids to know other than from recorded messages of past history. Something needs to be done.

It's critical, so very important. The inspiring, sustaining diversity of the wildlands needs to be preserved... and, better yet, enhanced. But how? We ask this question a thousand times, of ourselves and of each other.

"How do you encourage a connection, convince someone to love something whose subtleties, they have little comprehension of? How can they feel and understand when it is so remote, alien, or, in extreme cases, even nonexistent to them?"

To take someone by force or coercion and subject them to alien ways would only make things worse; it would traumatize them, which may have the effect of making those folks hate the wildlands instead of merely ignore them. This, of course, is far from our idea of introducing them to the love and understanding intended. There has to be a way to gently encourage a complementary connection.

If hate is born from trauma and fear, the wildlands could be wiped out in a heartbeat by the enormous power and energy of the vast sprawling cities. They have robotic machines, deadly poisons, and the organized willpower to change everything almost overnight, if it is deemed necessary or even merely desirable.

So, what's to be done for our struggling natural wildlands? We are learning complicated things now about money and the power structure of the human world. We can easily see that most people are not bad inside their hearts; it's just that people have let their unfeeling mechanical minds take over. This is the disconnect that somehow needs to be addressed and corrected. But again, how? Here is where the guidance of our parents' teachings and all the days spent at special conferences starts to make sense. We now have many city friends, and we know beyond a doubt that even though our friends don't entirely understand, they're fully capable of not only understanding, but of honest loving. They just need to be eased into it in a way that makes uncomplicated sense to them. Somehow we need to entertain, mesmerize, relax, and pacify the programmed fear of people's possessive minds long enough for their hearts to relearn the unrestrained freedom to start truly living and to interact with unrestricted, safe, and benevolent feelings again.

4. A Hatched Plan

Together we hatched a plan. Remember... we'd been encouraged from our youth to be open and appreciative, and we'd learned to be perceptive communicators.

It seems everyone knows my sister, Sarah. Now you're about to hear the plan she and I hatched, how we guided it, nurturing it to grow and prosper.

Sarah attended advanced business classes involving law and politics. At university, the boys (some pretending to be Neanderthals) were not all nice to her, but even the verbally repulsive ones did sometimes follow her around like lost puppies. She couldn't come out of her dorm room without some young man or woman, some not so young, seeking her attention. They were akin to paparazzi, always underfoot. At first, she liked and even encouraged the attention, but it soon became spooky, detrimental, and monotonous. We were both relieved the day she met Ged at a conference and he invited her to lunch. Ged is uncanny, not arrogant or forceful in the least, but he couldn't hide his reputation. His parents had enrolled him in martial arts classes when he was a boy. His instructors were well respected and he'd learned to enjoy the sport, winning a few trophies along the way. It was soon obvious to her persistent admirers that Sarah had a committed boyfriend and that did help her to develop boundaries, giving her a semblance of peace.

I'm Jim, Sarah's minutes-older twin brother. Sarah says I always wanted to be first in everything, but really I was just checking to make sure it was safe for her to come out into Earth's atmosphere. We all know how vulnerable and sensitive girls can be. I tried to protect her gentleness, not wanting her to be frightened or become hard like I imagine some pretty ladies do.

Sarah and I are a team. From the moment of our conception, she has always been the best part of me. I might have strength in muscles, but I believe I would've shriveled without the guidance of Sarah's wondrous heart and brains.

At university, I studied environmental biology, soil chemistry, and veterinary medicine. Some say I have more than a few problems that started in middle school. According to me, I have none and it's the girls who have the problems. They can't seem to get enough of me. They always want more than I can rightly give. I am already committed to my own ideas, my needs, and my wants, and there really is very little room in my life for any lady who does not fully understand or appreciate that. I'm not coldhearted, although I've been told I am by more than one teary-eyed, confused, and conflicted admirer.

It's just that I'm already committed to my own dreams. My heart is fully taken by the wildlands and I've not met one intelligent beauty, other than my dear sister Sarah, who understands the depth of that, but they do keep trying to win me over. I'm overflowing, hot-blooded, and I sure do enjoy their warmth, but I learned to keep my heart unavailable, and that's what fills the ladies' eyes with tears. It's not really my fault they keep trying and I can't resist, so it's all a big distraction, and it sometimes makes it frustratingly difficult to keep my concentration on my studies, yet somehow I manage to get my needed degrees.

It's not easy, but I need the knowledge and the respect that these degrees will give me to help implement Sarah's and my *plan*. We need to be able to convince intelligent experts and powerful people that *our plan* is sound. We need the support of many different people if we are to have a chance of success. It's good we learned the importance of communication skills, as these helped us develop respect for our own species.

A difficult part of our long education years is not to get so fully wrapped up that we forget who we are; luckily, we keep in touch with our parents back home, visiting briefly whenever we can. This contact with our childhood is very important to our well-being and symbiotically important to our longtime dream of enhancing our beloved wildlands.

Our dream now encompasses the city folks we've also learned to love, respect, and understand. Only now can we start to bring these living forces together into a state of mutual support.

If we'd known from the start how much time and effort it would take to accomplish all our dreams, we may have been discouraged and given up, resigning ourselves to becoming experts at ignoring our vanishing world. The nagging, the pulling at our heartstrings, might then have driven us to despair or anger, so it was well that we didn't know beforehand, and that we had gotten an educated start when we were young enough to have the time and energy ahead of us. It is also very helpful that we have our sanctuary, our childhood home base, with its many peaceful blessings.

5. Money, Power, and Politics

Sarah implemented the setting up of our businesses. We dreamed these would eventually be publicly owned and traded companies, so we had to do it right. Even national law and politics would be involved soon enough.

You might think it slightly strange, fortuitous even, how it came about, but our timing was right, our foundation was strong, and people were ready for a change, for connection, for adventurous fulfillment.

Sarah and I had luck on our side. I can say we recognized, flowed with, and enhanced our own luck as we progressed. Some say we're so perceptive and gracious that people like us and are happy to be of assistance. Of course, 'giving is always a two-way street,' but we give with our conversations, by teaching, and by sharing what we know of how to do things in better, easier ways. People appreciate us, opening doors normally closed. That's our way, and we use it not only for our own goals but somehow it always works out that whatever we instigate is to and for the benefit of all. The people we meet feel enlivened. Those who know us well say they often feel their own hearts swell with even a passing thought of my bubbly sister and me.

Unbeknown at the time to either of us—but if we could have fast forwarded into the future of our lives, we would have seen—not only would we be facilitators helping to bring back the natural wildness of the foothill plains, but we would also be involved with far lands, multinational companies, airships, special satellite drones, and many other modern technologies. All of these working together to enhance the wondrous diversity of Earth.

We have many friends in big cities, both young adults our own age and older folks, the professors who taught us, and the many business people we've been introduced to. It's not easy to say goodbye, but it's time. We all vowed to keep in close touch.

6. Back Home

Beckoned by what we love, we travel to the homeland of our blood and bones. It's comforting and inspiring, to be near our parents again—both of them still actively healthy, both still deeply in love with each other. It's uplifting to wake in the morning and hear laughter; it's good to see their smiles and be encompassed by their affections again. We'd missed it more than we knew.

Sarah and I saved a small nest egg from the teaching, modeling, and investing we managed to do between classes and our busy social lives. Neither of us are married yet. We have lovers, although none ready to commit to living in Wyoming. We've been gone almost ten years and it's now time to get some long-dreamed-of and serious work done.

Our horses are still in the home-place pasture, but they aren't as young as they used to be. They won't be able to do those thirty- or forty-mile days anymore. Maybe twenty, but just the same, they remember "Saaaaarah" and "Jiiiiiiiim..."

We brush them down good, trim their overgrown hooves, long tails, and manes. Soon we all go for short rides. It's not only our horses that have lost their riding muscles. Sarah and I sore up quick too; it takes a while to get back into saddle shape.

Short rides bring back vivid memories of our wondrously energetic, innocent, and playful youth. One of our favorite places to stop, on our rides long ago, was at a ranch twenty miles up the creek from our parents' place. On the second week home we make it there and, to our delight, nothing has changed much.

"Look, Sarah," I say, "mule deer in the hayfields, white-tails down along the creek bottom, a pair of mallards in the lowland grassy pond, even a flock of indigenous wild turkeys strutting through the yard, their fuzzy chicks in tow."

Sarah points to our trail. "These tracks look like they might be elk. Perhaps they've wandered down from Yellowstone, only a half day's eagle flight to the north."

The old couple is still here; they aren't bent, but they're moving real slow. Their steps liven up when they notice us ride in. Gramp tries to dance a little jig; Gram almost squeals in surprised delight. They're sure happy to see us, their favorite kids again.

"You gota stay for lunch," Gram chimes. "Take those saddles offa them horses and turn 'em into the corral. There's some good grass in there and fresh clean water. They be alright for a spell. You all come on in the house and tell us what you's bin up to."

It feels fuzzy-warm all the way around to be back with people we've long loved. It's been some years, but the feelings

HEVAN HERTH

We create our future. Let's be careful what we wish for!

are even stronger now. All the understanding we share this afternoon is enough to make an angel's heart light with joy, or even an Earth-man teary eyed with love's longing. We have four short hours to visit, talk, and get reacquainted before it's time to make tracks on the dirt road to home.

7. This Is What Was Said!

This old couple knows us younger folks well. We called them Gram and Gramp as we shared shaded hours under the big cottonwoods down by the creek on hot summer afternoons when we had rode through on youthful adventures. We sipped gallons of thirst-quenching, pucker-powered, and lightly sweetened hush-um juice there, hidden from the midday sun. It had been Gram and Gramp who, many years ago, nourished and encouraged the ungerminated seeds of what we talked of this day.

First, Sarah and I tell them highlights of our years away.

Then, Gramp wants to get right down to business.

Gram says, "Our health is failing fast, and we might not be around much longer." They never birthed any children of their own. Some problem with the reproductive works, they guessed, so they have no heirs. They don't want to sell their place to someone who doesn't give a damn and that's why they're still here, instead of some easy place closer to town. The ranch is a bit run-down from recent years of little maintenance, but it's a good self-sustaining place.

It's 4,000-acres of high-protein native bunchgrass grazing land, 200-acres of productive hayfield, flood-irrigated from the big spring up the hill, another flat eighty-acres sub-irrigated, its moisture wicking up from the meandering creek. The fences are in need of repair, the barn roof leaks, the old house could use a coat of paint, but the place is perfect for the start of what Sarah and I have in mind. We explain our grand plan to our old friends. At the end of four pleasant hours we've worked out a deal.

We ride for home to ask Dad if he'll pick up Gram and Gramp in the morning with his 4x4 and take them the forty miles into town.

Sarah says, "Let's all meet for lunch at the one restaurant."

This is a small village, with one bar, which also serves as a gas station. Funny combination, gasoline and alcohol, but that's the way it is in some streetlights-free, off-the-trail towns. There's a motel of sorts—nothing fancy, mind you—but other than a few weeds in the gravel parking lot it's clean and well-kept.

The lady who owns the motel refreshes our beliefs when she points out, "Those aren't weeds. They're volunteer flowers. Ain't they pretty?"

She smiles when we promise we won't drive over them.

There's a small convenience store in the office of her motel. There are also probably twenty-five houses scattered throughout this little village.

In one of these painted wooden houses lives a semiretired notary. He used to have a commercial practice in a bigger town but now only opens his business door a couple days a week, "unless you have something that needs doing right quick." There's a short gravel airstrip, but it hasn't been used much since the state built the big bypass, five miles yonder. If you need groceries you'll have to drive the interstate another eighty-miles into a real town.

Sarah and I drive, early morning, to this little village. We want to ask around before the locals disperse for their day. We locate a small but well-kept vacant house on the outskirts. It has leafy shade trees, a lazy creek out the back door, and a sidewalk along the front that the village maintenance guy keeps clear of snow in winter. A dial thermostat hangs on the wall for heat; there's hot and cold running water. No sign, but "Yahoo."

The neighbour says. "Sure it's for rent."

Sarah catches up to the owner just as he's leaving the filling station. Their handshake seals the deal—three hundred and fifty dollars change hands. Gram and Gramp have a warm home in town. Our company will keep the rent and services paid. After we eat lunch, Gram and Gramp and we twins make our way to the notary's office. The document that Sarah drew up last night needs witnessed signatures and an official's stamp.

Gram is tickled. They can keep their house on the ranch and visit whenever they like. Sarah and I rename their ranch Bison Leap, then it's turned over to the nonprofit, with us its principal managers. A nonprofit gives us many advantages to start, but we dream of expanding way beyond that. Sarah has other business setups too, but they wouldn't activate till necessary. Even when these other companies do come into play, this original ranch will remain under the protection of the nonprofit. The complex laws of business are not my expertise, but Sarah has that part of our plan well covered.

Dad knows a fellow not far away who, with his helpers, builds small but very cozy prefab cabins. He'll drop by our folks' home-place tomorrow to discuss our needs. Things are coming together nicely.

I tell Sarah, "It's still early spring, but we've much to do before the next snow flies, so best we get at it."

Our parents' place is wired with a landline phone but no internet. Bison Leap has neither, so communicating will be difficult till things get better developed. We help Gram and Gramp settle into the village house. To them, it's new, fully furnished, and it even has an electric fridge, so there'll be no more need to handle heavy propane bottles.

8. Six Directions

Tomorrow will be another long day, so we head home to rest. After much discussion tonight about what buildings we need to start, we agree that two identical cabins with roofed porches, an open living-room-kitchen combination, one bedroom, and a small bathroom will be plenty comfy enough for now.

Sarah wants hers on the little knoll facing the shady cottonwood creek. There's a fluffy black-dirt garden-spot nearby. Sarah likes the quiet, active meditation of nurturing plants, the fresh outdoor air, and communing with Mother Nature, watching life sprout, fill out, and grow, giving so willingly of its vibrancy to the needs of beast and man.

I'll place my cabin up on the bare rocky ridge; I like to look near and far in all six directions. The wind often plays on these high ridges. It's a comfort, a friend to me. It's the wind or perhaps only its child, a light pleasant breeze that brings stimulation to all things. I need to be careful in a rogue storm, don't want the wind blowing in through a window and out the door, leaving the kitchen table face down on the floor; to the plants, movement is breath, like the diaphragm of an animal helping its whole system function, exchanging converted gasses for renewing energy. Mostly, it sings to my ears sweet melodies, bringing voices from intimately close by or far, imagined lands. Sometimes it shocks and shakes our world with urgency, waking up strengths and rearranging weaknesses. When I let it blow through me, it clears my dusty cobwebs, bringing visions, inspiration, and images from whispering realms, painting pictures for me of swaying grass, fluttering leaves, and gently dancing trees. It is company on lonesome days, inspiring life just because it's forever in changing motion.

I can't see far down from this site. It's just a ridge, not a mountaintop, but all around I can view the awesome starry night, and daylight distance, almost forever.

We will need another building. Only vague ideas of how we'll afford it right now, but somehow it will have to get done. This one, we figure, should have four nice bedrooms, each with its own bathroom, one large lounge-dining room, and at one end a well-equipped kitchen.

"We need to find a Spanish pirate's hoard, a genie's vase to rub, or a leprechaun's rainbow's pot of shiny coins," says Sarah.

"Where will we find the money?" I wonder.

Dad figures he should run his little bulldozer up the dirt road to Bison Leap. A few heavy rocks have rolled down onto the road, and there are some places that over the years have sloughed in a bit.

"It'll take me a couple days," he says. "I oughta level off the cabin and guesthouse sights while I'm up there."

Thanking him, I volunteer, "I can run you up some lunch."

Dad and Mom ask us to start calling them by their names. They say it makes them feel old when they look at us, all grown up, and then hear our words, 'Dad and Mom'. They say they want to feel forever young, and it'll help if we treat them more like friends instead of parents. I believe, looking back, there was a lot more to it than what they stated. I assume they were encouraging us to be independent adults by thinking of them as equals instead of as parents. That, however, never diminished their love, respect, and support for us, which I am eternally grateful for. Sarah and I attempt to comply with their request. It'll take awhile to get used to, but if it will help them feel young, we'll give it a try.

Jake packs his own lunch. Samantha will haul a portable tidy tank of fuel to refill the crawler and meet Jake tonight for supper at Bison Leap. Maybe the job will take a few extra days, on top of the three already planned. Sarah and I are encouraged to find something else to do, while Samantha and Jake have themselves a little second honeymoon.

The cabin plans are settled on with the builder. We talk about the guesthouse too, but it can wait a bit. We have a few days to kill, so we take a freeway run into the big town to connect with high-speed internet.

It's been over two weeks since we've talked to our city friends. They'll be anxious for news, and both Sarah and I have interesting stories to tell. Two days in a not-so-fancy hotel eat a bigger hole in our wallet money than the month's rent we paid for the old couple's house, but we soon learn it was money well spent.

Sarah contacts a cell tower company about service to Bison Leap. The company will look into the cost and get back to her. The big surprise happens when we talk to friends via video. It's downright encouraging how excited everyone is. Of course, they all know about our crazy grand plan. They've often kidded us about our big dreams. It seems like it's really happening. Yes, they are excited and they want to be a part of it, asking, "What can we do to help?"

Sarah decides she'd better stay in town a few days to organize our new volunteers. I decide to go out to Bison Leap and see what shape the perimeter fence is in. Sarah reminds me to stay clear of the hayfield fence for now, "so the folks can have some peace and quiet."

The cabins won't arrive for a week or more. We have time to get a few other things done. I want to drive up to Yellowstone soon to talk about acquiring some yearling bison calves. I'd also like to talk to a rancher in northern Alberta about the wood bison he has—a subspecies of the plains bison of Yellowstone, but it'd be good to mix up the genes a bit. It has been way too many years of close breeding within the small isolated herds. It's desirable to inject some vigor and diversity back into the bloodlines. There's also a herd on an elite hunting preserve in Austria. It seems Buffalo Bill presented the monarchy of England with six young bison calves when he took his Wild West Show there, many decades back. She kept them for a while, till they got a bit difficult to handle, then gave them to a friend of her distant cousin who held an old world, private game preserve. The calves thrived and some of their descendants can now be shipped back to their native homeland.

We want all those that are young, healthy, and available. They'll have to be quarantined for six months, possibly a year, monitored by government veterinarians in both countries, to make sure they're disease and parasite free. These beasts are totally unrelated to either the northern Alberta-Yukon herd or the Montana herd, so they are of great interest to the gene pool. The new Bison Leap herd needs to be completely disease free, and have as diverse a gene pool as possible.

I think a little about the eastern North American species, gone the way of the passenger pigeon, the dodo bird, and countless other species. The last eastern bison was tracked down and fed hot lead in 1860. "Didn't want him bustin' fences, trampin' gardens, and makin' beefalo calves!" The eastern bison—maybe it had something to do with their high-protein winter diet of acorns, but they were a much taller, heavier species than the plains bison. I wish I could have seen one of them, but no sense lingering for long on thoughts like that. Thinking those thoughts is like milking the cow with a big hole in the bottom of the bucket. Best patch the hole first...

9. Video News

Sarah's been squirming with delight all day. She says, "A belly tickle warms my insides from all the excitement coming our way." In a few short days of high-speed communication, our friends and the thousands of their contacts pledge over a quarter million dollars to Bison Leap's nonprofit. A communications network is being set up in an office room of a close friend in Chicago. It's very encouraging to know so many people are genuinely interested in sustainable natural restoration.

It's rumored that a big multinational company wants in on our endeavors, but it'll have to be something other than a nonprofit first. It has paid off for Sarah and I to have shared our dreams with all those we met in our school years. Things are snowballing now; it's definitely time to get organized.

I drive Dad's old farm jeep up to Bison Leap. It doesn't have license plates, but it's mostly dirt road the whole way if I head out the back gate. I'll check the fence on foot.

It'll be good to have time to think a bit, and walking gives me a personal feel of this land. It's all of twelve miles, up and down around the perimeter fence, so I carry a little backpack with a bit of lunch, a thermos of tea, my Stetson, and a windbreaker, just in case. No tools are needed; I just want to have a good look.

There are small herds of bison here and there in both the U.S. and Canada, but they're pretty much domesticated from being enclosed within a fence for the last century-plus. I'm not entirely sure if their old natural instincts can be reawakened. Are they latently attached to the genetic makeup, or are they gone forever? I'm hoping the memories are still there and, if not, I hope they can be reinstated. Either way, I know it will help to have animals with their instincts intact to mix with the semi-domesticated ones we will also have to acquire to build the herd numbers up.

The ones we're most interested in are still awake with all their independent wildness. They don't hang around the fort waiting for somebody to baby them with a free meal. They're wanderers and, if they can, they'll follow their whims to wherever they sense something they need. They can smell water two, maybe three days away on a light breeze. Their bodies have the mysterious ability of being able to sense the mineral and healing properties of a plant from farther away than even I can imagine, but if something spooks them, like a grass fire or a hungry predator, they might end up in the next county or even state. There are no wolves or grizzlies around here yet; we don't need any right now, either! Someday there'll be a use for them, but not just yet.

The other intriguing thing about bison and most other wild animals and plants is they're light sensitive. Over the eons of their evolution, their genetic makeup has programmed when and when not to birth young. Their bodies can predict when the time of year will be most advantageous for new young to survive. This light sensitivity was discovered by modern scientists who conclude that most wild animals can automatically measure the difference in daylight hours against the hours of darkness. This stimulates them to ovulate to conceive for optimum offspring survival. This is all governed by the particular earth's latitude where the animal lives. What this means to Bison Leap and the bison is that the bison bulls and cows can be left together year round without danger of their calves being born out of season.

Domestic animals are selected by man to cycle year round, but this has many disadvantages, not the least of which is that domesticated males and females need to be kept separate except in human-wanted breeding season. If they're not separated, new life may be born in the middle of a dehydrating heat wave or a freezing snowstorm. This would be totally unacceptable for what Bison Leap has in mind, hence one of our concerns—that as many wild instincts as possible remain intact in the animals selected for Bison Leap's new herd.

The locals have killed the odd wolf or bear that has recently ventured down from Yellowstone, but just the same, the fences will need to be in good shape. I figure when the new herd starts arriving we'll enclose them on the hayfield for a while, where we can keep an eye on them till we know for sure they've settled down. We'll get the first cut off the field before they arrive. That should be more than enough hay to keep them well-fed this winter. The bison might not need any supplemental feed at all if it doesn't snow too much, but they'll mostly be young animals so we'll give them a bit anyhow, just to let them know where home is.

My walk around the perimeter fence takes most of the day, what with all the up and down, inspecting the land, and all the *dreaming* I'm doing. The wire is still all here; a few strands are broken where a deer or falling tree has hit it, but there are plenty of rotten posts, four or five hundred, I reckon. The fence will need re-stretching and new pickets wired onto the whole twelve miles. It'd be advantageous to string another wire on it too, to run some juice in. A good solar-charged electric fence will help teach any critter to respect a shiny wire.

I need to reawaken my hiking senses. I slip coming down a low-gradient rock face and take a bit of hide off my right shin and forearm. That hurts and it damn near makes me swear, but it's only skin, so I pay closer attention after that. Too many years of travel on flat city-sidewalks has made me a bit out of touch and clumsy. The cottonwood salve mother—Samantha—keeps on a kitchen shelf will take care of my scrapes.

10. Cottonwood Salve

Early spring, before the warming sun bursts new buds into leaf, Samantha meanders along the creek with her wicker picking basket and a broom handle stick. Her stick has a stiff wire vie-hook fastened to its end. The live tips of the cottonwood branches grow plump buds covered with sticky yellow sap. They smell lovely and have healing properties better than anything purchased in a drugstore. She reaches up with her hooked stick to pick a basketful, being careful not to take too many in any one spot, dumps them in a big pot, adds a little water, and simmers them on low heat on the side of her wood cookstove. As it simmers, she skims off the leafy bits that float to the top.

When it's done, she's left with sweet-smelling, thick, and creamy yellow salve. If she can get it, she stirs in a little balsam sap and a bit of melted beeswax, so it stays on healing skin longer. Either way, it works faster than anything we've ever found in town. Sarah and I used plenty when we were kids, and I'm glad Samantha still makes a fresh jar every spring. Some old habits are admirable, and I silently thank both her and the cottonwoods for their generosity.

Buffalo don't usually jump a fence like deer do, so the standard five-foot ranch fence is high enough, but they are strong, stubborn brutes. If the fence looks solid and it gives them a shock once in a while, they'll stay clear of it. I'm not quite sure how all this necessary fence work will get done, but long days of concentrated sweat will put a big dent in it. We don't have a post pounder, so we'll have to hire to get that done for sure, but the rest we'll manage somehow. I stop in quick to say hi to Samantha and Jake at the old couple's house before heading back down to the home place. I notice lots of healthy grass in the big pastures between Bison Leap and our home place. It appears it's not been eaten for a few years.

Next day, Sarah phones from town while I'm cooking my supper. She is bubbly and anxious to share good news. "We have money now to pay the prefab guy to start on the guesthouse, with plenty left over to hire someone in to contract the perimeter fence and build a brand new one around both hayfields."

We also need a strong set of sorting corrals and a processing building, but not for a while yet. It's just part of the incentive for our good-hearted contributors, but all those who donate to Bison Leap know they have a holiday destination and a private bedroom in the guesthouse whenever they wish. Besides being an abstract part of something grand, they will be able to hands-on participate in Bison Leap's endeavors.

Sarah has lots of news! Her boyfriend Ged is flying in from Toronto next week for a visit.

"He wants a tour of Bison Leap to see for himself what all the fuss is about," she says.

Ged is always busy, but he needs a holiday from his family's prosperous venture capital business.

He teases Sarah. "I can write my visit off as a business expense."

11. Ranch Realtor

Sarah meets with a ranch-lands realtor. She explains to the realtor, "We at Bison Leap are interested in good grazing land in this area. We'd like it to be at least twenty miles away from an oil refinery or coal-fired generator. We don't want anything with a rail line or public road cut through its middle. It needs good water, and the fences should be in decent shape. Bison Leap wants to stay clear, for now, of anything that's been fracked."

To make it especially clear that the realtor understands her, she continues. "Fracking is the latest desperate attempt to extract oil from underground porous rock, but it has the unsavory reputation of allowing the groundwater to mix with the oil and other extraction chemicals. This poisonous mix contaminates the groundwater and sometimes floats to the surface, rendering large areas of what was once pristine productive land into unusable wasteland. It will take hundreds or maybe even thousands of years for this land to heal itself, and BL wants no part in perpetuating that." She drives her point home. "Maybe those with the greed and foolishness to condone this type of degradation will realize their errors before vast stretches of unusable land and water become unsalable. That will surely haunt their unconscionably padded bank accounts.

"We'd like a long-term lease payable at the end of each year but will consider buying if the price is right. If the current owners would like to remain living there, put up the hay, and feed it out as needed in the winter, they'll be welcomed and compensated. It'd be negotiable. BL is open to suggestions and possibilities. Keep your ear open for a warehouse type building. This," Sarah explains, "won't be needed for a year or two but best to get the word out, so it'll be available when the time comes. This building must be very clean, have a smooth cement floor, office rooms, and the whole building should have easy airport and interstate access and be well insulated."

The realtor winks, telling her, "My wife is out of town and I hate to eat alone, so will you dine with me tonight to discuss all your needs in greater detail?"

Sarah thanks him for his offer, explains she's very busy and has many things to do before her boyfriend flies in, so perhaps they could meet for lunch at a restaurant "when he has business news for BL."

A few days later, this realtor calls to say the Bar X, a monstrous place, has grassland they might be interested in leasing out. The back end of this ranch is all the land, two miles wide, running along both sides of the creek, from our parents' place to Gram and Gramp's ranch, Bison Leap. It's everything one mile either side of the creek and the full twenty miles long.

A total of almost forty square miles! In land speak, one square mile is termed a section, six hundred and forty acres, and there are forty sections. Converted to metric this would be over ten thousand hectares, more than three kilometers wide by thirty kilometers long. It's covered with healthy bunchgrass that hasn't been pastured for two years. This is all freehold land (private deeded), but the Bar X also holds grazing leases on a large tract of adjacent state land they would also like to include with a deal.

Bison like to wander much more than domestic cows, so meetings should be set up with the grazing branch of the forest service and the state revenue department. It will also be best to notify all the environmental groups to get their approvals and support. It's time to have meetings with the Native Band landholders in the area.

It makes sense to keep our meetings small, with individual interest holders working out concerns before it goes to often-conflicted open public forums. A lot of explaining needs to be done among many varying points of view. These groups will need to give their full support for us to have a chance of success. It's absolutely necessary that local people participate in our project.

This Bar X pasture is the same grass that had amazed, and to my dismay had made me a little envious, when I passed through a few days before. A half dozen retired ranch horses graze here, but other than these and wildlife, it hasn't been touched. The horses can go with the place as long as they'll be looked after. The dirt road Dad cleaned up with his steel-tracked crawler runs lengthways through its middle. The owners of the Bar X have done some major business restructuring. The wife got sick a few years back, and they've since sold the biggest part of their commercial cattle herd, keeping back a select five hundred they'll pasture closer to home. This small bunch can be managed by the husband and his one longtime cowboy. The couple has three grown children, but they all live in the city with their respective families and careers. Although they do help with branding and roundups, none of them are interested in taking over the ranch.

Sarah and I drive over to the Bar X headquarters to see what arrangements can be made. We work out a mutually beneficial agreement; because the Bar X had a large influx of cash from their recent cattle sale, it will be prudent, tax-wise, for the Bar X to hold future shares in Sarah's Bison Leap Two Company, rather than giving half away to the IRS. Sarah will get proper papers drawn up.

"Perhaps the tax attorney and accounting firm in town would like this job?"

12. Serious Stuff

It looks like neither Sarah nor I will be having much time to enjoy either the wind or the birdsong. We'll be spending more time in airplanes and at business meetings than time on the land, but our plan is now becoming much more than an ethereal dream. This is very serious stuff, and we need to start getting some expert help on board.

I recruit Dad to find a fencing contractor. Jake will also oversee the prefab company's progress and installation of the two cabins, the guesthouse, and now a fourth building. Because everything is proceeding much faster than expected, we decide to go ahead with the processing facility. We need a sanitary building for butchering the tons of meat Bison Leap will produce in the years to come. This dream of ours must be run as a money-making business if it's to succeed.

Now, some may believe it's so wrong to think of a wild majestic animal as money in the bank, but if these animals cannot be thought of as monetarily profitable by the business world then they will not be allowed to reproduce. We considered this as part of our original *grand plan*.

I board a plane to visit distant herds we hope to acquire. We need to locate quarantined sites to hold them before they're transported to Bison Leap. Every single animal will need documented testing. I decide it'll be best to have them inspected by three experienced vets. Each animal can be initially done in one handling, so as not to stress them out too much. I want all three vets to each take a blood sample of every critter. Each vet will then send his samples to a separate lab. The result will be that each individual bison will have its blood analyzed by three different labs, for health and DNA recording.

It seems a little overkill to Sarah, but I assure her, "This will catch any mistakes or inconsistencies and prevent them from haunting BL's future."

Each animal will be implanted with a small microchip just under the hide behind the shoulder blade. These little chips are about the size of a grain of rice; they do not transmit but have an individual bar code, readable remotely with a scanner. This chip identifies individuals, and their blood sample will be recorded to the chip. Any amount of info on each animal can be entered into the database for future needs, and individual animals can be located if need be. The complete medical record of every individual will be data attached to their chip, but the main reason I want it done is so we can find any specific animal showing superior traits in their offspring, as far as genetic diversity is concerned. BL can match bulls with unrelated cows and vice versa. This is important because of the small gene pool we're left to work with. Once the herd gets built up to sufficient numbers it'll not be such a concern. I'm a little worried right now that we might have to sort out some inbreeding defects. BL did not invent these procedures; we just enhanced the system already established by the cattle industry.

Our business is not only about recreating the freedom of the past but also about science and economics. All this data collection is needed to preserve and enhance the world of nature while leading industrialized man to his senses, so on the surface it appears complicated, but with a little study it's really quite simple. If done right, it'll be an all round win-win situation.

13. Temple Grandin's Students

Sarah contacted Temple Grandin's school of animal psychology to inquire if they could and would design both a corral and handling facility specifically for bison. Their school has accomplished wonders in the past with new, more humane handling systems for cattle, and hopefully they're up for another challenge.

Sarah meets Ged—monogamous nine years now—tomorrow in town. On the way, she stops by the office of the semiretired notary, who also acts as the village's tax collector-service co-ordinator. They agree that if Bison Leap foots the bill, he'll get the maintenance man to ready the little airstrip for use. Ged and Sarah spend the night in the fanciest room in town. They arise late next morning, and soon after brunch a taxi drives them to the airport.

A four-seat helicopter is warmed up and waiting. They set down between the house and garden at Samantha and

Jake's. The squawking chickens run for cover, thinking it's the baddest hawk they've ever seen.

"No eggs tomorrow," Samantha proclaims.

Samantha smiles when Sarah pleads, "Come for a ride with us."

A quick cup of rose hip tea and they lift off to get an overview of Bison Leap and our newly acquired pasture of the Bar X.

Ged's distracted. He's been lost in deep thought all morning. He later tells Sarah, "I've been thinking of buying one of those nice yellow diamonds the miners are now finding in the Yukon. They aren't covered in human conflict blood like the African ones. Some tundra modification is attached to them, but other than that, they're clean." He adds, "Would you be pleased with one on your finger?"

Sarah smiled, "I was wondering when you'd realize that's our destiny."

The stunning views bring him back to the here and now. Before they land again, he's decided he'll put a proposal in front of his company as soon as he gets back to Toronto. He doesn't want to miss this opportunity! He's known both Sarah and me for many years. He knows how dedicated, honest, and business savvy we are.

Ged tells Samantha, "If there's anybody on the whole planet who can pull something like this off, it will be Sarah and Jim."

He calculates about thirty million will be a good start. There's lots more where that comes from, but this, he knows, will be all he can swing until Bison Leap shows a profit. Sarah comes near to fainting when, just before he boards the big plane back to T.O., he whispers in her ear what his business plan is. Part of this plan is that all the venture capital funds his company invests in our grand plan will go toward leasing or buying usable land, equipment, or bison to expand BL's operation. These assets will be held under one of Sarah's company setups other than the nonprofit.

When my sister relays this news to me, I twirl her in a bear hug with both her feet swinging clear off the ground, till she's much too dizzy to stand on her own.

When we both come back to our senses, I ask, "Will you head right back into town and get the law firm to set up a trust account for the veterinarians to draw on?"

The Temple Grandin school has left a return message: "We have a group of our best graduate students who will be delighted to design bison handling corrals." Sarah thinks it'll be an appreciated gesture to transfer a little money into the school's account. The pledges collected from the Chicago office are still rolling in.

This reminds us of the time, a few years before, when a new start-up electric car company set a world sales record when they unveiled their newest model. It's all in the timing, and it seems this is the right time for Bison Leap. We are on our way to putting together by far the biggest free-range bison herd North America has seen in well over a hundred years.

14. Air Miles

I'll get on a plane tomorrow for Yellowstone. I want to finalize discussions I've had with park management. We learned this park has been randomly tranq-darting their bison for many years. Not all their tests for tuberculosis and brucellosis have been negative, but the Montana bison will be the future nucleus of Bison Leap's new herd. Both these contagious diseases, like the common cold, have been imported to this continent and are difficult to control.

I was told the park would like to part, this fall, with one hundred and fifty young animals, but Bison Leap needs many approvals first. The critters can be captured the first of September if the paperwork is all signed before then. We have some talking to do.

I ask Sarah to inquire if a lady friend's public relations firm can be hired to do this job.

Sarah explains all the details to them. That frees me up to first fly to Northern Alberta and the Yukon, then on to

Austria. I need to see these animals up close and personal before any major decisions are made. There are two genetically unique herds in Utah that are claimed to be disease free. I ask for the numbers available.

The Yukon-Alberta wood bison have a few cases of both brucellosis and tuberculosis, so they will have to be carefully sorted and quarantined for at least six months. The cattlemen's association has been trying for years to get this herd exterminated, from fear they'll spread their disease back to commercial cattle. Their proposals have been narrowly voted down a number of times. There are still some people who don't want to see another irreplaceable species go extinct. Maybe Sarah and I can help satisfy everybody's concerns. We have many cards in our favor.

We enquire about locating an isolated farm in northern Alberta to hold bison for the quarantine duration. We need a place the vets can fly into. Sarah asks Temple's students to design a transportable handling system for this job. Perhaps all the handling systems should be transportable. That will save our company some expensive outlay in the future.

On my way to Austria, I set down in Gander, Newfoundland. An island near there has an old Canadian government quarantine station. It was used for cattle importation quarantine, but hasn't seen any activity for many years. I enquire if it's still available. Any animals flown over from Austria will have to land in Gander, and then be boated over to the island. It will be a hard trip for the bison, but necessary just the same. They'll need special, individual wooden crates built for the transport. We'll contract the crates built in Austria when the animals are ready. These critters are checked every year by Austrian government vets and are known to be free of all disease, but they still need to stay on the quarantine island for six months. It's the law and, from our perspective, we understand it as a good law. Nobody needs diseases spread from one continent to another. There has been much heartache and loss from that in the past, so it's best to be sure of these things right from the start.

When I ask Sarah how she's handling all her paperwork, she replies, "It does take discipline". I'm very proud of my sister and so glad we're the best of friends. I hope she and Ged marry someday, even if Ged has never been on a horse. Maybe I'll get him on one of them old ranch horses. They've all put in many years with good cowboys on their backs and won't hurt you, even if you're flopping like a sack of spuds, upside down and backwards. For sure, I'll somehow get Ged on a slow one, even if Sarah has to help me be devious and trick him into it!

15. Ranch Plans

I've been thinking lately about the small privately owned herds of bison scattered all across North America and a few even beyond. I wonder how much effort it would be to find them all and get a genetic registry set up. We might have to put a few dollars aside to get that one done, but it could pay off in the end. I'll ask Sarah to look into that when I get back home. For now, I'm really enjoying this trip and the new friends I'm meeting. They're good people, these lovers of the shaggy beasts. They have a funny way of not only looking back in time, but also of being able to see far ahead, and they are, every one of them, a hundred percent behind Bison Leap. They help make it easy, and I feel some days like I need to put rocks in my pockets to keep from bumping my head on the clouds. Life is good and yet it keeps getting better every day. I hope it stays this way forever, but even though I'm a dreamer and so enjoy it, I know I need to keep my wits or BL could get blindsided from any little thing we've overlooked. Life's funny sometimes—not *funny* funny, just surprisingly weird—so I do carry a rock in my pocket to remind myself.

In Austria, I learn that forty years ago a select bunch from this herd was sent to another hunting preserve in Romania. I figure I'd best go check to see if Count Dracula left any blood in them. To my delight, I find two hundred fine, healthy specimens. I put a request in for any of these that become available.

Three weeks on the road and now it's time for a long nap in my cabin on the ridge. It'll be good to see the family again. Maybe Jake and I can sneak away together and entice a trout. We'll take a frypan and matches in case we get lucky. It's been way too long since Dad and I had a fresh trout on a creekside fire. I can smell it cooking, and it makes my mouth water just thinking of it.

I'm looking down over the old place after I've had a quiet cabin rest and I think, with all the money coming in, we'd better reseed this hayfield. Over the years, the quack grass has got so root-bound it's choked out all the other plants. It should be loosened up and new seed planted. The bison from Yellowstone won't arrive until September, so if we get right on it there'll be enough time to get the field reworked and still get one good cut of hay. This field has been ditch irrigated from the big spring that flows up out of the ground right below my cabin. The small water ditches traversing the whole field make for a slow, bumpy ride on the haying equipment, so it'd be nice to smooth it all out and put in a pivot system. A state of the art pivot uses way less water than this old ditch system, spreads it out more evenly for better growth, less erosion, and it'd be almost no work once installed. The water will gravity feed itself into the pivot pipe, so no pump is necessary. We'll have to put in a little catchment pond in the flow-bed of the spring, some solar panels, and lithium storage batteries to power the wheels that move the pivot, and lay out some cash, but when it's all done it'll be an awesome system. The whole field has very good soil with a nice buildup of humus from many years of proper management. It also has no rocks in sight, so it'll be worth our effort and expense. I'll run all this by Dad tomorrow at the fishing hole to hear his thoughts. In the years to come, BL will need the extra hay this field could produce.

BL will have bison coming out our ears before long. I figure it'd be best to get another building to house all the batteries and electrical components and do it so we'll have enough power for everything that'll be needed here in the future. We'll get someone who knows what they're doing to come have a look. The irrigation company in town may be happy to get the work. Perhaps the boys who Da— I mean, Jake—hired to fix the fence know someone who'd like to work up and reseed the field.

The machines here on the ranch are old, small, and mostly worn out. It'd take half the summer to get it done with them, so it'd be best to find somebody who has the equipment and time to do it fast. We'll get a nice cut of hay if it's seeded before the summer sun gets too hot. It'd be worth spending a little extra to put a rush order on this job. I hope there are locals looking for work; we have lots of jobs and not enough time to do them ourselves. Sarah and I will be spending most of this summer in meetings and will be lucky even to get to sleep in our cabins once in a while. Such is life when you've made yourself wanted.

Ged calls Sarah. "The thirty mil has been released and is on its way. It'll be in BL's account tomorrow." He wants Sarah to get the cell tower installed at Bison Leap as soon as possible. He says his company has conditions for the investment, the financial proceedings of BL need to be open for scrutiny, he needs to be able to get ahold of her 24/7, and she needs to carry her phone with her at all times.

Before he hangs up, he adds, "There are other recommendations too. Can you meet me in Chicago next week to discuss them?"

16. Meetings

Sarah and I are both feeling out the deep waters, the sometimes erratic winds of opinion. We need to know, intimately, all the many points of view on the subject of wildlife and wildlands. Where each particular opinion is centered, we would like a personal rapport with each party, group, and organization even remotely interested.

The gauntlet of public opinion runs between two extremes. "Nobody has a right to interfere, in any way, with wildlife. They should be left alone to do what they know best; they survived on their own before man came along and will continue to do so. They should not be monitored, restricted, or subjected in any shape or form."

And its opposite: "The damn things are obsolete, they're in the way of progress, and they're spreading disease. We don't need them anyhow."

All these words—rational and emotional—apply not only to the big, visible, and sometimes dangerous critters, but also to the plants, scenery, birds, bugs, and—lest we forget—microscopic organisms as well. People are funny in their habitual attachments, which they assert as being knowledgeable and correct.

Bison Leap has a hard row to hoe. We'll need luck on our side if we are to have any possibility of bringing a mutual understanding to these sometimes contradictory and often closed trains of thought and emotion.

I have specific ideas of my own, but Sarah says, "It'd probably be best to keep most of them temporarily up your sleeve."

Just getting people to accept the surface of BL's proposals will be plenty for now. It would be prudent for BL to get all the visible aspects of this venture understood and accepted; the rest of the plan will eventually become universally understood, admired, and appreciated if we can get over these first big hurdles.

Sarah, Ged, and I talk all this over, via video. We agree on a number of things. Except for the grazing lease on state forest-land that BL holds in trust for the Bar X, we are not subject to control by public opinion. Of course, BL wants public opinion, as well as scientific, government, and financial institutions on our side, but we have time. It will take a few years to build the herd numbers up to the point where they'll need roaming access to more country, and even though all three of us are excellent communicators, BL needs to get a professional relations firm in on this from the start.

A reputable company headquartered in Denver might be interested. They're close, which would cut down on travel expenses, and they have an already developed understanding of the issues and area. They have smoothed out similar, although simpler, things such as this in the past and left all the involved parties with a sense of respect because of their honesty and integrity, so they are given the opportunity of taking on the job. This PR firm will send a representative to camp in the guesthouse at BL, along with a film and audio crew later in the fall to document the arrival of our first bison.

A full-length, informative, and entertaining documentary should be put together to air in people's homes. If it were made in an artistic, tasteful manner, it'd go a long way toward bringing an understanding and acceptance to our project.

Ged agrees. "Although the film isn't needed right away, it'd be best to start preparations soon."

Sarah puts effort into getting filming organized.

I keep busy with genetics, arrangements for live capture, shipping, and quarantine. It also falls to me to get the BL land holdings developed for the coming herd. Jake takes care of ranch details, but it's still my responsibility to make informed decisions.

A lot of people are becoming involved with BL; so far, all of them understand and are completely supportive of our dream. As more people come on board there'll need to be more time allotted for conversations so everyone has a clear view. This dream is about manipulation, but it is not about greed, force, or coercion. Communication will bring understanding and co-operation.

Temple's scholars have completed their map of the psychological differences between cattle and bison and are now in the first stages of design. They haul prototypes to an actual bison farm to observe animal reaction, working out bugs before developing the final BL handling system. Sarah gives them the go-ahead to send a representative to many different small bison farms to glean info on subtle inventions they could incorporate into their designs.

"Nothing like a hands-on look to see what works and what don't," she says.

It'd save a lot of time if they can pick the brains of people who've been at it for years. They still have a couple months before they need to submit final plans for fabrication.

The hayfields at BL are worked up and ready to reseed, the pivots and electrical system are on the way, the fencing is almost finished, and it's time to take a step back and admire our accomplishments. Sarah got a cell tower installed on a high ridge point. We'll be able to receive fast internet in all our buildings; cell phone reception covers the rest of this place except the bottom of one deep coulee. The fence crew built a high double line of strong heavy fence around the tower to keep the big saggy beasts from rubbing on it. In the spring, when their winter coat is starting to loosen, they get itchy and can rub the bark off a tree if there're no large boulders to scratch on. BL sure doesn't want them near the cell tower.

Too high a concentration of grazers can devastate a landscape, including trees. That would not be good for the bisons' reputation. Since about 1950, a few huge multinational logging companies have cornered a monopoly on timber harvest. They spent millions convincing people that trees need to be everywhere. They put out all the fires and the trees grew, covering the wildlands. As the century closed and the earth warmed, the timber harvesters had new propaganda for their interests.

They claimed, "Trees capture carbon and this will help cool the earth."

More trees grew and smothered all the smaller plants in the limited areas the wild grazers have been forced to take refuge into. Wildlife populations plummet because they have nothing to eat. The tree monoculture has devastated their food supply. Even the bugs, birds, and bees suffer.

I understand all the healthy smaller plants capture carbon too. They do not lock it in suspension as long as a tree does, but they recycle it, yearly, back into organic soil. An acre of mixed herbs and grasses capture as much carbon as an acre of trees in any given time. The trees are beautiful and a very necessary part of the environment, but, like everything else, they need to be in balance. Any monoculture stifles diversity (this includes everything from lawn chairs to airplanes, from insects to elephants, from grass to trees) and that is not good for any environment's health. I will do my best to encourage all things to stay in balance to enhance diversity, diversity, diversity!

Sarah plants her garden with salad greens and a few hardy vegetables. I promise not to let it dry out while she's in Chicago. I look forward to a bit of quiet time. My little cabin is intimately comfy, I have some thinking to do, and many other things I'd like to get caught up on. My spirit cries out for some alone time with the land, and it's time to honor that. I plan to sit on my porch for a couple days and do *nothing.* One of my favorite things to do is to do nothing. I've met few people who can do nothing for very long. I have a natural knack for it. I'm not lazy, not by a long shot, it's just that I like to feel everything through before I jump in with both feet. I'd rather be doing nothing than messing something up because I haven't felt it through, so nothing it is for two days.

17. Jim's Dream

While Sarah is counting money and her other blessings in Chicago, I'm counting my blessings on the porch. I have a funny way sometimes. I imagine things. I can't see the present much, except for things I can touch, but occasionally I can see the future. It's not like it's a gift—I have to work at it—but if I sit quiet with my eyes closed, I start to dream. I don't fall asleep; it's more like I get these little glimpses of things, images, like I can watch my imagination. First there will be glimpses, scenes, and then if I'm not distracted or disturbed, these single images start to form like a movie. I have to work at it, all right, but if I stay with it, it'll be like I'm creating a moving, living world in front of my very eyes. Sometimes I can even hear it, but mostly it's just visual.

Sarah's talent is different because she's more people oriented than I. She's good at seeing into people, and that's scary for me, but we do make a good team.

On the second day of my porch sit, I glimpse a woman with a little boy. Their image is fleeting but I feel love. Then I start seeing open prairie. I view it all the way from northern Alberta and Saskatchewan, south into Montana, North and South Dakota, Wyoming, Colorado, Nebraska, Western Kansas, Oklahoma, Texas, and down into northern old Mexico, then back north again, into Arizona and New Mexico, as well as parts of California, Utah, Nevada, Idaho, Oregon, and even some of Washington.

It's a beautiful land: mountains, rivers, open prairies, wind-carved rock of many shapes and colors, some of it covered with cactus, some so hot and dry not even cactus can grow. There's more, lush with grass and rolling hills, some just rocky barrens; trees, creeks, rivers, lakes, and vast green meadows interspersed with rainbow-colored wildflowers, and my heart longs for it all.

There are small villages and roads, cities both big and small—not big like New York or Chicago, but they are there. There's good, productive cultivated land, and I can see farmhouses scattered here and there. It's a very good land. Some of it challenging for man or beast, but interesting all the same. As I look, I can see the land covered with wildlife. There's an abundance of deer and elk, antelope and bison, vibrant wildflowers and plants—not everywhere, but there are many. Large flocks of wild bighorn sheep in the rough country, mountain goats on the rocky crags, a few burly grizzlies, and here's a wolf pack cleaning up the carcass of a bison bull. This bull probably got a horn stuck through his ribs by one of his sparring buddies. As I watch, the fences start disappearing, and then slowly the roads change...

I can see what looks like two transparent, parallel, round hollow snakes with peopled things zipping back and forth in them. These hollow tubes have dirt bridges built over them at close intervals for critters to pass. The houses are all still here, the villages and the cities. Some new small cities are being built... they're intriguingly different, unique... interesting...

At this moment, the irrigation guy drives up on his broken muffler quad to ask if I will lend a hand for a bit!

That is one of the most vivid and intriguing realistic dreams I've ever had, and I long to get back to it, but I satisfy myself with an old saying: "Before enlightenment you spend much of your time chopping wood and packing water; then after enlightenment you still spend much of your time chopping wood and packing water." I've had a refreshing rest and inspiring visions, so now it's time for wood and water.

The crew is hoisting the pivot sections into place and need an operator on the second boom truck. I spend the afternoon helping in the field. Tomorrow, we plan to open the twelve-inch screw valve and test the new system with gravity-pressurized water. We use a gas-powered electric generator to power the pivot wheel's rotational movement because the solar panels and lithium battery system are not completely finished yet, but it's all looking fine.

The new field seed is poking up and it, too, looks like a healthy catch. We planted a mixture—red clover, four kinds of alfalfa, timothy, brome, orchard grass, oats, and about ten percent of the total mix are wild native grasses. The seed company tried to talk us out of the native grass mix 'cause it's so expensive.

"It's difficult to harvest the seed," they said, but we wanted it anyhow, so that's what we got. I'm thinking it'll be good when some wild herbal plant seeds—some call them weeds—land in the field. I have an idea the critters will enjoy the diversity of taste and the medicinal properties of wild plants mixed in with their hay.

I ask if I can catch a ride out with one of the crew tomorrow. I want to visit the folks and maybe ride my saddle horse back up to BL. The old gelding will be happy in the small pasture between the barn and creek. I'll lead Sarah's saddle horse up too, and I want to have a better look at the retired cow horses BL has inherited. Maybe I'll borrow Jake's pickup truck and take a drive over to the Bar X headquarters for a visit.

I like these people; they're hardworking, honest, and fair. Their land has been in the wife's family for three generations, and they know just about every ranch family for five hundred miles in all four directions. They figure they know quite a few in the other two directions as well, and they do have some stories to tell. You'll never catch them bad-mouthing anybody. I love to hear about the history of this country and its people, and listening to these folks talk is better'n reading any book. I heard they're screwing new tin on their barn roof so I'll give them a helping hand this afternoon.

The country folk around here are like that: you don't show up for supper, popcorn, and a movie; you come and pitch in a bit; it makes everybody's life a lot easier and forms bonds that last forever. Besides, I want to know more about these horses and talk some about the old irrigation ditches that run out of the cottonwood creek onto the flats between

BL and the folks' place. The Chinese workers must have had a hand in digging them after they finished with the old transcontinental rail lines. Those people know how to get water to just about run uphill. They've been doing it in their homeland for thousands of years, and they helped transform this country into what it is today. Water on these dry flats will sure boost the carrying capacity of BL's range. I ask Sarah to check if the state water licenses are still intact. We won't dry up the creek, but there's a lot of extra snowmelt early in the spring that could be soaked into the ground to mitigate summer drought.

We'll make that valley green again if we can find somebody with the inclination. I ask Jake to level off a short airstrip on the long flat bench between the hayfield and my cabin. Perhaps we can hire the county road-grader operator to smooth it out after the little bulldozer has knocked the worst of the humps off. There should be plenty of power from our off-the-grid electrical system to run a string of LED lights down both sides of the strip and the fencing crew are still here, so we'll hire them to close it in to keep the critters from getting in the way of any incoming. I sure am feeling good about the way things are fitting together. As every day passes it seems like I can see my dream of the future a little nearer, a little clearer.

18. New Markets

I check with the vet crew to learn how they're making out with the genetic research of the bison lineages. The bison themselves are relatively inexpensive because most of the small herds (except the northern wood bison) are overpopulated for their limited fenced-in pastures. There's no decent market developed for them, but the capture, transport, and quarantine are going to put a hole in our bank account. Maybe Sarah has more good news?

A significant reason no market has developed for bison, or for that matter any other wild farmed game animals, is that the government health department demands all animals—both domesticated and wild—that are to be sold as meat to the public need to be killed in a federally approved and inspected facility. This is partly because, through the political lobbying of big corporations, they've managed to get a monopoly on the entire meat industry with their assurance that no unhealthy products will get to market.

That usually works fine for docile domesticated animals, but when you try to load an independent critter like a deer, elk, or bison on a highway transport truck, ship them down the road, then stand them in line at the killing plant, it's not good at all. The wild animals are so stressed out from all this handling, they're pumped full of adrenaline, bruised up, and some even have broken bones. By the time the meat gets to the consumer, it smells a bit like a skunk and chews like an old tractor tire. You'll need to get your teeth sharpened and put a clothespin on your nose before you bite into a piece of that!

We have ideas on how to change this around. It makes a whole lot more sense—environmentally, economically, and morally—to do it the way we envision. BL will start out small, working all the bugs out of our new system and helping to build a world that not only has never been seen before on planet earth, but also a world everyone can and will feel proud to be a part of.

Samantha and Jake are tired of the highway job, so Jake puts his resignation in and takes us up on our offer of looking after BL's farming and water systems. Jake knows a young couple in the village who will enjoy dedicating themselves as his helpers. BL set up a prefab cabin for them on one of the old run-down vacant homesteads along the creek. It's a pretty spot about halfway to BL. A perfect place to start a new family, especially this time of year when the grass is green, wildflowers are in bloom, and the baby birds are hatching. I ask the fencing crew to pound posts and string some wire around this couple acres on their way out from B.L.

The summer passes quickly, and there's not been much rest for either Sarah or me. We've been busy with all the preparations for the coming years of Bison Leap. Support for our new company continues to energize and inspire us. The small office that Sarah originally set up in Chicago has now moved to Denver with its expanding employees. A whole floor of office space is leased in the same building that houses the public relations firm. BL isn't using all this space yet, but judging by the way things are proceeding, it won't be long before even it will be bursting at its seams.

Sarah is sporting a pretty Yukon stone set in gorgeous Outback opal. It looks like the Milky Way on a dreamy night. Her wedding takes place at Bison Leap early next summer, just after the bison calves are due to be born. Samantha is making plans for a wondrous celebration. The little airstrip will be active for a few days.

19. Winter Feed

Jake and the young couple put up a big stack of sweet-smelling, not rained on, round-baled hay from the pivot field. They planned to cut the lower sub-irrigated field too, but because it is enclosed within its own fence, they decide it's a good pasture to let the new arrivals settle down in.

Jake says, "We'll let the pivot field grow to give the new seed a chance to get a strong root before the cold weather sets in."

We have more than enough hay to overwinter the small herd that will be at BL this year. We'll keep them close and well fed so they won't wander too far.

These first critters will teach every herd that comes after them where home is, so Jake wants to tame them by keeping their bellies full and talking to them a bit. The Yellowstone bison are familiar with people and have never been hunted, but it'll be a different story with some of the imports that are to follow next year.

The Alberta-Yukon bunch will be the wildest; more often than not every time they've seen a human they're being shot at, so it'll be good to mingle them with a quiet bunch. Perhaps the quarantine farm we've located for them will help settle them down, but they need to be tested monthly, which won't help much in building their tolerance of people.

The steel fabricator calls. He has a set of handling corrals welded up and ready to install.

I ask them, "Can you make two more complete sets?" One of which will be sent on freight trucks, to the quarantine farm in northern Alberta. The third set can be moved around as need be. These are strong corrals, and, from what I've seen, the bison move through them like they're at home. Temple sure knows her stuff, and we are more than impressed with her students' accomplishments. The fabrication company is also praised for their fine work. BL will make sure they're all thanked with a freezer full of tender bison from our first harvest.

The cabin-prefab company is commissioned to build a shooting tower at the far end of the pivot field. It wouldn't see any use for at least another year, but BL has the funds, so best build it now. We also build a climate-controlled cool house for hanging carcasses and another attached sterile building for further processing. This has industrial walk-in coolers and freezers, stainless steel counters, band saws, microwave dryers, commercial kitchen, office rooms, showers, and a separate room with cots for harvest helpers to sleep.

Sarah's realtor locates the industrial building she requested.

"It's being used now but will be available next year," he tells her.

He also has two large ranches just listed he thinks we should take a look at. Ged will be flying in soon for a visit, so Sarah will wait for him, and the two of them, along with the realtor, can jump in a helicopter for an overview.

I teasingly tell her, "If you'd learn to astral travel you wouldn't need no chopper."

Sarah replies, "Ged is afraid of that kind of flight, so I guess a noisy chopper will have to do."

20. Pemmican

Samantha—her heart is indeed blessed—is working on recipes for our new products. This is one she plans to serve at Sarah and Ged's wedding.

BISON LEAP, PREMIUM QUALITY HEALTHY FOOD

PEMMICAN

Meat from wild free-range bison,
raised on the vast open plains of North America.
ALL INGREDIENTS CERTIFIED ORGANIC
SOURCED FROM FAIR TRADE FARMS.
STONE GROUND
---BISON, raised naturally, ethically, and with considerate care, inspected and processed by certified personnel
---cocoa powder from Ecuador
---sugarcane juice from Cuba

---maple syrup from Ontario
---cooked, dried wild rice from Manitoba
---blueberries from British Columbia
---almonds from California
---pinion nuts from the mountains of New Mexico and Colorado
---cranberries from Quebec
---wildflower honey from Georgia and Alabama
---sesame seeds from Africa and India
---dried apples from Washington
---ground quinoa from Peru
---blue corn flour from old Mexico
---dried, powdered pineapple from Hawaii
---dried bananas from Guatemala
---cold-pressed olive oil from Italy and Spain
---kiwi juice from Australia and New Zealand
---dried peaches from South Carolina
---apricots from West Virginia
---sea kelp from Nova Scotia and Norway
---pinch of potassium salt from Saskatchewan
---pinch of red chili from Bolivia
---wild rose hips from Oregon
---taste of hush-um berries from Idaho
---pecans from Louisiana
---sweet nutritional yeast from Tennessee
---dried green mint from Wisconsin
Ready to eat, excellent mixed into soups and stews, or sprinkled on salads.
Tasty high protein food for athletes, adventurers, busy executives,

and/or couch potatoes.
You can't afford to eat anything less.
ENJOY! For questions or comments contact BISON LEAP
at www... DENVER, COLORADO, USA

Ged presents both Sarah and me—via email, and paid from his own personal account—flying lessons at the airport in town, to be taken at our convenience.

"I don't want you to have any excuses for not flying to meet me if I'm in the area," is how he puts it.

Ged has an idea that he might give Sarah some wings for a wedding present, but he makes me promise to keep that for his personal surprise.

Ged tells me a story... There is a bank across from his office, and one day it has a number of police cars and fire trucks parked outside. As he walks to his car he passes a couple homeless guys gawkin' and talking.

He overhears one guy ask the other, "What's going on?"

His buddy says, "Fire in the bank."

First guy says, "Somebody burnin' money again."

Second guy proclaims, "That'd be a stupid way of trying to smuggle it out."

Ged learns later what actually happened—the bank roof was getting a new coat of tar and it caught fire from an over-applied torch. No damage done. Perhaps the torch-man was distracted, daydreaming about all that cash below.

21. Chronic Wasting Disease (CWD)

A big concern reared its ugly head among government game biologists, food producers, and cattle industry representatives. Chronic wasting disease and its close relative BSE (also known as mad cow disease) could or maybe even would spread within any group of wild animals, getting into the human food chain. It was thought that animals in close proximity to each other would contract this devastating condition simply because of their so-called overpopulation. It was now known that this weird protein complex could be transferred to humans who consumed the meat of infected animals. There are a few people who, although they admit no ill-will toward the meat eaters, believe that any human who eats the flesh of animals probably already has a degenerative brain-heart disorder.

"It's a shame, but really, no big loss."

"The disease is probably for the best anyhow."

"Just karma taking its course."

"Maybe now everyone will see the light and convert to vegetarianism," they say.

Some of these beliefs are based in logic, with scientific facts behind them, so they do have growing public support for everyone becoming vegetarians, but the answers—to all the questions concerning the morality of meat eating, along with the reasoning that it takes too much space and resources to convert plant protein into meat protein—are not quite so simple.

Of course, in some countries and cultures, where the human population or use of resources have outstripped the natural carrying capacity of the land, it makes some sense for these people to be vegetarians. They are correct that four times the number of people can be fed from the same land by eating plant protein than can be fed by converting that same plant protein into meat. But do these people really have a right to let their population get so high, or use so much of the natural resources? They've displaced other species that had called this environment home. These are sentient beings that have been displaced, and so the argument of not killing animals on moral grounds is full of holes. You see, to take an animal's environment is to not only kill one animal but also to kill every one of what would have been its future offspring. That is genocide in a blind, deaf, and dumb way.

Another view, presented by both meat eaters and vegetarians, asserts that "there is much land that could but should not be cultivated for human plant food, and it'd be best left in its natural state for erosion reasons and as a home for its nonhuman species."

There are many views, and they all have their merits, but in general there's not much agreement on what should be done to address these opposing opinions. The conflict of interests sometimes gets heated; after all, it can boil down to being able (or not) to feed and space you and yours!

From the beginning of mankind's time, there's been bloodshed over territory to house and feed one's family and even now, in this time, the conflicts have not been resolved. People, even though they see themselves as much more civilized than their predecessors, are still capable of killing each other in sophisticated and ever more morbid ways, in order to house, comfort, and feed themselves.

These important and volatile issues directly affect Bison Leap's future plans. We need to address each and every opinion on a grand scale to get a mutually understood and accepted consensus in order to proceed. Of course, this need not all be done at once, but it will need to be done just the same. This is part of our original grand plan.

It's a very good thing that BL's public relations firm is onboard and able to understand all these intricacies. It's necessary to explain our extraordinary concepts in a positive, clear, concise, truthful, and comprehensible fashion, not only to the affected people in the immediate area of BL's startup ranch, but also to the general public, along with politicians, lawmakers, and economic powerhouses. Bison Leap needs help. The search is on for visionaries, communicators, and all those who can understand these intricate concepts without allowing personal biases to interfere with clear knowledge implementation. This will be the start of a whole new way of being, interacting, and living—not just for humans, but for all the other organisms as well.

Communicating is a project in itself, but everyone agrees that even though it will take a lot of dedicated time and effort, it not only can be done but it needs to be done. When it is thought through to its conclusion, it is our consensus that there really is no alternative. This is a life or death situation, not only for humans but for many other species as well! It could well mean the very existence of planet earth as a semisolid gem, rotating within its solar system as it has for incomprehensible time, rather than as dust specks within our galaxy, the Milky Way!

Some of the best medical research scientists in the world have spent years studying these abnormal protein complexes that are only now coming into mainstream human awareness. In light of the fact that the cannibalistic head hunters of Papua New Guinea often contract the human variant of BSE, it is widely believed that the closer you eat to your own species, the more likely you are to having your brain waste away. Now there is some truth to all this, but it's soon revealed that it's not the whole truth.

It hits international news. A large group of healthy vegetarians near San Diego all come down with this disease, seemingly all at once. These people have been vegans their entire lives, and most have never let even a morsel of meat pass their lips. This fact gives a whole new perspective to this devastating disease. It doesn't take the World Health Organization long to funnel investigative and research money toward discovering what is going on. If vegans can acquire this disease, then maybe it's a bigger problem than previously thought. This could turn into an epidemic!

It is discovered, by the same scientists who've been studying prions for the last many years, that these vegans have all eaten produce from a reputable organic farm in Arizona. Upon further investigation, it is learned that a month prior, some migrating geese had flown down from the northern tundra of Canada, pooping in the field where the produce was grown. It seems the protein complex had gotten into the soil, been transported systemically up into the plant leaves, and had then been consumed by these vegans. On their flight south, these same geese had eaten wheatgrass from a field that CWD-infected whitetail deer are known to frequent. It is soon discovered that this protein is common in much of the world's soils and that maybe plants naturally take it up as a sort of unconscious defense against being eaten.

"Oh my," thought some, "what a fix we're in. Every species on the planet has turned against us. The next carrot we eat may take its revenge upon us. Must we become airatarians?"

The scientists had never noticed the worldwide prevalence of this protein complex before. It is such a tiny inconspicuous particle that it'd been overlooked. It seems normally it has no effect on warm-blooded animals, but under certain unique circumstances it can propagate its ugly self. Including humans, any animals that die from this have a prolonged and morbid death.

It can't be killed in the soil. The scientists take a sample of contaminated soil, soak it in concentrated chlorine, dry it in a microwave oven till it is over one hundred degrees Celsius (two hundred and twelve degrees Fahrenheit), and then hit it with ultraviolet light. It is still capable of completing its life function.

"Damn, what is this thing?" frets one scientist.

22. Jumping the Gun

Hell, in the '90s a few meat eaters in Great Britain came down with Creutzfeldt-Jakob disease, the human variant. Four point five million innocent cows, horses, and sheep took misdirected blame. Machines dug huge pits, riflemen fired till their barrels were too hot to touch; these critters then soaked in diesel; matches were tossed.

To some, the boom of guns, fires, and terrible smells brought back atrocious memories of times elsewhere in Europe, not long past. It reminded others of deeds and forsaken places where barbarism still occurs.

We've done many terrible things because of our naivety, but we're still plenty self-righteous. Maybe this protein complex has always been here. Maybe it existed before us and will continue when we're gone. There really is no way of knowing.

Sarah, our PR firm, the vets, and I are keeping ourselves informed about what's now being discovered. This could ruin our dedicated work and put an end to our lifelong dream! The Bison Leap investors are getting worried. It is decided we must go for broke! The public relations firm suggests that thirty of the best medical research scientists from twenty different countries be given plane tickets to San Diego. The World Heath Organization (WHO) put up a lot of money too, but this could well be about the world's food supply, or lack of it, so money is no object. These specialists are given everything they need to find answers, and quickly! It's becoming common knowledge this thing is just about everywhere on the planet, probably even in the oceans. You sure can't kill it without making stardust of the whole place, so there has to be another way. Our lives hang on hopes of success!

Why it shows up sometimes and in some places and not others when it seems to be so common in soils is one of its mysteries. Another is the discovery that some animals get it, while seemingly similar acquaintances of theirs don't.

A small flock of domestic sheep and goats reside on a mountainous Native American reservation in Nevada and come down with CWD. All but one nanny goat and her offspring show advanced symptoms. Through DNA analysis it is learned this particular goat has a wild Rocky Mountain goat ancestor somewhere in her past. Upon further study, the research scientists find that even though the protein complex is within this nanny, it is not negatively affecting her. Somehow she has immunity, as do her kids!

Now we have to find out why. The researchers conclude that this nanny is "a Naturally Genetically Modified Organism." A rarity for sure, but natural mutants do occur from time to time. In the lab they prove that CWD cannot pass on its traits because of a very minute quirk in the hereditary makeup of this nanny. The scientists are not entirely sure, but they have an idea that the genetics of the CWD protein and its variant cousins may also be recent mutants. Not all genetic mutants are made by devious humans, and on rare occasions natural mutants have been evolutionarily positive, as in the creation of a new species to fit with environmental change. Usually they fizzle out on their own because they do not fit with their environment, but some that do fit in survive and prosper.

It is unclear whether these odd protein complexes are natural or manmade, but under the circumstances it is felt we really have no choice but to fight one mutation with another, so that is exactly what we do. The intricacies of the genetic code are way too complicated for all but dedicated geneticists to fully understand, but somehow these lab geneticists come up with a simple synthetic injection that passes the mutant-hybrid goat immunity on to any warm-blooded critter.

Some conspiracy theorists assume this weird complex was a sabotage attempt by ruthless forces, or at the very least an experiment escaped from a mad scientist's lab, the same as they figured the AIDS virus had been in the past. If there is anyone who knows for sure, they are not saying. Either way, it needs to be dealt with as soon as possible. Further investigation can be carried out as time allows, but for now the medics need to put all their effort and resources into stopping its spread.

Humans are encouraged to take a refined variant of this immunization. People line up for their shots. No one gets sudden uncontrollable urges to climb rocky cliffs and there are no other surprise side effects, so it's a boost for our cause of co-operation.

Bison Leap immunizes every bison that can be captured. All the cattle in North America are injected, and then every animal on the planet that can be is given the same. It takes some years but everyone agrees, it's a job well done. There are still wild critters running around that should be done, but most of these you'd just about have to kill to catch, so they are left alone for now. A few dolphins, whales, and seals are discovered to have died of CWD. An attempt is made to inoculate their species, but it is tricky work. Better tools are needed to help the ocean mammals.

The technology is developing at an astounding rate. If you go holidaying for a week, it'll take you two days to catch up on what is new on the market. If you don't want to get left in the dust, you'll have to really be paying attention! The world is changing fast. Any and every good idea spreads around the whole planet in a matter of days instead of the decades or centuries it had taken in the past.

There are those who've always proclaimed that "anyone can read the ethereal consciousness of everyone on the whole planet, so any individual can know everything that any and all people know" (sometimes called 'reading the Akashic record'), but the fact is, there are few who can actually do this. That seemed to change with the global internet. Some say the computer internet system is based on the same principles as the Akashic records system, but the mechanical computer is far inferior to the natural human system because you are depending on sensitive, easily broken machines instead of a self-repairing organism.

I remember an unorthodox teacher I once had who told us of an obscure diary, written soon after the first English sailships landed on the shores of Australia. It seems one of the sailors took leave for an extended walkabout. In time, he learned the Aboriginal language. His diary records that "the Aborigines somehow know the whereabouts and doings of all their acquaintances even though they may be untold distances apart." In his diary he implied that these people were almost as connected to each other as a normal person is connected to him or herself.

Anyhow, even though the computer is a machine it does give people the ability to change our world in a hurry. Not all the changes are for the good, but that is more a matter of people's choices than the fault of the machines. The good thing is, if there are a hundred people all thinking of the same concept, and each one of them has only one little piece of the whole puzzle, then the machine can instantly give everyone all the other little pieces, so all one hundred people have complete access to every little piece previously held in individual isolation. So that is what fuels this exponential growth in new knowledge and technology! It will be very good when people start transferring emotional intelligence with the same fervor that we now share mechanical knowledge.

23. Yellowstone to Bison Leap

So that we don't get too far ahead of ourselves, let's get back to the bison. One hundred and fifty—mixed sex, big calves, long yearlings, and bred two-year-olds—arrive on the first trucks from Yellowstone. The Temple corrals and handling system had been erected only the week before. Its first use is fluid, without flaw. The film crew sets up cameras to record the unloading and the young bisons' first investigations of their new fenced-in pasture. The cameras take a chopper ride to film a bird's-eye view of all the present lands of Bison Leap. This is the start of an entertaining and educational film that will prove to be so useful in the near future. The crew stays a few days to capture playful antics, especially of these comical calves, on film. They also film the buildings and add narration back at their studio. They return many times to film as things progress. The little airstrip is well used.

The bison settle in quickly to their new home. They walk the fence looking for a way out, but lush, nutritious grass, shade trees, and the flowing creek soon convince them this is a welcoming place to stay awhile. It's time to leave them alone for a few weeks and let them recover from their capture, the vet checks, and the truck ride. Not one of them has been injured, and that is mostly attributed to Temple's great design. The corral system is situated so the bison have to walk through it, from the field to water and back again. This accustoms them to the corrals, making it so much easier to sort or check them when that needs to be done.

No one is ever to harass or chase these animals, so it must be learned how to move them in such a way that they calmly and willingly go where we human guardians need them to. These are to be the nucleus of the new herd, so any habits or attitudes, both good and bad, will be symbiotically transferred to the next arrivals.

I can easily sit for hours watching the bison moving about or being as lazy as I.

It is nearing time to invite the public to enjoy our herd. First, Sarah invites the neighbors and village folk. When it seems people are satisfied as to the safety and professional manner in which Bison Leap is being run, invitations are hand-delivered to all the schools within bus range. Two smaller four-wheel drive buses are purchased and parked at Samantha and Jake's place. Our buses together can carry the occupants of one large bus. Schools are invited to send one large busload of students at a time, with two drivers. The drivers transfer their passengers to our small buses for the narrow dirt road to Bison Leap. Every visitor is provided a free lunch from our guesthouse kitchen, a choice of drinks, a fifteen minute video, and an easy walking tour of the grounds and bison herd. At first, the lady of the young couple who'd been hired to help Jake with the irrigating and farming is recruited to make lunches and give the guided tour. It is soon realized that another cabin needs to be built to house a full-time employee for this busy service. An extra room is added to this cabin, equipped with a first aid post. The air ambulance service in town allows us a priority connection through BL's communication network, just in case.

These bison are not aggressive animals, except when they have new young or if you meet an old bull on a trail, where you'd best step aside and let him have unrestricted passage. The visitors are never allowed to wander on their own, but it is good to be prepared for any unforeseen event. It could happen that a medical emergency arises unconnected to BL or our bison herd. Bison Leap wants to be known as an enjoyable, informative, and safe place to visit.

24. Quadcopter

A business investor with his teenage son drives in one afternoon for a visit. This investor has heard about BL and is "always on the lookout to diversify," so he thought he might get acquainted with our new operation. His son brought a quadcopter to get a bird's-eye view. It's a small, very fancy toy.

"Can I fly it over the field where the bison graze?" he asks.

"I'm not sure about that thing," I tell him. But the young man gives me a demonstration, in the yard by the guesthouse. It flies silently and its pilot has excellent control.

This young man equipped it with a minute video camera that relays back to his control monitor. The monitor has a viewing screen and two joysticks, all in miniature. This is suspended in front with a shoulder harness. He also installed a two-way speaker-transmitter that he enjoys playing tricks on his friends with.

I allow him to fly it as long as he promises not to spook the herd. The young man's dad and I watch awhile. Then we get involved with business talk. The young man, Doug, unnoticed by either Doug's dad or I, wanders down closer to the field. I notice the bison forming a group, and then as one they move toward the corral. This is odd; it's not the time of day the bison usually go for water.

I say, "I'd better have a look."

As Doug's dad and I get closer, we notice Doug near the fence. We are too far away to hear clearly, but it appears Doug is animated. The bison are being talked to through the speaker on the quadcopter. This is new and very interesting. We watch without interfering. I can see that Doug is not a herdsman, but he does have amazing control of his talking flying machine. The bison are responding to the noises they're hearing. I hear a low growl once in a while as the copter darts this way and that behind and around the sides of the herd. When the bison near the corral, Doug has the sense to back off, letting them go through in ones and twos.

We walk up beside Doug and I make eye contact.

This young man has a very guilty look on his face; he is sure he's in trouble.

I smile and all three of us stand still while the bison drink from the creek.

When they've had their fill I ask Doug, "Can you bring them back?"

Doug comes to life; his copter darts into the big cottonwoods. It's moving faster than I can keep track of it! We hear a bark and a growl come from the trees. The bison start to move toward the corral. I signal Doug to slow down, and we again watch as the bison calmly make their way through the corral and back into the big field. Doug's copter darts back into the trees to make sure none have been missed. Two more come out with the copter hovering above and behind them. These two join the rest of the herd, and Doug brings the copter to rest on the ground near where we stand. I am intrigued, impressed, and have many questions to ask. We wait awhile, by the fence, to make sure the bison are not upset, then head up to the guesthouse for a bite and chat. I want to know more about this flying machine.

Doug explains that he bought a kit for the main body of the quadcopter, then sourced the video camera-viewing screen and speaker-mike system from bits and pieces from many different suppliers.

"Can a GPS be mounted on board, and how far can it fly?" I ask.

Doug replies, "If you can dream up what you want, it can be built. It'll just take time, money, and help from my friends." He explains that he knows tech people at Google, and he also knows an old engineer just retired from Apple who is setting up a little specialty company of his own.

Doug continues. "This quadcopter has a limited flight time because it can carry only so many batteries and they need recharging, but a fixed wing drone can go just about forever and the two can be made to work together." Doug also states, "If the cell tower is used to boost the signal, then both the fixed wing and the quadcopter can be controlled from many miles away. A slow-flying bi-winged drone could be configured to carry, deploy, and recharge a quadcopter."

My gears are smoking with the possibilities. This needs further investigation.

I've been playing in my spare time with the retired ranch horses. They all get a good brush, have their feet trimmed, and I deworm them. After checking their teeth I figure they range between twelve and twenty years of age. There is one with a calcium bump on its right knee, another has a back leg tendon stretched a bit from a previous injury, and the oldest one has a sag in its backline. I take short rides on them all; they are soft mouthed and responsive, like good cow horses should be. You could ride any one of them with nothing on its face, just lean forward and they move out, shift your weight back and they stop, twist your body slightly one way or the other and they respond by turning for you. They'll make fine guest horses. Other than the three with minor problems they'll all put in as many miles a day as any greenhorn will ask of them. Even the two injured ones and the swayback will easy do a five-mile day. I'll round up some saddles and tack for any guest who wants to ride.

The old barn gets a new tin roof and a few other repairs—new windows, new doors, energy miser LED lights throughout, a rodent-proof tack room, and a chicken coop out back with a large run.

Sarah smiles. "Nothing like farm-fresh eggs."

25. Late Fall

An early morning chill in the air warns of winter not far off. The cottonwood leaves transform from their sun-absorbing deep green to paler shades of yellow. Early flocks of Canada geese honk their passing on their way farther south, some of them soon to get their names changed to Mexican geese. People are generally a possessive bunch. No one seems to realize the geese give no allegiance to any governing authority except for their motherland, planet earth, and its freely given guidance. They are a lot like the bison in that respect.

I like fall as much as any other season. It's a busy time of year preparing for the coming winter. It is also a time to appreciate all we've accomplished. We've done amazing things in our short while at Bison Leap. Everyone involved feels pride in the way things seem to naturally fit into place. We have a good company—co-operative, energetic, progressive, and insightful. BL is attracting associates who are visionaries with a well-developed sense of tolerance and support. There is no competition among ourselves other than each individual demanding the best of their own personal abilities. We talk a lot, sharing ideas and dreams of a future we are creating. Things seem to get done with little effort, and it's heartening when true compliments from peers flow freely.

The bison are doing well. They've made this place their home, but Jake notices the grass in the creek pasture is eaten down and ready for a rest.

"It's time to open the gates and let the bison wander a bit," he says.

"I hope they don't go far," I answer.

We'll have to keep an eye on them somehow. It's good we have a few horses around, but I can't quit thinking about young Doug's quadcopter. We invite him to Bison Leap to discuss possibilities.

Bus tours are winding down for the year. The young lady who's been giving tours decides she will move to Denver for the winter to help in the office there.

An old cowboy who rides some for the Bar X breezes in one afternoon to have a look at our wild critters. Some call him a saddle-tramp, but there's no welfare recipient in this guy. He's just independent and likes to move around a bit. New country is always whispering to him.

"I never been around bison much, but think I might like them shaggy beasts," he says to Jake, adding, "I'll keep an eye on them wanderin' buggers this winter, if I can camp in the vacant cabin."

He asks for "a tin of snus, a little fuel for my old truck, and a bag of groceries once a week. That and the cabin is all the pay I'll need to keep track of them bison." He has his own saddle. "I'll give them horses attention and exercise. You won't have to worry none about them buffs gettin' through the fence and inta the next county."

26. Copters and Drones

Doug asserts, "I had enough schooling," and would like to come stay in BL's guesthouse till he figures out his career options. He just wants to fly his quadcopter. He's been playing with electronics since he was old enough to walk, and he's good at it. He and I will spend a lot of time around the guesthouse table. Mostly it's Doug educating me on what can be done with electronic flight as it concerns Bison Leap's future needs. After much discussion between Doug, Doug's acquaintances, and me, a plan emerges.

In one of the office rooms at BL, we will set up a large high-resolution viewing screen. This will be hooked, via satellite, to real-time imagery of a vast area on and around BL's range holdings. When you're looking at the screen it will appear as if you are actually flying or hovering in person. You can look down from high up or come close to the ground, you can move miles in seconds, or stay suspended in one spot as long as you like. You can focus close enough to see a songbird sitting on a fence post or broaden your perspective to take in many square miles at once. GPS will show, on the big screen, exactly where you are in relation to the landscape at all times. This will all be routed through our cell tower so it'll have no lag time.

One quadcopter or many at once can be sent out to observe, investigate, or herd the bison. A copter can carry, all in newly developed miniaturized versions, GPS units, infrared, radar, ultrasound, video, and audio systems. They'll relay all this info through the cell tower, back to the monitor-control room at the office, along with their remaining flight time and travel distance, predicted by the remaining battery charge and wind conditions. These copters will show their positions on the screen and can superimpose their view as an overlay.

Doug figures he can reconfigure and reprogram microchip scanners to send back identities of specific animals or search for a particular one that needs locating. Doug's friends are working on getting the copters to override human control, self-returning to the nearest charging station when their batteries run low. They also have a start on getting smallish bi-winged drones, which can be used for longer range flights, to carry a number of copters, releasing and accepting them back as asked for.

These drones will be capable of quick charging a returned copter and readying it for another flight. It won't be needed for a few years, but all this real-time data and control could be relayed to Denver or anywhere else by simple upgrades to our existing system. Everything will be made of separate components, so fixing or adding will be quick, simple, and cheap. The old saddle tramp chuckles, shakes his head, then turns, and with his bowed legs slowly shuffles away when Doug tries to show him how easy it is to operate.

He reckons he likes his livin' flesh-and-blood horse better. He tells Doug, "A horse got his own brain and senses. Once he gets to know what you want of him, he'll show you things that no machine ever could."

Doug will have to teach other pilots how to operate this complicated system, and he already has a young lady in mind. I have to admit, she's much more than a little cute. Melinda seems intelligent, but she's too young for me. Besides, Doug's sweet on her. Maybe Melinda has an older sister?

The old saddle-tramp—his friends call him Here-n-There—warns Doug and Melinda, "You best not be spyin' on me when I'm waterin' a tree, getting rid of some beans, or havin' a nap on a sunny sidehill, or we be findin' out if these flyin' contraptions can duck lead."

He's smiling when he says it, but just the same, Doug and Melinda take note and Doug assures him, "We might check on you once in a while, just to make sure you're not dead yet, but other than that you'll have your horse and solitude all to yourself."

Sarah has been doing plenty of flying between Toronto and Denver processing stacks of documents, political hob-nobbing, attending everything from public meetings with the relations firm, Native Band council meetings, as well as realtor, law firm, and accountant meetings. She is busy getting things all lined out for BL's future. Sarah and I talk lots on our cell phones, trying to keep informed of all the other is up to, but so much is happening now that only the highlights are discussed. Sarah has found a few nice places that we will have to look at.

Ged and Sarah are happy spending time together in their Toronto apartment.

Ged told Sarah, "I could do most of my family business just as easy out of Denver, or Boulder. Maybe see what's available there with a view and an easy drive to the airport."

He believes Sarah would like Boulder better with its cloud-piercing mountains, and it's only a half-hour drive to Denver international, then three hours to Toronto, if that's where he's headed. A lot of his family's business is in the U.S., so it'll really be no inconvenience for him to move from T.O. He'll keep his little apartment so he can have a place there a few days a month. That'll be much easier than hauling his luggage back and forth and it'd be a good place for his friends to lay up if they are in town.

Sarah finds an apartment in Boulder, two big bedrooms, a windowed office, hardwood floors, a large balcony already set up for a therapeutic garden, awesome views, and close to downtown. It has private underground parking with a quick charge station for Ged's electric Roadster, and a greenbelt bike and walking trail just out back. She'll use the smaller bedroom for her office, and Ged can have the bigger office. With the mountains close they will be good skiers by winter's end. Sarah has her small plane license now, and she wants to ask Doug or Melinda to teach her how to fly these quadcopters.

It's a short flight from Boulder to the little landing strip at BL, and Sarah comments, "It'd be nice to spend more time in my cabin."

Jake finds a decent gravel seam a ways down the dirt road a mile from her cabin.

Sarah asks him, "Can you get your old road buddies in to screen enough for the landing strip, get it hauled, spread, and graded before the ground freezes too hard?"

A smooth, dry, and solid year-round strip would make visiting much easier. From what she's been hearing, we'll need it for those fixed-wing drones soon anyhow. She can rent a small plane from the local airport anytime she likes, so it's all rather convenient. Sarah likes to hear the stories Here-n-There gets to telling when he's in the mood. Maybe she'll ride a little with him before it gets real cold. She has not spent much time with the bison and wants to get to know them better. Sarah says she could learn a few things from Here-n-There—a couple days on her horse with the cool fall breezes, grass, and bison would be better for her spirit than a fancy spa. She likes to be in closer touch with the land than what can be had out her office window, an electronic big screen, or the windscreen of an airplane.

27. Possibilities

Doug, the three Bison Leap vets, and I, along with a group of the medical research scientists who'd worked on the CWD campaign, meet for a conference in Santa Fe.

We asked the scientists, "Can you develop a complete vaccine combination that could be injected, along with a microchip, as a one-shot deal?"

The vets, after seeing the control that is possible with the quadcopters, are thinking it might be possible to vaccinate and microchip all the new calves on the range without bringing them into the corrals for handling. This would be the ultimate way of protecting them without the detrimental stresses of interfering. The vets and Doug have talked about the possibilities.

The discussion goes: "The infrared sensors can detect any warm-blooded animal from afar. As the copter gets closer it can single out an animal that does not have a bar code chip already implanted. With a critter located, ultrasound, guided by video imagery, could pinpoint an injection site behind the shoulder blade, then the chip—with an attached vaccine—could be fired with high-pressure air (like a miniature Amazonian blowgun). Of course, the copter would have to be nearly silent.

"Perhaps a special ultra small copter would need to be developed specifically for this."

"It would need to be fast and get in close, without disturbing the animal. All the critter would feel is a little fly-bite-like sensation."

The real challenge is this: "Can multiple vaccines be combined into one small capsule without jeopardizing their effectiveness, and then can a capsule be attached to a microchip in a dart-like projectile?"

It will be tricky work to accomplish all that, but these specialists, Doug included, will collaborate to figure it out.

Like everybody involved with BL, they know that *where there's a will there's a way.* If this can be accomplished, it'll make it so much easier on the bison and on us too. The herds can stay out on their calving range with every newborn calf vaccinated and identified without having to be rounded up, sorted, separated, or injected by hand.

In days of old, instinct, predators, and natural immunity helped keep the herds healthy, but there are now international diseases around that these critters have no resistance to, and even in days past there were often massive die-offs from naturally occurring pathogens. We need our herds to be healthy and productive with a minimum of predators or human interference.

This is heady stuff. The conference ends with everyone feeling adventurous and lighthearted. Doug, with a devilish twinkle in his eye, tells me on our flight back to Denver, "Perhaps Here-n-There might like to be first for a copter-injected vaccine/chip combo."

I remind him, "You better make sure you're well out of arm's reach when you mention it."

Ged's business is expanding to include information and research on investors who might be interested in the long-term goals of the great and prosperous Bison Leap corporation. His office now fills the previously unused space of Sarah's communications floor in the relations building. Bison Leap administration is considering acquiring the whole office tower for our fast-expanding needs.

One of the things the veterinarians and I are a bit concerned about is, other than the very remote herds in the Yukon, most of the remaining bison have a small percentage of domestic cow genetics in them. The DNA analysis is showing that it is common for the seemingly wild bison to have varying percentages of domestic cow parentage in their lineage. Our concern is that this percentage might be enough to encourage some bison to cycle year round rather than the normal late-summer, early-fall cycle. If it becomes a problem, those that cycle out of season could be sorted out and shipped farther south where that will not have such a detrimental effect on calf survival rates. Bison Leap should prepare for this and acquire rangeland in southern Texas,

Arizona, New Mexico, or northern old Mexico. The realtors in Albuquerque, Tucson, El Paso, and Chihuahua are asked, "Be on the lookout for suitable bison grazing land."

The small herd at Bison Leap has been making rounds on the range. They've investigated every ridge and coulee but they come back near the farm fields every few days for a visit and a lick of the molasses mineral blocks we set out for them. Here-n-There follows them around like he's their momma. Doug and Melinda keep an eye on them from above.

The old cowboy figures he knows every trail of Bison Leap "better'n he knows his cabin kitchen." He suggests, "It's time to open the gates and let the herd wander onto the Bar X creek pasture. It'd be good to let 'em get some trails made so when the big herds start arriving in the early spring they'll all know where home is."

After talking it over with Jake, I tell Here-n-There, "Go ahead, but I'd like a daily report via cell phone." The cell phone that he's now encouraged to carry.

Doug has started to shorten Here-n-There's name.

He says, "That old guy don't need such a long, formal name," so he starts calling him Here when he's close and There when he's far away.

The old saddle-tramp likes Doug's sense of humor, so he lets it stand. Soon everybody catches on, and so he becomes Here, sometimes, and other times he becomes There.

Here notices something. "When a snowstorm is on its way those shaggy beasts don't start bawlin' for extra food like a cow does. They eat a lot before the storm gets to them, then when it hits they turn face-first into the wind, and go into a semi-hibernation."

Their heartbeat slows, their body temperature lowers, and they just stay that way, conserving energy till the storm passes. He watches them in over two feet of snow.

As he tells it, "They just lower their big ole shaggy heads till you can't see their ears no more and walk along munchin' grass like it's summer." His voice changes when he talks of the bison. He'll never admit it, but everyone knows he has a soft spot for these critters.

In January, a chinook blows in, it gets sunny warm for a few days, and then the temperature plunges. The weather change forms a two-inch hard ice crust on top of deep snow. A person can walk on top of this crust without leaving so much as a footprint. It's time to open up the haystack and start feeding. It's cold enough that Jake's little diesel crawler doesn't want to start. The oil in its crankcase is thick as molasses, and its diesel fuel is gelled so it won't flow. Jake left it for us to use, parked in a work shed attached to the back of the old barn. We start a fire in the wood-stove and let it thaw out for half a day, hook the charger to its battery, and it fires right up. There breaks a trail to the herd with Jake's crawler, while Doug and Melinda use their copters to start the herd for home. The bison are fed on the pivot field for two months till the snow starts to melt, and then they want to wander again. Plenty of hay is still left in the stack and the field is covered with good manure.

Jake says, "It'll grow fine next year with all this bison fertilizer."

The herd has a few three- and four-year-olds, so Bison Leap will get some calves late spring after the grass greens up nice. Traditionally, the wild grazers have their young late spring, early summer. Besides being pleasant weather, this gives the unborn calf or fawn an extra boost of nutrients, from fresh greens, in their last burst of gestation growth, and gives the mother rich abundant milk for her new young, while the growing plants give the young a secure place to hide from watchful predators.

28. More Bison

The vets have eleven hundred bison, all under five-years-old, health cleared and scheduled to land at Bison Leap this coming spring and summer. The arrivals will be spread out a few truckloads at a time because they need to be held in the fenced-in creek pasture till it's sure they've recovered from their trip and settled down. The pregnant ones will arrive first so they can calve at Bison Leap. A few weeks in the creek-field, then they'll be turned out to mingle with our original bunch before the next loads arrive. Doug and Melinda will test their vaccine-chip copters on any new calves born. Doug will move in front, to distract the bison with his copter, while Melinda sneaks in beside the animal with hers to administer the shot.

Melinda is an ace pilot. She's actually much better at moving and working the bison than Doug because she has a subtle sense of knowing just where to be at the right time. It is all in reading the animal before it actually makes its own mind up. Once these bison have their minds set to do something or go somewhere it is very difficult to convince them otherwise. The trick is to read their body indications before they're in motion and then make it seem, to the bison, that they have other plans. This all needs to be done without upsetting or exciting them, and it takes a lot of experience to develop that skill. Even people who've done it lots sometimes don't seem able to get the hang of it. Melinda is a natural herdswoman. She grew up riding on her family's ranch. Since she's been knee high to a grasshopper she spent most every day of her summers horseback with the cowboys moving cattle around. She does not understand the flight technology like Doug does, but when it comes time to fly to the herd, Doug hangs back a bit and lets her take the lead. They work well together, these two, and are fun to be around. Sometimes, when Here isn't There, he sits with them in the control room, not because he likes quadcopters, but just because he likes the company of these two energetic tricksters.

Doug spends more of his time co-ordinating research and development of the flight machines, while Melinda is the specialist at actual flight interactions with the herd. They will both teach new recruits the fine art of flight, but when it comes time to work with the bison, Melinda will take over the teaching.

Sarah and I get little time to visit with Gram and Gramp, but whenever Here gets There he stops for a coffee and keeps the old folks informed of what's new at BL. They're tickled pink and say they'd like one more visit to the old place as soon as the calves hit the ground. That will be at Sarah's wedding, and then Here can move his bedroll into their old ranch house because they wouldn't be needing it anymore. Here-n-There's cabin can again be used for the guest guide if she'd like to move back up for the summer.

The county road-grader man suggests, "Maybe I ought to widen the road out a bit for all that traffic that'll be stirrin' up dust gettin' there this summer."

Jake says, "It'd be a shame to tear up too much grass, but for safety reasons we could widen it a little and put in a few pullout spots."

We build a booth at the entrance gate, near where we keep the buses parked. It has a sign-in-and-out register, pamphlets on bison etiquette, and safety recommendations. Doug installed a transmitter at the gate to notify control of any incoming visitors, and he can send a drone down to have a look, or a copter to give them 'a talking to' if need be.

Sarah is finding, through realtors, word of mouth, and interested contacts, plenty of good bison-raising land stretching all the way from the northern Canadian prairies through the U.S. and into northern Mexico. Except for a bit of southern land for any critters that cycle out of season, we are only interested, for now, in land close to Bison Leap's home place. It wouldn't be good to get spread out too thin without having more infrastructure in place, but the possibilities seem almost endless.

Wyoming itself is easily capable of supporting over three million head of bison, and it will be a long time, if ever, that

Bison Leap's herd will be anywhere near that number. Sarah files all this land and contact info away and concentrates closer to home. There are possibilities of incorporating more land already bordering BL, but we have many details to work out. Her pilot's license is handy to view and visit some of these vast areas, and she's beginning to see a pattern in the lay of the land. It interests her the way the rivers run and the many contours of the high country.

Sarah wants to convince Here-n-There to fly with her, for him to see what he feels will be a natural way for the bison to wander without fences or forced herding. Where will they be at what time of year if left to choose on their own? These are questions for the old saddle tramp who's come to love the bison. The highways have changed the migration routes wild critters once used, but it's interesting just the same. This old cowboy is about as shaggy as the bison beasts, and he thinks a lot like them, so he'll be able to see and tell—if we can just get him up in the air—where the next best place to expand the grazing range for BL's critters will be.

Meeting Ged is one of the best things that ever happened in Sarah's life, and soon they'll be officially committed till death do them part. She is feeling like they will be together long after that. They have a supporting love that is rare these days, and she now thinks she knows how Mom and Dad feel about each other.

The bison wander up and down the creek all the way from Samantha and Jake's place to as far the other side of the pivot field as they can get. They never seem to be in a hurry, but they can cover a lot of ground with their steady grazing pace. They stay together in a loose-knit, spread-out fashion.

Sarah notices when flying over that a bunch of twenty-five or so have separated themselves from the main herd and are off on their own.

Here says, "They's the ones gonna calve soon."

Doug sends a copter to read their chips; sure enough, the whole bunch is all mature cows. Melinda records a few minutes of a bison cow's stomach skin jumping from the soon-to-be-born calf kicking inside. Sandy-colored calves will be on the ground soon. The mother cows want a little peace and quiet away from the main herd.

Doug thinks it'd be nice to have a small hangar off the side of the runway.

Sarah votes yes on that. "It's time the air machines have a place out of the wind and weather."

29. Sarah's Wedding

At the end of May, twenty-five strong healthy calves are birthed within two weeks of each other. All from twenty-six young cows. We are pleased to see this group of bison have all cycled together like nature intended. These calves are on their wobbly legs in twenty minutes, bunting for a warm mother's tit. One calf was born dead, but the cow pushed him out without assistance. I want to do an autopsy on that calf, but the cow stands protective, never leaving its side for three days. By this time, it's stinky and only the coyotes, ravens, and eagles are interested. They are attentive moms, these bison.

A verbal warning circulates with an addendum attached to the guest pamphlet. "Do not go anywhere near these cute calves, or for sure the cow will tromp you into the ground." Old Here-n-There rides up close to them, but they've become familiar friends. Doug's copter microphone sometimes picks up There's voice jabbering away to them critters. He won't get off his horse close to them, but they don't mind him riding by and saying hello.

For Ged and Sarah's wedding feast, Jake and Samantha sacrifice a chunky two-year-old bull that Here says is "too lazy to make a good herd bull." We save the tenderest, juiciest cuts for the barbecue and the rest of it Samantha makes into pemmican.

Ged's parents fly down from Toronto for the ceremony, all the neighbors from miles around attend, and many of Sarah's and my friends make their way out from distant cities. Most of the business associates of Bison Leap are on-site, and other than a few clouds that drift by, the sun shines all day. The little airstrip is a busy place.

Just as the ceremony finishes a small plane flies over, dipping its wings. It makes no noise, and everyone holds their breath, suspecting the pilot has lost his engine, but it banks under power, makes a tight circle, showing off with wiggles, dips, and steep climbs, and then lands smoothly on the little airstrip. The pilot climbs out, bows, ties a wild-rose pink ribbon on the door handle, struts himself down to the loaded table of food and begins helping himself. He seems to be enjoying the juicy bison steak. When Sarah walks by, he says (with a mouthful of tender bison), "This bison tastes as good as you look." He winks, kisses her on the cheek a little close to her ear, and with juicy lips wet. Sarah recoils, blushing, but then he hands her an envelope with Ged's note on its front saying, "I Love You." Sarah rips it open and on the inside she finds ownership papers filled out in her name.

Ged has given her a fresh off the line electric plane, recently made in France by the Airbus company! The interactive electronic owner's manual tells her in its robotic voice: "We cruise at one hundred and sixty miles an hour, have a range of four hundred miles, we'll take off and land on the shortest of runways, our stall speed is less than forty miles an hour, I'm almost totally silent and can be recharged in under one hour."

Ged smiles and laughs when Sarah takes off running up the hill, to inspect her new baby.

Doug will need to get an upgrade on the charging station in the hangar and make sure a bay is left open for Sarah's new pet; he checks into those new artistically designed wind turbines being developed in Denmark for cloudy windy days. They have vertical spiral veins rather than the long propellers that are usually seen. They don't make that unsettling *woop-woop* noise, and the flying critters are not as harmed by them. It seems that when small birds or bats pass close to the propped turbines the contrasting difference in air pressure between the windward and the leeward sides bursts their tender eardrums and they fall dead shortly after.

Doug can get a turbine installed up on the point of the hill near the cell tower. Depending on how often Sarah will be dropping in for a charge. But Doug doesn't want to be short on juice. Maybe he'll get a few extra solar panels installed too, and more lithium storage batteries.

30. Newborn Calves and Visitors

With new calves on the ground and the ranch's reputation as an inspirational outing, Bison Leap expects a lot of visitors this summer. We welcome our guests and go out of our way to assure everyone is in awe, or at least content and smiling. The second busload of school visitors this spring is from a reservation clear across the other side of the state. It's too far for them to make the return trip in one day, so they've brought basic camping gear to overnight somewhere along their route.

I suggest that they set up in the yard space near the old house, but warn their guardians, "Do not let the youngsters wander because of the very protective and potentially dangerous new calf mothers."

"Our home reserve has a small herd of bison, and all the kids are well aware of the dangers," the teacher-guardians explain. This puts a whole new perspective on their visit and makes it easy for everyone to relax and enjoy each other and our surroundings.

Sarah happens to be here this day and is delighted to help the kids feel comfortable. Their teacher-guardians organize the kids' camp in a big circle, and they build a cozy fire in the middle with their tents set well back. The open space between the tents and fire is for social gathering. They seem very interested, not only in Bison Leap's way of looking after our big shaggy beasts, but in our plans for the future. Sarah, Doug, Melinda, Samantha, Jake, and even Here-n-There, along with a few other Bison Leap associates, and I, mingle with the visitors. When the sun starts to set we gather around the campfire, trading stories late into the night. The kids talk of old legends, bygone days, before the Europeans discovered there was a continent here. They tell of how the big herds of bison wandered free, and of the hunts for winter food, where every able-bodied person from their tribe gathered in a confining circle around a herd and stampeded them over a cliff, killing enough to keep the village well-fed for the coming cold winter months.

It was a cruel death for the bison, but it had to be done if the indigenous people were to live through the winter. They told of how, when the Spanish brought horses, they learned to ride and could now travel to chase the bison, killing them from running horseback with spears or arrows. This brought fresh meat to the village more often than the old hunts, but when the bison ran from the hunters, calves got trampled or separated from their mothers, and the herds would be scattered and confused. They also told of when the steel rail lines were being built, how the riflemen would kill hundreds or even thousands of bison and leave them, horrendous, in a stinking mess to rot, sometimes cutting out their tongues, layering them with salt in wooden barrels, or maybe taking the hides to freight them back to towns far away. The big free-roaming herds were long gone now, and the kids ask, "What does Bison Leap have planned?" The youngsters seem genuinely interested.

Perhaps this is not just a holiday for them. All BL people in attendance are asked by the kids' teachers if they will explain, to the kids, a little of their day to day jobs. The youngsters are especially thrilled with Doug and Melinda's talk, and a hands-on demonstration is planned for the following day.

The kids are excited and sleep is far from their minds, but the teachers insist, "Get to bed, as it's been a long day and you will need to be wide awake tomorrow if you want to fly a quadcopter!"

The kids scurry to bed, whisper and giggle for a while, then fall into silence.

Sarah and I, two of the kids' teachers, and an old white-haired man are left around the fire.

"What are the goals of BL?" a teacher asks.

I tell of my dreams and visions while the teacher listens attentively without interruption. When I finish, the other teacher asks Sarah how we intend to accomplish such a feat? As best as she can, without going into a lot of technical legal jargon, Sarah explains BL's plan from a business perspective. Again, the audience is silent, listening attentively. Everyone now sits in contented silence, enjoying the night air, the dancing of the fire, and the presence of each other's company.

The old man, whose two long white braids hang nearly to his waist and who came on the bus with the kids, hasn't spoken all day; he smiles once in a while, and I notice he sometimes gets a faraway look in his eyes. Now he clears his throat, and asks if he can speak, then sits silent again.

"We will be honored to listen to your words," Sarah tells him, and we all move a little closer to hear the almost distant sounds that flow, rumbling deep from within his depths. A solitary tear runs down his weathered cheek when he tells us how pleased he is to have met us, how honored he is to have heard our words, and how proud he will feel if we honor him again with our presence at the Grand Chiefs Council, to be held at Cheyenne, this coming August.

Sarah and I both gasp for breath, our hearts beat loudly in our ears, and our chests swell with a pleasing warmth.

"Yes, yes, of course we will be there," Sarah answers at last. "Would you mind if we bring a few of our helping associates?"

We all say good night, for the kids will be up early tomorrow, and make our way to bed, except for the old man, who sits by the fire, alone, a while, before he turns in.

Early the next morning I ask Here, "Visually pick out another nice young bull, and recruit Doug or Melinda to identify him by his chip so we can find him when the time comes."

I call Samantha to make sure she has enough of the imported pemmican ingredients left over to do another whole animal. The commercial kitchen in the fourth building is seeing use sooner than we imagined. Sarah calls the office in Denver to fill them in on the night, and asks that they start preparations for the Grand Chiefs Council in August.

31. Pinion's Sounds

The kids wake at the soft light of dawn and soon have their fire crackling, anxiously awaiting this coming day. Doug has readied a half dozen small, simplified quadcopters for occasions such as this. They have basic cameras but none of the other more expensive features of the working copters. Melinda and Doug have an active day planned for the kids, but they will have to take turns, only two kids at a time: one under Melinda's guidance and the other under Doug's. The pivot field is chosen as the fly area. It's close, has no obstructions, and its perimeter fence marks the flight boundary. The kids are surprisingly talented; some are better pilots than others, but they all say it's like playing a video game, only for real! One copter brushes a cottonwood branch, and then bites the dust. Doug has spares and he'll be able to fix this one, so no real harm done.

A little girl, who is near the last to take her turn, is a sensitive pilot. She whispers in Melinda's ear, "Can we fly to the bison?"

"Right after lunch, come to the control room," Melinda whispers back, as she slyly points toward the big building.

The little girl warms Melinda with her smile, kisses her lightly on the cheek, and hop-skips away.

After lunch, Sarah takes all the kids, except for this little girl, up the hill to show them her silent airplane. Then they will hike up the creek a ways before it's time to board the buses. The little girl—whose parents named her Pinion, because "She's small and oh, so sweet"—races to the control room as soon as her classmates have left.

As promised, Melinda waits for sweet little Pinion. When they are seated at the control console, Melinda explains, "We have a special job to do." She tells Pinion about the tender young bull they will find and identify, shows her a little of the complicated sensors on the working copter, and sends it for a warm-up around the field.

With Pinion in rapt attention, Melinda flies it high over Sarah and the other kids, then heads out to the herd. Here-n-There is camped on his horse a ways back from the bison, and Melinda swoops in close 'for a chat'. She is always careful never to come up on him from behind and always waits to see his wave before approaching too close, but this time he's waiting patiently for her.

They 'talk' briefly and then Here points out a fat young bull on the far side of the herd. Melinda is instructed to fly across the herd and Here will guide her with his cell phone, letting her know when the copter is above the chosen bull.

When Melinda gets the "word" from Here she records the bull's chip code and then zips back to say "goodbye."

It is Pinion's turn at the controls. This copter is similar to the ones the kids flew earlier but is much more sophisticated. It has a camera, chip scanner, audio, radar, ultrasound, and infrared.

Melinda instructs Pinion, "Take it easy, because Doug will be upset if his favorite copter gets broke," so Pinion does exactly that. She flies it slow over the range, up over ridges, down through coulees, brings it back over the control building, and then high above the trees she heads up the creek.

"Can we find the new calves?" Pinion asks.

Melinda gives her the go-ahead signal and off she flies. At first she climbs high, pauses, then looks all around. Pinion can see a small group two miles away, almost hidden from view on a flat green bench. It looks like it has its own small water spring. Pinion, with her sharp eyes, can just make out the little sandy-colored calves near the bigger bison. She darts closer for a better look.

Still high above them, she clearly sees the calves. Pinion's eyes sparkle as she smiles and glances at Melinda; it seems okay, so she slowly lowers the silent copter; the bison cows and their calves are lying abstractly, calmly enjoying the afternoon sun. Pinion inches her way down till she is five feet above the ground and a hundred feet from the nearest calf. Melinda has been much closer many times, and as long as you go easy the cows do not seem to mind. Pinion stays motionless, hovering, scanning with her camera.

A minute later, a cow jumps up and, without warning, she charges the copter, coming fast! Melinda doesn't know why—perhaps Doug has been teasing them again, or maybe the cow is simply having a bad day—but the mother bison is covering ground fast, and in another second she'll have a horn through one of Doug's favorite copters! Melinda takes her eyes off the screen and glances at Pinion. Pinion hasn't flinched at the charge. The cow is fifteen feet away now, and she puts on her brakes, skidding almost within touching distance of the copter; she quivers a little, then stands still. Melinda again glances at Pinion; she hasn't moved her control sticks and the copter is still stationary. Melinda notices Pinion's mouth is changing shapes and her throat is vibrating slightly; the audio light is on but no sounds can be heard other than the cow's deep breathing. Melinda does not want to speak for fear of exciting the cow, but she motions to Pinion to lift up. When Pinion is hovering, safely, one hundred yards above the bison, Melinda asks, in a dismayed but quiet voice, "What happened?"

"Sorry, I didn't mean to upset her." Pinion looks at her with big sad eyes.

Melinda is baffled. "Why did that cow stop?"

"I had to stop her; she surprised me. I forgot how to make the copter move, so I made sounds," Pinion explains.

"What sounds?" Melinda had heard no sounds.

They watch the cows and calves a bit longer, before Pinion brings the copter home.

Melinda wants to know about the sounds—she heard nothing and doesn't understand what Pinion is trying to say.

"You've done nothing wrong," she assures the young girl, but Melinda does want an explanation because she's never seen any bison, ever, stop a charge once they've started.

Pinion is only five, almost six, and she's not used to telling stories, especially to big people, but because she likes and trusts Melinda she talks. She tells about the time when she was four and the big black dog chased her. She was in an open field a long ways from her house, and the starving dog came to bite her. She knew it was too far to run and the dog was mean and fast, so she froze and made sounds in her throat that stopped the dog! The sounds hurt his ears and he went away.

She practices sometimes on her brother's horse. She can "wake him up or put him to sleep, make him shake his head and go away, make him come or stay where he is. It's like talking but different."

The land of her home reservation is almost the same, except for a few dusty dirt roads, as it was hundreds of years ago. The government built them houses and there are not as many wild animals around as there used to be, but there are still some. Like all the other kids in her village, she is never told not to wander, so she often does. In her excursions, she gets very close to deer and the few bison that roam her reservation. She's spent many days practicing her sounds on these critters, for fun, just to see what they'd do. She likes these animals. They're her special friends, and she's learned many things from observing them.

"Every animal is different," Pinion explains. "I can make lots of sounds for different animals and for different reasons. No big people can hear my sounds and only a few of my friends can, but all the animals do, except for some that are really old. I made a bear go away from my berry patch last summer with a special sound, and he never came back!"

Melinda gives Pinion a warm cuddly hug and asks her, "Will you tell your story again to a special friend?"

Melinda then calls me and demands, "Please hurry to the control room!"

The kids have to board the bus soon, and this is important news. Pinion is shy with me but Melinda coaches her, so she talks a little about her sounds. Melinda tells her she will tell me the rest.

"Can Melinda and I visit you someday at your home?" I ask this wee girl. "I promise I'll ask Doug to make a little copter for you and bring it when we come."

Pinion kisses me lightly on the cheek and runs for the bus, but she turns back and whispers, "Come soon."

I am absolutely spellbound as Melinda tells Pinion's story in detail. I ask to hear every word again, and then we call Sarah. Melinda has to tell the story for the third time!

I decide the copter we'll ask Doug to make will have both video and audio, and a console light enough for a wonderful little girl to carry. It will be presented to her in a shockproof carry case with her name in bold print and a hand drawing of a bison cow and calf imprinted on the case front.

Not only do I want Doug to get started on Pinion's copter soon, but I also ask Doug to do a little research to find the best sound experts available for consultation and ask them if they have time to spend a few days in eastern Wyoming to hear things that will amaze them. Doug is instructed to assure any expert interested that they will be well compensated for their time.

Doug thinks about this awhile, and then suggests, "Perhaps we should involve the public relations office to locate sound specialists that can spend time with Pinion before the audio engineers take over." This will need some delicate human finesse and perhaps the first step would be to send someone like a singer, a throat specialist, since Doug isn't sure but he thinks the engineers will be a little much for the young girl.

"We should explain to Pinion's parents what we want to do, and perhaps the old white-haired Chief can put a word in for us," Sarah suggests, adding, "I will fly there myself in a few days to talk with him."

The relations firm is consulted on how to proceed with Doug's suggestion, and Doug gives his audio engineers a heads-up. Sarah talks this all over with Ged to get his professional opinion, and we will proceed from there.

32. Melinda

Melinda vaccinates and implants the new calves with the blowgun injector that has been recently developed at Bison Leap's request. Ged is getting orders from both private business and government agencies for this new tool and its projectiles. He helps set up another company to manufacture and distribute it. This will be a very useful source of income for BL, and because our name is on the products it also helps give us worldwide recognition and respect.

Doug can outfly Melinda with the copters, but because he's not inclined to learn the subtle art of "reading the bison," the job of injections falls solely to Melinda, except with the occasional spooky animal, when she'll ask Doug, "Help me. You distract them with your copter."

There are twenty-five calves from the first herd to do and another two hundred from the early loads that arrived this spring. Melinda can easily handle these, but next year there will be at least five hundred calves to do, quite possibly a lot more. Melinda really loves her job, and she is not one to complain, but the vets have recently informed us that every bison needs a yearly update on their vaccine shots. Each shot needs to be recorded with its recipient and all records kept up to date. The calves need to be located, injected, their codes recorded, and cross-referenced to their dam. Most of this recording is all done automatically with computers, but it still takes time and she has many other jobs as well, so somehow other prospective pilots need to be found and trained. These prospective pilots do not need outstanding people skills, but they will need to be able to read animals well, be fluent in computer operation, and be very co-ordinated with the flight of the copters.

Our Denver office is asked to locate young people who have grown up working livestock, are computer literate, and who would also like to learn flight. They also need to be willing to relocate to the ranch. Melinda imagines that someday flight control and deployment could be headquartered in an easier to access place, but for now her ranch console is fine.

Here-n-There talks about the herd, how we have way more bulls than what is needed or desired. Each bull can easily cover twenty cows during mating season.

"If there's more bulls than that, they spend their time fighting," he adds, "with injuries and death a result. Besides, the extra bulls will be taking up space and eating pasture without any benefit to the herd."

BL accepted more bulls than we needed for breeding purposes just to get the females wanted, but it is now time to think of sorting them out. There meanders on horseback through the herd, visually inspecting them, keeping his eye open for any unneeded bulls that could be harvested. We decide that only bulls over two years of age, those with injuries, or those with obvious defects will be chosen. Melinda or sometimes Doug hovers to identify the coded chips and record any that Here selects. That complete, we will have a count on the obvious numbers, and then if more are needed, There will select ones he deems to be of lesser quality. In the end, BL wants to be left with one excellent quality bull, over age two, for every twenty cows. The other bulls (except for those under two) will go for meat.

We also decide that in future, any animal—cow or bull—that is showing signs of inferior reproductive abilities will be taken from the herd. These inferior traits would, if left to nature, eventually eliminate themselves, but that could take hundreds of years, and it will be advantageous to all concerned to scientifically expedite the process. To do this properly takes a lot of observation and knowledge, but BL is up to the task.

One thing I want to see figured out is how to take a blood sample in the field without disturbing the donor. The blood sample would be matched to the chip, DNA'd for parentage, checked for disease, and any mineral deficiencies in a pasture could be addressed with supplements. Knowing the DNA parentage of a calf will also indicate which bulls are superior and let us know if any individual bull needs to be culled because of sterility or genetically passed-on defects. Sterile bulls will show themselves with no calves on the ground.

I ask if Doug and Melinda can figure out how to take blood samples with the copters. If so, then roundups, corrals, and stressful handling will become a thing of the past. The animals could be allowed to happily wander without detrimental interference, they would be healthy and productive, the range would be utilized without fences, and more meat per acre could be produced with much less effort, expense, or environmental impact than what is done on today's farms and ranches. This all adds up to dollars in the pocket, and that is what will build a positive, sustainable environment not only for man, but also for beast, flower, bird, and bug.

33. Lights-Out

By Melinda and There's count, forty-two bulls over two years of age should be culled this fall, maybe more if fight injuries occur; the one cow that birthed a dead calf is forgiven this year, but her chip record is updated and if it happens again the computer will red flag her for meat. There's one young bull and two young heifers with leg injuries. These will also be taken.

We intended to bring the herd in every October for vaccinations and to sort out the ones for slaughter, but the quadcopters have changed our way of thinking. We are discussing that it might be possible in the near future to take blood samples in the field, and if that were so, then it might also be possible to cull selected animals without bringing in the whole herd or disturbing them in any way. That is something worth thinking about.

We resign ourselves to bringing in the herd this fall and sorting them through Temple's corrals. Disturbing the bison with a round-up is very stressful for these freedom-loving animals. Separating, sorting, and confinement are not things the bison take to lightly, not to mention the time spent on our parts. Perhaps next year we will find an easier way.

We will use the tower in the pivot field for an expert marksman with a silenced rifle to kill the forty-two selected bulls. His target is small. Even though a bison's head looks big, his brain is quite tiny—about the size of two little oranges stacked one on top of the other. The marksman will need to hit this precise spot without fail. No exceptions. No excuses. The chosen critters will die calmly while munching on good feed and melt to the ground, as if they went to sleep. No fuss, no struggle, no pain, and no adrenaline. They'll be fine-tasting, tender animals.

Doug asks his team of engineers to work on a tiny vacuum tube projectile with a short needle on its nose that could be tethered to a copter and reeled back with a blood sample. We name it the Moskito. Doug is also intrigued with another interesting suggestion: another small device, fired again with a burst of highly compressed air, only this time with a small diameter projectile with a detonation tip designed to blow after an inch of penetration. The detonation need not be very large if the accuracy is precise. The guidance sensors have to be as good as or better than the sensors used to implant the microchips. This is to be used for culling and will need to be able to hit a gently moving Ping-Pong-ball-sized target at thirty yards. A machine accuracy capability of fifty yards would be better, but with a good pilot thirty will suffice. If Pinion's sounds can be used to calm or mesmerize the animal, then the cull projectile could be much smaller because the sounds will allow a pilot to get in close, feet rather than yards, without disturbing the target. Could Pinion's sounds also be used for the Moskito and vaccine-chip injections?

"This thing definitely needs to be licensed, monitored, and locked away when not in use," says Doug. He calls it Lights-Out.

We realize that if we get Lights-Out operational we will be able to kill animals when they are in their prime, probably late summer, wherever the animals happen to be. This poses the problem of transporting them back to a butchering facility.

"Could the Lights-Out copter work in tandem with a large air balloon to lift the heavy critters?" Doug asks the engineers. "Could you think on that one this winter?"

But for now we have other pressing tasks.

34. Licensed Facilities

Bison Leap's facilities have passed the inspection and paperwork approval and are now licensed—by state, federal, and world health authorities—to process meat for public consumption. These approvals are granted partly because of BL's outstanding contributions during the CWD campaign. These agencies are also impressed with our accounting and record-keeping as far as health, cleanliness of facilities, and business transparency are concerned. Inspectors are encouraged to visit BL at their discretion and convenience. The inspector's job is to monitor all public food producing-handling facilities, but we make it as easy as we can for them to visit us, as they are experts in their field. When treated with the respect they deserve, they are most helpful with suggestions and insights to make our job easier and our product as safe, health-wise, as humanly possible. It is all hands on deck to process the forty-two animals, and a few other hands need to be found to help as well.

Jake digs a large compost pit above and beyond the pivot field for the grassy stomach contents and cleaned ground bones of the butchered bison. In time, this compost will be used to help fertilize the fields. The inedible parts from the carcasses are preserved frozen for now, but once the edible meat is processed it will also be dried, ground, then sold for pet food, except some that is kept on hand for dispersal in the coldest weather and at calving time to keep the scavengers' and predators' bellies content so they will not be as interested in harassing the new calves. The bison hides are salted, dried, and shipped to tanneries and then go for shoes, car seats, and furniture coverings.

The choicest cuts of steak and roasts from the tenderest animals are frozen for shipment to consumers and the rest, which is most of the meat, is made into pemmican according to Samantha's well-received recipe. This year's processing is all done at the ranch. In the coming years, only the preliminary drying will be done on-site, to reduce transport weight; then the products will be further finished at the bigger facility in town.

Sarah has not been using her cabin much. She suggests that Doug and Melinda might like to move in there. Sarah can stay at the guesthouse the few times she overnights at the ranch. It's a short flight to head back to Boulder in her electric plane. Almost as quiet as a glider in the air, it has no emissions, and it costs close to nothing to recharge from the sun's energy. Her airplane and Ged's Roadster are similar, except Ged's car has four wheels that work best if they maintain a grip on the ground, and Sarah's plane has two fans that love the freedom of the skies.

Sarah has a heartfelt meeting with the old white-haired Chief and the engineers now work on sounds that Pinion has taught them. They are being challenged to program their computers to convert a normal human word into a sound that only an animal can hear. The computer needs to interpret the meaning of the normal word and then translate it into an inaudible sound, with all its subtle inflections and innuendos, so that the operator will only have to tell the animal what is wanted (as if the person is talking to another person), but the animal will be hearing sounds that have meaning only to it. This is complicated stuff, but if they get it right it might be used for many different applications.

The audio engineers hope Pinion's ears remain sensitive enough for her to guide and correct them for a few more years. They assume that when Pinion reaches puberty, or maybe even before, her ears will desensitize and she will lose this gift. They work as fast as they can, in case they are right, for without Pinion's guidance they will be stumbling in the dark and may never be able to attain the subtle variations or the intuitive talents she has.

The Grand Chiefs Council is coming up soon. The relations firm and film crew complete a half-hour film to highlight Bison Leap's objectives, and then Sarah and I will answer any questions the Chiefs have. This is an important meeting, and we are so glad we have plenty of Samantha's pemmican to distribute there.

35. Elk Tracks

At the end of the elk tracks, Sarah and I saw on our first ride up the creek last year, stand six healthy adults with three new calves. They are proud, majestic beasts, and because BL cannot allow hunting near our buildings, these elk have become tame. They are part of the attraction for visitors, but they are fast becoming a nuisance. The five-foot fence around the hayfield is no deterrent to them, and although there are only six, Jake says these elk have trampled enough hay to feed fifty bison this winter.

Sometimes they are seen on the airstrip. Sarah aborted a landing one afternoon for fear of a collision, and the white-tail deer that hang out along the creek bottom have nibbled down to nothing every plant in her garden.

BL does not want to build eight-foot fences all over the place; that would be expensive, would go against our natural freedom philosophy, and besides, those fences are down-right ugly—but *something* needs to be done. Doug is given permission to train these critters, but it's suggested we should vaccinate and microchip them first. Once we start on the training, the copters won't be able to get close. It's a shame to harass them, but at the moment it'll be for the best.

The elk are easy enough to chip, but the skittish whitetails prove a challenge. Melinda is the pilot who gets the whitetails, and she does the mule deer while she's at it. The fish and game department are interested in this. They'll be able to monitor them through our system without capture or radio collars, so they are quite pleased.

Doug is now ready to start the training. He makes irregular checks of the areas of concern, and if there is a trespassing critter he swoops in to "growl them" out of the area. It is a little harder to do at night, but the copters are equipped with infrared so the warm-blooded critters show up on the monitor. The copter's radar and sonar alerts the pilot to possible collisions with hills, rocks, or trees. Doug is having his fun, nipping at their rumps, but it takes time and it makes the sharp-eyed and sharp-eared critters afraid of the copters. Everyone realizes a different solution needs to be found.

Some progress is being made with Pinion's sounds, and Melinda is testing the preliminary prototypes, but they have a ways to go yet before they'll be satisfied with the results.

The Grand Chiefs are honored with Bison Leap's presentation at the Council. They are in awe of BL's accomplishments and inspired by our future plans. They ask to be kept informed of all BL's proceedings and hope that a BL spokesperson can be sent around to tribal schools and village meetings to inform and educate those who will listen. The Grand Chiefs will do everything they can to "help prepare BL's trail."

BL's stocks continue to climb because of the excellent work our PR people have been doing. The firm passed its previous clients on to its associates and is now dedicating its time and resources toward BL's goals. Most of the PR employees have invested in BL, as has the firm.

Sarah located another large tract of land east of the home ranch. Its far boundary is the Green River; between its near boundary and the home place is only a short flight. A large ranch is in between the two places, and when she finally convinces Here-n-There to fly with her, he points out obscure trails the bison would use, if given a chance. With a few fences removed, the lay of the land is perfect to join the places and Here advises Sarah to "buy that in-between place, no matter the cost!"

If these vast plains are managed as they could be, we believe the great Serengeti of Africa will be outdone by the splendor that is possible here!

Sarah calls a meeting with all the investors to solicit their approval. The present owners of this in-between place are not in much of a hurry to sell. But they do have school-age kids, and because of the distance and road conditions into their ranch, their kids have to board in town during the school week. They suggest that perhaps BL should buy them a good place with easier school access and make a trade.

36. Here-n-There's Walkabout

Here and I get to swapping stories sitting around the fire pit one night.

Here says, "I got a long one for you, Jim." Then, after a quiet spell, he proceeds. "One spring, long ago, when I was still half full of piss and vinegar, I points my good buckskin south. We ride for months, campin' under the stars every night, wherever we happen to find ourselves in the evenin'. Come near fall, we's all the way into old northern Mexico. My buckskin is gettin' a little trail weary, and so is I. One mornin', near the big blue Pacifico, we come upon a neat an' tidy hacienda. They have plenty of well-fed cows and their horses are all fine fleshed, well-bred animals. One of the vaqueros takes a likin' to my fine buckskin, and I know he'll treat him good, so I part with my fine horse and I sell my saddle too.

"In a few days, I'm on a coastal freighter bound for eastern Argentina. I don't like this rockin', rollin' ship much, especially when we gets down around the south tip of Chile and we gets sideswiped by a cold howlin' storm, blowin' north off the ice of Antarctica. In between gettin' seasick and wishin' for dry land, I keep busy helpin' the crew and afore I knowed, we's docked in Buenos Aires. After I help them Spaniards unload that monster ship and fill her up again, I take a small riverboat up the Rio Paraná. I disembark at Rosario and ride for a month, helpin' some gauchos round up a big herd of snortin', tails-straight-up-in-the-air horned cattle.

"Them gauchos is sure fine horsemen, but they ride them old high-backed saddles. Back home we call them damn things bear traps 'cause you can't get out of them if you needs to in a hurry. I's scared my bronc will stumble chasin' them wild cattle across that rough ground, and I'll be stuck in that high-backed contraption, so's when we get enough cattle gathered to fill the trucks they has comin', I takes a slow, rattly train west. We crawl up the east side of the Andes. You know, Jim, them's some mighty high jagged peaks. We make it over the top and start headin' down, back toward the Pacifico agin. I'm sure glad we's over the top 'cause they's not much to breathe way up there. I figure that engineer drivin' this train is about plumb light in the head, 'cause we's pickin' up more'n enough speed comin' down some of these steep grades that places I figure we's about to fly right off the track and be floatin' right alongside a condor on them switchback corners. We make it to Santiago near the coast and I's glad of that, but I ain't ready to point for home yet.

"I had enough of wobbly, cold, wet, and windy seasick ships and I never been on one of them airplanes afore, so

I gets me a ticket all the way across the big blue Pacific to Auckland, New Zealand. I must've hit her the wrong time of the year 'cause I's there more'n two weeks and it never lets up rainin' once. I figure to get outta there before that island lifts anchor an starts floatin' off like that ship I didn't like so much, so I buys me another ticket to someplace I can get dried out and warmed up in.

"Next I know'd I lands in Sydney, Australia, with them there kangaroos and wallaballabies. I don't take a hankerin' to cities much 'cause it seems you ain't welcome anywhere less'n you got money to spend. Not like in the country where you do about anythin' you want and it nary cost ya a dime, less'n you want somethin' store bought, but it weren't more'n a couple days an I gets lucky agin an catch a ride with a fellow pullin' one of them I-ain't-stoppin'-for-nothin' long-heavy road-trains, all the way across the dusty outback to Darwin.

"That outback is sure some hot, dry country, and just about everythin' there wanna bite, scratch, or poke a fella, but I sure enough got warmed up an' dried out. The speed that truck-train traveled we stayed ahead of our dust cloud alright, but most everything in our way became scavenger lunch. When we finally rolls into Darwin, I buys that driver and myself a good hot meal and a few pints, maybe one more than I shoulda, but after dehydratin' on that long stretch of outback, that good cold Aussie beer wet our whistles with its fine taste. Then I wanders, walkin' a bit crooked-like, along one of them slow, lazy rivers that flows out brown, right into the deep-blue Timor Sea.

"First driftwood log I come too I's gonna sit a spell an' rest my full belly, an' maybe have me a peaceful nap. I's just about to plunk myself down when this log wiggles, gets up on four short legs, an' starts after me. Damned if it ain't one of them big ole saltwater crocs and he seems a mite hungry too. I can tell you for sure, I weren't sleepin' on this beach. I looks around some for a week or so, an I's startin' to miss this country agin, and my money I saved was dryin' up a bit, so I thinks I better start hightailin' it for home.

"It's six of one or a half-dozen of the other whether to go back easterly the way I come, or keep pointin' west an' right clean around this whole grand earth, back to home. I opt for right clean around and that's what I done. I stop off in Austria partway, and have me a good look at those Alps that everybody makin' so much talk about. When my belly's full and I have a few good beer they looks pretty enough, with clear rivers and all them little green farms scattered all across the mountainsides, but when I's thirsty an hungry I figure the mountains round here is just as nice, and maybe some of them is even a mite prettier. Besides, everybody round here talks bout the same's me, so most days, if'n I tries a bit, I can find somebody to jaw with some.

"I soon buys me another ticket and the next solid ground I touch is New York. I gets more'n a bit lost there, tryin' to get from the airport to the train station. I musta wore a half-inch off both bootheels walkin' them many miles on hard cement. My ears is about deaf from all them car horns afore I find the train station. Almost seems like there's always somebody in somebody else's way and those folks ain't a bit shy about complainin' about it, or lettin' everybody know how many important things they gotta get done right now. I have a little time to do some rememberin', while I was wearin' down my bootheels. Some of the things I seen and heard that I kinda wished maybe I never seen or heard reminds me of another story I've been known to tell a time or two, about rats in a barrel, trapped; they wait, semi-dazed, until their captors pressure them beyond tolerance. Then, because they have no other recourse, they lash out at each other till few remain. But best we save that story for another starry night fire.

"I come prid-near straight home after I gets outta the Big Apple. I never have a hankerin' to be in a big city, on a jumbo airplane, or an ocean boat since. I knows I like my horses an' my old-rusty-rattlin'-truck, but I's glad I gots some idea how big an' grand is this pretty earth, and I's also more than a little glad an' proud to be sittin' right here, around this fire, with you, Jim. Can't say's if'n I ever had better company."

Here's story had kept me entertained; I was tickle touched, and that was enough storytelling for one night.

After Here goes for an inline flight with Sarah in her electric plane, he begins to get 'whisperings in his ears'. He talks it over with me and asks if we'd be all right calling him There for a spell. He'd like to take the two best horses for a walkabout. He's not sure how long, but he'll "be back for the buff harvest."

First, he rides over to the Bar X headquarters for a visit, and then he rides north till he hits the mountains; he turns east by southeast and follows the foothills till he comes to the Green River. Camping along the river, he meanders south till he figures he's about due east of the home place. He lingers a few days just to savor the sights he seen, and then heads for home. He's been gone a few weeks and maybe this has been his last long ride, but his spirit is light and he has great hopes for the future. He visits some of the old ranches he rode for in the past, telling stories to friends he's not seen in years. Other than opening and closing hundreds of gates in all the fences he crossed, he has an enjoyable trip.

There praises the bison every chance he gets and teases his friends for "still being slaves to them needy domestic cows." He invites them all to "stop by Bison Leap and have a look at some critters that'll let you take a holiday whenever you like."

Here is happy to be home again. After he pulls the shoes off these two good horses, turns them out with the bison for a well-deserved rest, he carries a soft chair down by the creek, and under the shade of a big cottonwood he sits, communing with the creek as it gurgles by. No one disturbs him and he's content for a few days.

Doug smiles when he says, "That old man sure knows how to whittle away the time," but of course, he has no way of knowing what is going on in the old saddle tramp's heart or mind. Here helps with the bison harvest, then he goes to sleep.

I notice an owl, hiding from the light of day in a thick spruce down by the creek, and then I hear a crow *caw, caw, caw*, and it brings back the memory of a dream I had a few nights before...

I'd been lulled to sleep by the soft hooting of an owl who perched himself in a nearby ponderosa pine. In the shortness between night and early morning, a noisy crow woke me from my dream. I can remember bits of it, but it seems the crow scattered it into disjointed pieces.

In this dream, we float in space, suspended on the twilight side of the moon.

Here whispers, "Look, Jim. Look at the earth."

I can see this whole blue-green planet, alive with a light, aware of itself. And then another voice, resonant, benevolent, not someone I can see, but mesmerized, I listen.

I hear the voice coaxing me. "Look closely. See the vibrant lines of light surrounding her! She's alive, a sentient being, but see those broken lines? She's in trouble, Jim!

"These broken lines are chaos, created by the accumulated negative thought patterns of the many suicidal humans on earth. Together they have power.

"These life-lines hold her circular, spinning predictably, helping to keep things constant, vibrant. If more lines break, the earth will go out of round, wobble, shaking off Earth's organic life. This has happened six times in Earth's history. Life has had to start from almost nothing and build up again. This is totally unnecessary. Earth is now in a precarious state. You can help change it, Jim. Give people a reason to live, help them to have positive thoughts, connections, feelings of aliveness.

"Their positive energy can heal the earth! You got to try, Jim! Remember your dreams! ... We'll help you..."

There are more details, but the urgency of that crow has distracted the connection and I can't get it all.

Melinda finds There, in his bed, with a peaceful face, like he's dreaming of vibrant new grass on a sunny spring day, but his undomesticated old heartbeat is now, only *memory*.

We dress him in his favorite well-worn clothes, wrap him in a newly tanned young bull bison hide that I had gotten specially made for a bedspread, and lay him in the back of his old rusty truck for one last ride into town. We take him to the crematorium, mix a pinch of Samantha's best pemmican with his ashes, and with fluttering hearts and blurry eyes, Sarah and Melinda fly him high, on a cloudless breezy afternoon, and let him drift over the grasslands of Bison Leap.

Melinda sets his empty unglazed clay urn on an ancient boulder near the fire pit. That was one of his favorite places to be when he wasn't out wandering. As I build a wood fire in the pit, I *remember*. When Here-n-There first showed up at Bison Leap, I built a big fire in this same pit. He looked at me with questioning eyes.

"White man build big fire, sit way back. Indian build little fire, sit up close." I built lots of smaller fires after that.

We gather around the cozy fire. Melinda voices what we all feel.

"We've been blessed by this man's presence. We'll miss you, you shaggy old tramp."

We also know Here-n-There will forever whisper to us on the wind, smile at us with the sunshine, and be in the vibrant blades of growing grass that pop up every spring for the earth's critters to eat.

I look at Sarah across the fire. I haven't seen such sadness in her eyes since right before I punched that boy Derin in the nose, such a long time ago. Sarah lifts Here-n-There's urn from the boulder and sets it gently in the fire's center. She sobs.

"We release you, old man."

When the red coals heat the urn, it cracks into many pieces. After the fire cools, wet from our warm tears, we each pick a piece of unglazed clay. I set mine in front of the little mirror resting on the mantel above my cabin fireplace. Sarah picks two pieces. I notice later, Sarah keeps one on prominent display in her Boulder apartment; the other she glues on the inside of her airplane windscreen.

I park Here-n-There's old truck on the next ridge over from my cabin. It's funny, the bison make a well-worn trail to that old truck, and to this day they still enjoy rubbing on it.

37. Sarah's Story

Sarah speaks at the native schools and presents the PR firm's film. The students are skeptical, proclaiming, "We'll have nothing to do with any white man's business."

"They don't play fair," and "They change the rules as they go."

She tries to change their minds with a little story.

"They are as many as the stars in a clear night sky, and each has the strength of a grizzly, the speed of a falcon, the eyes of an eagle, the stamina of the best young bull bison. They can hear and see each other on opposite sides of the earth, they can move like a panther through the night, or fly to the moon where no bird has ever gone! They have the brain of the fastest computer, they can focus on the smallest insect from a hundred miles away, or see the whole planet at once, as if they were holding it in their hands, but their hearts are sometimes as hard as winter granite and the sharpest arrow launched their way will shatter and fall useless to the ground, so they are our masters, and we must not antagonize them. But... *that does not imply that we cannot have a say in the world we will help them create*!"

This seems to get the kids' attention. They listen and decide Sarah is correct, and they give their support to Bison Leap.

Doug helps with the bison harvest. After loading forty-two heavy beasts onto a wagon with the tractor loader and hauling them a few at a time through the hayfield to the hanging shed, Doug huffs, "There's gotta be an easier way."

The hayfield is flattened wherever the tractor has gone and it's been slow, tedious work. He sure doesn't want to be doing that out on the open range with five hundred or more beasts.

Half-jokingly, I make an odd suggestion in passing. "We need a big balloon to lift and haul these critters."

"I'll do some research this winter to see if that is possible," says Doug.

No point in selectively killing bison scattered all over the many miles if they need to be gathered with a slow, bumpy tractor that squishes all the plants everywhere it goes. Besides, Doug likes the idea of another flying machine. He doesn't think much of slow, cumbersome balloons either, but maybe he can put a motor on one.

It doesn't take long for Doug to get something done once he puts his mind to it. In a few weeks, he figures he has a solution. He discovers, with the help of the internet, that a well-known multinational company has recently developed airships for hauling heavy freight in roadless environments. These ships are made in all sizes, from one-man minis to monstrous things that can lift and carry the biggest of heavy equipment. They can be fitted with lightweight rechargeable lithium batteries to power their small control impellers, and are set up to be fully integrated with the latest remote and/or onboard pilot controls. With lithium-powered electric motors, they are as quiet as the quadcopters and can be charged with BL's existing system. He puts together an information package and turns it over to BL's administration.

Doug's dad, Dave, has always been curious about BL's business and now, after being kept informed by his son and doing investigations of his own, he is suitably impressed. He liquidates a good portion of his interests in other companies and is now a substantial shareholder in BL. He prides himself on being able to get a foot in the door of a good thing before it becomes common public knowledge. He tells Doug that he feels this is one of those rare opportunities that only a fool would pass up. Doug is glad he'll be seeing his dad more often now, even though his dad keeps nagging him to "smarten up and marry that girl." His dad is a little old-fashioned that way, but even so, Doug knows he is right.

Doug tells Dave about some interesting news he discovered online.

A time ago, between the great wars, the leading scientists of the day had been working on discovering renewable energy sources—one being fusion, the other fission. It was reported that the scientists were leaning toward fusion, but the money behind their research and development demanded they develop fission instead. With fission, an extremely terrorizing bomb can be made. The authorities really wanted, saying they needed, this bomb, so all the research on fusion was shelved in dark, dusty vaults.

Fission is about splitting atoms, which releases huge amounts of direct-able energy, but it also radiates an energy that kills or mutates every organic cell it contacts. This detrimental radiation, at the time, was deemed to be an acceptable risk because of fission's other energy benefits. After the bomb, many large electrical generating facilities were built. Over the following years, these nuclear generators gained a bad reputation for occasionally malfunctioning and contaminating our environment.

There seemed to be no other alternatives to producing the huge amounts of energy needed. Some suggested burning coal, but it is understood that if you live near a coal-fired generator, you will get lung cancer from breathing the emissions. Another alternative is large water dams, but they too have adverse environmental effects. There are wind and tidal turbines, solar panels, and geothermal generators, but these are also inadequate for various reasons. Can you imagine what the birds will do if all our ocean coasts are lined with big windmills?

It seems most people have forgotten about the old research concerning fusion.

Doug explains. "Fusion is not about splitting atoms, it's about pressing atoms together so they fuse together into one.

That's exactly what happens from the massive gravitational pressure in the center of the sun. This fusion releases many times more energy than fission does without the long-term detrimental radioactive side effects."

So what is happening now, that Doug wants to give his dad the heads-up on?

"There're folks who've rediscovered the old forgotten fusion research. They're now in the process of developing a fusion reactor. These fusion reactors, because they are relatively safe, can be made in small semi-portable units and can be set up wherever heat or electrical energy is required. These, when ready to market, will change the future of planet Earth! Anyone who has a hand at bringing them into production will be well rewarded indeed!"

Dave thanks his son for this advice and says he'll look into this interesting new development. If it is as incredible as Doug suggests, Dave wants in on it. He'll do his own investigation, and if it looks promising he will back the research and development as best he can.

Doug reminds his dad, "When this generator comes online I want one to help keep my flying machines charged."

38. Company Growth

We have a growing number of companies under BL's umbrella. First, there's the land holdings, then the bison herd, the corral-handling systems, all the inventions associated with the quadcopters, the one-shot vaccine combination, many features of the flight control console, microchips and their data collection and monitoring systems, Pinion's sound company, the PR firm, accounting and law firms, and a growing group of public stockholders. The pemmican products are not yet profitable, but their reputation is building, and soon, when the herd numbers grow, they will bring in a substantial portion of BL's income.

Sarah, Ged, and I talked a lot, in the beginning, on how to set up and guide our company so that it would grow on its own. We were never impressed with the standard company model where a few top people control all assets, enjoying the rewards, hogging the glory, while the majority of company contributors—even though they are the backbone, the muscle, and the blood of the company, and most often are the inventors of new company products—are relegated to receiving only enough to survive on. Enough to house and feed themselves so they can come back to work the next day. One of the many troubles with that setup is the so-called employees have very little incentive to put their hearts and minds into their job, and often are even considered fools to be taken advantage of if they do.

Bison Leap does not operate in any standard fashion. All the people associated with BL are encouraged to invest in the company, not just in time or money, but in their personal ideas, their strengths. For that, they're given a profit share, an ownership in the assets, a say in the company's direction, and a sense of family pride.

We're a big family; we breathe the same air, have the same red blood running through our veins, the same hopes, dreams, and goals. We also have something unique, but it's contagious. It's a way of being, a way of interacting with our fellow humans and with the rest of our world.

Bison Leap has a knack, from our very beginning, of being able to shy away from people, companies, and situations that are competitive. It's known that none of us are cowards; in fact, the opposite is closer to the truth. We're a group of brave, courageous souls. We have vision, inspiration, strength, hope, and, yes, even love. These energizing and admirable traits give us the power and the knowledge to accomplish our goals without force or coercion, and we attract people of the same inclination. As Bison Leap grows in material and human assets, it becomes increasingly obvious to those we encounter that this company and its people are different. One does not have to be guarded to work with BL. Any and all contributions will be appreciated and acknowledged.

People find this a rare commodity.

"It's attractive, uplifting, and inspirational," they say.

Common, ordinary people and businesses alike find it a pleasure to be affiliated with all and everything Bison Leap has a hand in. All this business and personal interaction gives Bison Leap a reputation as a trustworthy organization.

It's the ultimate culmination of Samantha and Jake's parenting, Sarah and my many wise and bighearted mentors, Ged's extraordinary business sense, and, of course, the latent desires of all our friends and acquaintances to do something fulfilling with their lives. Every human has it in them to live in a positive, sustainable matter, other than in isolated unique situations, it'd just never been given much of a chance before. This is different—this is a growing, flourishing, profitable, and publicly visible company. It seems everyone wants in on the action. People are searching their hearts, minds, and pockets to find ways to be affiliated with Bison Leap. Most people have never even gotten a taste of Samantha's pemmican yet, but they've tasted the inspirational words, the dreams, and the visible business interactions of Bison Leap, and they think, *Yes, what can we do to help ourselves become a part of this*?

A ruthless few still wait, like blind scavenging vultures, for Bison Leap to implode, so they can pick up the pieces, but this is not a wishy-washy conglomerate of misfits that under pressure will lose the inspiration of their dreams. This is a group of dedicated, educated, energetic, thoughtful, and intelligent people, none of whom are held together by some individual's philosophy. We've come together from well-thought-out, personally experienced observations and a mutual desire to live to the best of human possibilities. We are strong, capable individuals, and even though we're independent thinkers and feelers, we know the value of co-operation, shared knowledge, and mutual support. We follow no one blindly and put effort into personally distilling everything to its essence so that we can make indisputably correct decisions.

39. State Biologists

The few elk and deer that Doug and Melinda vaccinated and chipped are, through BL's observation and data collection system, being monitored by state biologists. With effortless movements of their fingers, the biologists observe these animals from their home or office computers. It's cheap, easy, and informative. Never before have they been able to obtain so much documented information so easily, and it is changing the way they think about their jobs.

They ask, "Could BL set us up with a system, and teach us how to use it, to vaccinate and chip all the wild critters that are under the state's guardianship, and if so, what would it cost? What does BL foresee as the benefits, to the state and to its publicly owned wildlife be, of such a system?"

In Wyoming, the biologists have many indigenous animals to look after.

"There seems to be no shortage of conflicting views as to how our job is to be done. We have bighorn sheep, mountain goats, antelope, moose, whitetail and mule deer, bison, elk, grizzly and black bear, cougar, wolves, many species of birds, fish, and other smaller critters under our care."

Some people want all undomesticated animals confined, controlled, and even exterminated.

Others want them totally unmolested, protected. What this usually boils down to is that the politicians and lawmakers implement and enforce laws that bring the most taxation and licensing fees into the government coffers, as is deemed their mandate. The implementation of that objective is often forced to be very shortsighted and detrimental in the long term. Usually the wildlife and natural environment pay the price for all these compromises.

It is becoming increasingly obvious to most people that the detrimental side effects of the present way of doing things are also detrimental to human society's end objective of becoming healthy and happy.

Bison Leap suggests the benefits of our system to the biologists that will not only help the biologists accomplish their personal goals but will also satisfy the many differing public opinions, and also put an abundance of much-needed money into the coffers of government administrators and public works institutions. BL's well-thought-out plan is not the common way of thinking, and will take some quantum leaps in understanding to implement, but BL is now well on its way to becoming experts in the fine art of public relations and education—so, with the biologists' support, the original grand plan will soon become the grand plan of the general public!

It is the biologists' job to monitor the health and population numbers of the many animals, making recommendations to lawmakers and enforcement officers as to how many critters in each area should be protected or harvested. This is all subject to the pressure the politicians receive from public interest groups. There are farmers who will not be able to pay their taxes if a herd of elk destroys their hayfields, auto insurance companies who receive too many claims from collisions, hunters who want higher animal populations for public harvest, and tourist operators who need more critters for photo opportunities. It all boils down to money, and that does need to be considered.

The list of potentially conflicting needs and opinions are almost endless, and the biologists are stuck in the middle, not being able to satisfy anyone's needs or use the science they have learned. These are the same issues that Sarah and I have been wrestling with since we were old enough to think. It will be subtle work, but Bison Leap's recommendations to the biologists are similar to what we are implementing with BL's company proceedings. A branch of Bison Leap will work closely with the government biologists to enhance the wildlife populations, while at the same time addressing the many conflicting concerns and needs of both the public and private businesses. Bison Leap has had this in mind from its inception. It will not be easy. We do not have all the answers yet, but it can certainly be done.

40. Administration and Doug

After much deliberation, Bison Leap's administration gets back to Doug. "Go ahead, you may order an airship." The accountants will arrange lease payments. Their recommendation is: "The ship should be able to safely and comfortably carry twenty school-age children, together with five adults, have a return flight range of one hundred miles, and be fully updateable and integrated with BL's present control system. It should be able to transport and recharge a winged drone that is also of a size capable of carrying at least two quadcopters, and, when needed, it should also be able to lift and transport a minimum of ten tons of freight."

Doug is thrilled! He will have a mother ship to not only carry his copters far and wide, but he'll also be able to ride in person. Trouble is, can he fly all these machines himself at the same time? That could be done with the help of sophisticated computer programming, but it'd be a lot more fun to have additional pilots.

The PR firm is interviewing prospective pilots and has narrowed its choices down to ten applicants—five males and five females, all under the age of twenty-five. BL wants mature young people with sharp responsive senses and clear minds who can pick up new skills quickly. Doug and Melinda will train and evaluate these newcomers over the next few months. We'd like a minimum of two more pilots, and if the presentation to the government biologists goes well, a number of pilots can be directed there. It'll be fun to have some new faces around to liven things up. Not that Doug is bored, but he's a young, energetic, social critter, so a party once in a while is welcomed.

They'll take two students at a time; Doug will teach them technical skills, and Melinda will evaluate their subtle abilities to be able to work around the bison without disturbance. They draw up a numbered checklist to rate these students. Each student's preliminary training and evaluation will last two weeks, and then two more students will be brought in.

A male student decides, after three days, that he would rather be back on the family ranch working with his dogs and horses.

A female student, after five days, decides the isolation of the BL ranch is a little much for her. That leaves eight prospects, and it is looking like they all might make the cut.

Doug and Melinda are both noticing, in general, that the males are better at technical aspects of flight and the females are better at working in close with the beasts. Two female students are exceptional at both the flight and in close working of the stock. Bison Leap will hire them. A young man is an exceptional technician but seems antsy when he gets in close to the big shaggy beasts. He will make an excellent pilot for the airship when it arrives.

Melinda notices the bison are getting nervous when the quadcopters approach them. She realizes that it seems to the bison that every time one of these things is around they get a sting, so all the pilots are instructed to spend their free time flying near the bison. The bison will eventually learn to ignore the copters and treat them as they would any other nonthreatening bird. The extra flight time will sharpen the pilots' abilities and also help them to personally get to know the bison and the landscape.

We need one person with qualities that may be lacking in the students chosen so far. We need a triggerman. Someone who can kill without cruelty or remorse. This pilot will need to be calm and clear, their reading of an animal will have to be excellent, and their timing will need to be precise. No mistakes are tolerated on this particular job!

Melinda asks, "Are there any volunteers?"

One young man, not one of the three chosen so far, states he's always hunted with his dad.

"We kill our own beef every year on the farm. I know how to kill without the animal feeling a thing. I don't find it enjoyable, but if there's a good reason to do it, then I'm okay with that."

He's not a flashy pilot, but he won't need to be. He is actually rather slow, confident, and meticulous.

Melinda and Doug agree he's perfect for this job. The other pilots are all acceptable, but BL does not need them right now. They are told of the plans to work with the government biologists, and that they will be called back in and given further training when the time is near.

"Would any of you like to fill other job openings BL has in the meantime?" asks Doug.

All five are happy to take whatever BL has available and would like to learn as much about the company as possible. They will move around to different jobs as needed, to get as large a view of the company as they can. These are the kind of people that BL needs. Our PR firm has done an excellent job finding them.

41. News

A newsletter is now being sent to BL employees and investors to keep everyone up to date on all proceedings. Everybody is encouraged to add to the letter. It's not censored or edited in any way, and it helps to give everyone concerned a clear picture of the whole operation without them having to be on-site. Aside from the business perspective that this gives, it also helps to knit all BL associates into a supportive, understanding family.

It is important that everyone knows as much as possible about what is happening in their surroundings. This knowledge gives us all a sense of community, allows input for future direction, lets people know of others' dreams and wishes, makes gossip unnecessary, and keeps unwanted surprises to a minimum. This business is about interacting with friends, about relationships between people and their environment, so it's good to stay in touch.

The newsletter will help. Today it reads, in part:

Bison Leap News

- Airship arriving tomorrow, technician to accompany and assemble ship and train pilots. He requests bison steak for supper and pemmican soup for lunch every day of his stay—Doug
- Band council meeting packed, crowd responsive and encouraging, next meeting in two weeks, need bigger hall to accommodate expected attendees—Sarah
- Progress being made with Pinion's sounds; she is a sweetheart and her parents very helpful—audio engineer
- Green River land acquisition progressing as planned, should be able to turn buffs in there soon, residents have agreed to stay and put up hay, must we build more fence or will the sound towers be ready? Don't want bison in hayfield this time of year. Will update tomorrow—Jim
- Ditches all cleaned and expect to turn water onto creek flats tomorrow—irrigation crew
- Six new calves today. Eighty calves vaccinated/chipped so far this spring, everyone healthy. Jim's mineral supplement well-received, must order more—Melinda
- High pressure gun ready to test on quadcopter, lab tests promising but need pilot and Ping-Pong targets, any pilot available to test in Austin must bring copter to retrofit, reply ASAP. Quadcopter must have air expulsion out its back to counteract ejecta (air & detonator) to keep copter from flipping. Detonator weighs only one and a half grams but the 2000psi is a destabilizing kickback. Testing at lab is extensive, first firing without active detonation tip flipped copter, so stabilizing backblast was added. All systems seem in order now.

Need working copter and experienced pilot for final tests—Austin engineers

- Irrigation pivot needs realignment, company to send rep tomorrow—Jake
- Nice ranch located for the "in-between place" trade. Will meet them there tomorrow for viewing and approval. They're getting a good place—ranchlands Realtor
- 500 more quality bison to arrive from South Dakota next week. Can portable corrals be set up, to unload trucks at Samantha and Jake's?—wandering vets
- Computer says total bison headcount at BL now 2,567—Melinda
- Flight leaves Hong Kong tomorrow, will be good to see home again—Ged
- Have green light to vaccinate and chip all bighorn sheep in Wyoming, best to plan for February/March, on low elevation wintering grounds—government biologist

42. Expansion

With the expansion of BL's range I'm thinking I'd like to have one of those silent planes like Ged gifted Sarah. I'd like mine to be a single-seater with two sets of wings, so I can land and takeoff from about anywhere. It wouldn't be fast or fancy like Sarah's, but it'd be perfect for having a look around. The console in the control room is designed to look around, but I still like to have a more personal touch with the land; besides, I've been spending far too much time in a pickup truck, and I have far more important things to do than waste most of my day kicking up dust from one side of BL to the other.

The bison are spreading out and wandering; sometimes there's a mile or so between bunches. I'm still not sure what's going on in those critters' minds, but I am starting to see patterns in their behaviors and movements. It'll all become clear to me one day, but I sure wish Here-n-There could've stuck around a bit longer to teach me more of his intuitive knowledge of these critters' ways. That old man had become family, and he is sorely missed...

Doug and his sound engineers are teasing me again, with a novel idea of building little sound towers to act as fences. They will be moveable, set on tripod legs about ten feet high, spaced one hundred yards apart, and will transmit the frequency of sounds that Pinion has been coaching them on. These will keep the bison out of the hayfields and anywhere else they're not wanted. The little towers can be picked up or set out by hand or with the airship, moved around as needed; they'll turn themselves on and off with motion sensors, be self-grounded in case of lightning strikes, be lightweight and stackable, and will be charged with their own little solar panels. With Ged's manufacturing facility connections, they can be made by the thousands. In bulk numbers they'll be cheaper than a fencepost. No barbed wire, no holes in the ground, no bulldozed fence lines; they're portable, have long lifespans, and take very little time or labor to set out.

This is impressive, and every chance I get I push the engineers to build them.

"Start on the towers now," I say. "We'll add the sounds later."

I'm seeing the part of my dream where the wire fences are coming down, and I'm pleased with the thought that maybe my other visions are possible, maybe dreams really can be brought from the place of *imagination* to this place of physical touch.

Here-n-There would like this fence—no more gates to open and close, no more broken wires, no more fawns tangled up. He'd just need to carry a little on-off switch so the sounds wouldn't hurt his horse's ears when he passes through.

The Wyoming biologists have plans. They don't spread the news yet, but they're talking among themselves of more than just bighorn sheep. They'll start with the sheep because they have a high monetary value placed on them, but these other critters are, in the biologists' eyes, just as valuable.

Ged finds time to help co-ordinate the project, liaising between the computer engineers, electronics experts, technical manufacturers, and all the other companies and professionals needed to complete this endeavor. BL's law and accounting firms, and the public relations department, will also lend their expert talents. Doug and Melinda are free to train systems operators and pilots.

Bison Leap will have a hand in changing the landscape of Wyoming into something that will be the envy of every state in this great Union! Perhaps Canada, Mexico, and other countries will be impressed too. Bison Leap will make sure this system gets built right and is operator-friendly. I will use a little of our income and order that one-man, double-winged plane I've been dreaming of.

At one of the local cattlemen's meetings a rancher expresses his concerns about "them bison getting through the fence, breeding his purebred cows, and goring his valuable bulls." He states he will have no choice but to shoot any bison that trespasses, and Bison Leap will need to compensate him for any damages the bison might cause.

We need to be on excellent terms with our neighbors, so we assure the rancher, "BL will keep an eye on the fences and willingly pay any damages that may occur."

This is another reason the sound engineers need to get those fences operational. That is now a priority, and any resources they think might expedite the project are at their disposal.

43. Southern Range and Seed Stock

BL secured Native rangeland in the rough country of southern Arizona for any bison that shows signs of cycling out of season. The Band has irrigated hayfields they can use for supplemental feed in times of extreme drought. BL retains ownership of half the bull calf crop for pemmican, and the Band will have the rest for themselves, for food. Another win-win situation. The fair and just business operations of BL have built a reputation that now precedes us, and many requests for seed stock are being received. Bison Leap will work with anyone interested, but there are conditions involved.

These conditions as written are:

- no individual can claim ownership,
- all animals are to be considered as wards of the people in the immediate area,

- the bison cannot be branded, but will need to be microchipped and vaccinated,
- meticulous records are to be kept,
- any animal restricted in its movements in any way needs free access to clean water and will not be allowed to go hungry,
- no animal is to be abused or treated unfairly,
- the land the bison are to graze on will not be allowed to become overused,
- only humane killing methods will be tolerated,
- BL will give guidance and assistance wherever wanted or needed. BL retains the right to inspect all aforementioned animals without prior notice.
- The interpretation of these conditions remains at BL's discretion.

If any of the above conditions are violated Bison Leap retains the option of taking possession of all the original animals and any or all of their offspring. Legal papers will be drawn up to assure compliance. All parties involved need to sign to recognize that they have read, understood, and agreed to these conditions.

44. Here-n-There Visits

One evening, Melinda and I are enjoying the fire pit.

"I miss old Here-n-There," I tell her. "I'd trade my new plane for another day of Here's company."

Melinda knows Here-n-There had become a special friend of mine: a mentor, an inspiration, and family.

She smiles, telling me, "I've got a special gift for you, Jim. Sometimes when There was Here, he visited the control room and he'd get to telling his stories. I wanted to remember everything Here told me, so many times I flicked the recording mike on without Here knowing. I'll make a disk copy of one of his stories and give it to you tomorrow."

When I'm quiet on my cabin porch a few days later, I play it. It feels good, listening to Here's voice again.

"I wants to tell you a story of *seeing* trees. I suspect the deer, elk, and buffs can *see* 'em too, but I's pretty sure no domestic cow ever *seen* nothin' so grand. They's just too focused on keepin' their bellies full. Now, just listen and ask no questions till I's done or I'll forget where I is in dis story.

"You thinks trees is alive, you thinks they's more'n just shade, firewood, an' boards? There's some says trees can feel. Me, I's not entirely sure what feelin's is, but I's sure trees are livin' bein's. They've a vibrant energy they radiate and interact with. It's warm, fillin' energy an' easy to *see*. Now when I say *see*, I don't mean you *sees* it with you eyes, although it first appears thata ways. I say at first 'cause after a while you can *sees* just as easy an' maybe even better with you eyes closed. You *sees* it with somethin' else besides you eyes, and no, it ain't your mind, 'cause you mind gotta take a holiday while you *seein'*, so it's somethin' else that *sees* it.

"I tells you my story of *seein'* trees, so you be convinced, that you can *see* 'em too, 'cause they gots a deep beauty, just like the grass an' all them other plants, an' they give to you till you be all filled up with life an' warmth.

"First time I *see* this it ain't 'cause I try to, but I sure glad it happen. You know, I was cryin', both eyes filled fulla tears, my heart was broke, my world didn't make no sense at all no more. So when I's feelin' this way, I coulda gots drunk an' real sad or I coulda got mean an' mad, but instead I's *stopped the world*, I stilled them thoughts, some folks says *no mind*.

"Anyhow, what happens is the mind goes on holidays an' other senses now got some energy, what was before all used up with the busy mind.

"So my world stops, everything I thought I knew just quit, an' that was good 'cause it didn't make any sense nohow, an' then, in front of me is this radiant energy of a tree. My mind comes back quick, an' I first think maybe I's crazy, but you only goes crazy in you mind an' my mind already went on that holiday while I's *seein'* this. I checked my mind when it come back and it's okay, so I knows I not crazy. I couldn't be sad no more 'cause all that beauty right there in front of me. Too quick, I's thinkin' again an' my *seein'* goes away, but I wants to *see* it again, an' I look at the tree an' I see just a fuzzy line along its edge, up against the sky. First I thinks my eyes goin' funny, but my eyes okay, so I keeps lookin' at that fuzzy line, an' it grows, gettin' lighter, an' turns into that same beauty I *sees* before. Soon's I think about this, it all goes away an' it just a plain ole tree agin. But I just keeps at it, an' soon I knows that *any time I stop thinking I can sees it*, an same's all them other plants, but some's got more light than others. So all you needs ta do is quiet them thoughts an' give the rest of you free reign, an' you *see* it too.

"Just unfocus you eyes an' don't try too hard like you's thinkin', more like you startin' to go to sleep but you gotta stay awake. You try, you *see*, an' one day you know 'bout all the life, an' beauty, an' warmth that supports you and it's all around wherever you go.

"I tell you this 'cause I want you to *see* it too, an I knows you can. I knows if'n an old dumbass lazy nobody like me can *sees* it, then for sure a smart, full of life girl like you can *sees* it too. All you gots ta do is stop thinkin' for a bit. An' don't you worry none about you mind 'cause it always gonna be there an' it be fine if'n it gets a holiday while the best of you wakes up.

"You know what I thinks is real funny? At first you mind gonna be scared 'cause it thinks it not gonna be the boss no more if'n it rests an' lets you *sees*, but after a bit it's so full of appreciation that it starts to helpin' you, 'cause it enjoys the view too."

After I listened to the disk I knew there was a lot more to old Here-n-There than he'd ever let on. I'll give the story a try sometime. *Maybe There is still Here and he, like nature, has unintentionally fooled us all? Or is it just us, wrapped in knots, playing ourselves for fools?*

I ask Melinda, "Do you have any more of them stories?"

"I've got a few; some are short and some are long ones."

"Have you tried what Here-n-There talked about?" I ask her.

Melinda pauses, gets a radiant smile on her face.

"You just got to practice, Jim." She laughs gently, then dismisses me, before commencing her work.

45. Sarah's Flights

Sarah flies often from BL's home place to Boulder. It's about a two-hour trip in her fast little plane. She is starting to recognize all the many rivers, mountains, and outstanding contours of this vast country—some of it very dry and rugged, some green and productive farmland, some mountain goat country. Along the river valley bottoms is rich, black soil supporting lush plant growth. A few areas are heavily populated with small cities and big towns; other places there doesn't seem to be a human soul for a hundred miles.

Large ranches are scattered here and there, wherever there is water and enough flat land to grow some winter feed on. There is one particular ranch she flies over that always manages to capture her imagination. It straddles the Wyoming-Colorado border, has good creeks running through it, and on one side flows a wide, wild river. This ranch backs up onto high rugged mountains, is about halfway between BL and Boulder. It's huge, an inviting place. She guesses about how big it is by the run of the fences and the size of its log-corrals. Those corrals will hold a lot of cattle at roundup time, and there must be at least a thousand acres of irrigated hayfields. It is a big place, all right, and Sarah wonders who owns it. A good airstrip lies just below its buildings, so she plans to land there one day when she has a little extra time.

Sarah does get a little extra time a few weeks later. Well, it's not actually extra time but she manages to leave Bison Leap with daylight to spare, so when she gets to that ranch, she circles once, high over the airstrip, waves her wings to say hello, and sets up to land. Her wheels haven't yet touched the ground when she notices a big plume of dust coming down the gravel laneway from the buildings. When she climbs out of her plane, a grinning boy sitting on his quad asks, "Is you lost?"

Smiling, Sarah tells him, "I'm not exactly lost but not exactly sure where I am either."

"You's on one of the biggest and best cattle ranches this side of Chicago," the boy replies in a go-get-'em voice. "And you's a woman! You know my mom says she ain't seen no woman for two weeks now, and she sure would like to talk to one. She says men just never learned how to talk proper and she sure misses female company. I thinks you should come up the house and get her smilin'. You can just jump right on the back here with me, and I'll give you a lift."

Well, Sarah guesses there's no saying no to that, so she gets a fast, bumpy ride the half-mile up to the house.

The mom is overjoyed to have company. After a short introduction and Sarah's trip to the ladies' room, the mom makes a pot of tea and brings out fresh-baked goods.

She wants to know everything.

Sarah gives her highlights, tells her a little of Ged, talks a bit about her plane and, briefly, a little of BL's future plans.

Out of the blue, the lady says, "I was in the corral the other day helping the boys, and one of the young fellows asks my husband how come he's so grouchy, well my, I'm afraid my husband will send him halfway to Pluto, but he don't, he just gets real quiet for a bit and then he replies to that young man, 'You follow them stupid damn cows around for as long as I have an' you'll be grouchy too!' Well, you know I never heard my husband talk like that before, you know he was born right there in that bedroom, and his daddy was born up in that little ole house right up on that there hill."

She pours Sarah another cup of tea, and continues talking.

"I been thinkin' for the last two days now, if'n he feels thataways how come he still doin' it? He don't need to, you know. If he was to sell all them cows he been collectin', and them ones his daddy collected before him, we could fly around the world a hundred times and still have lots left over! So why would he still be followin' them cows around?"

"I can't say I know the answer to that," Sarah replies, gently. "I've got to get back to Boulder before the sun goes down. I've so much enjoyed our visit. May I drop in again sometime?"

The lady gives Sarah a friendly hug.

"Give Sarah a ride back to her plane," she tells her boy. "And don't you be drivin' so fast!"

She makes Sarah promise to come back soon.

Sarah circles once, waves her wings, and heads east by southeast to Boulder.

She tells Ged all about her day, and then she calls me, telling me about the ranch.

I say, "If you drop in there again, take them cowboys a twenty-pound box of Mom's best pemmican."

It's all formed into little round cakes, like a hockey puck, only smaller, about the size of a can of snus. It's just right to have a puck or two of that in your pocket on a long ride, or when you are bouncing in the tractor all day, making circles in the hayfield.

I tell Sarah, "We'll cheer them cowboys up, and give them something to think about."

I want to know exactly where it is, so I can have a look with the satellite connection. Sarah gives me the ranch's GPS co-ordinates.

46. Satellite View

Next day, I take a couple hours and have a look. There is a big river, blue water, fast and cold, right from the mountains, and all these hayfields! There are still wheel lines on some of the fields, while others are upgraded to pivots, but it'd take two people a long day, every day, to change those many wheel moves. There are plenty of smaller creeks and springs coming down from the high country. The hayfields, airstrip, and buildings are on the first big bench up from the river, but they don't use the river water for irrigating. All the irrigation is gravity fed from the mountain creeks, so no pumps are needed. Looks like they use a diesel generator for electric power, and the buildings are in decent shape. All of them have tin roofs and the house is stucco, so no danger of it burning in a grass fire. A gravel pit is below the airstrip, which they've used to build their own roads with.

Along the river and on the hills above the building site is open bunchgrass country. As the hills climb there are big flats with green meadows, some of them wetland sedge grass, with scattered trees. Up higher, there are many small lakes where the beavers have dammed up the creeks and, still higher, the trees thicken into tall, straight green beauties. Nice if you ever need to make lumber for building. Up above these trees is high alpine country, open with lots of green plants and small bushes, then rocky peaks: goat habitat.

To the west of the airstrip, the land flattens out, the valley broadens into miles of broken country, but more flats than coulees, and it too has healthy grass cover. It looks to me like the place probably carries four thousand head, and it is not overgrazed. A well-built fence runs up both sides, from the river all the way to the top, above the last tree growth. It's close to ten miles from the river to the timber line and it runs at least twenty-five miles along the wild, blue river. A nice place with some mountain goats on top, bighorn sheep a little lower, elk and mule deer in the semi-open trees, and whitetails in the willow bottoms. I'm sure I spotted a cow and calf moose, but they moved under tree cover before I could zoom in on them.

The place is split up into different pastures, with cross fences running here and there. In a big pasture east of the house, probably two thousand acres, roams a large horse herd—fifty, maybe sixty head. Them old ranchers are sure attached to their pets. At one time, a cowboy could wear out a good horse in a few years with all the miles they put on them, camping right with the cows and sleeping under a tree all summer, but these days horses don't get used much. Now, a cowboy loads up a horse in a trailer in the morning, drives for an hour till he gets near where he needs to be, unloads the horse, rides a few miles, then loads him back up again and heads for home.

Probably only a half dozen of that herd gets rode at all. I admire horses just fine, and they are sure handy sometimes, but they are also hard on pasture. There were no horses in either North or South America until the Conquistadors brought them over on their tall-mast sail-ships, so they aren't a natural part of the landscape; there's room for them alright, but like everything else there needs to be balance.

Some anthropologists are convinced it was overgrazing by horses, donkeys, and goats that turned large parts of Africa and the Middle East into deserts. Areas that used to be green and lush are now just windblown sand! The thing is, if they're overpopulated, the goats eat all the bark off the trees, and then the horses and donkeys come along with their top and bottom teeth and eat the grass right down to its roots. Once the greenery is all killed out like that, then everything just dries up and blows away. Cows, bison, elk, sheep, and deer don't have top teeth, so they can't eat it down that far. They'd starve to death before they killed all the grass out, not like a horse—there wouldn't be nothing green left alive before a horse starved. I have seen places that horses pawed the grass roots right out of the ground. Even though I like horses, I know too many of them is not good for the land, so if this place is under my management, some of them horses will have to go.

I could spend all day examining this place, but I have other things wanting my attention. I like it, it is a very good place, and the buffs will like it too. I sure hope them cowboys take a liking to Samantha's pemmican.

47. Natural Environment

As my day progresses, I think about all the animals I've seen in my life, all the things I've heard other people say about grazers, the schooling I've had on the subject, and I realize that to be a healthy country you need a vast diversity of animals.

Some critters like the wild goats live on the steepest rocky ground, eating small plants, twigs, and very little grass. They keep the high country renewed with tender fresh growth, keeping the plants from getting too old and woody. The bighorn sheep like rocky country too, but not as steep as the goats. They like flowering plants; they'll eat a bit of grass sometimes, but they prefer anything that gets a flower. The plants don't need to be in flower, they just need to be genetically capable of flowering. Sheep will eat your roses and get in your alfalfa field, but mostly they like herbs and weeds, so they'll nibble on them and keep that kind of plant from taking over the landscape. The elk do a little browsing, but they are true grazers, meaning their main diet is grass. They move around a lot, so no place is ever eaten down too much. They also keep the plants fresh and healthy by cleaning up the mature growth and turning it back into fertilizer for the new young plants. The moose and whitetails like to stay in the thick stuff, keeping the willows and other bushes trimmed, preventing them from becoming a tangle of dead dry wood. The bison prefer open country, eating mostly grasses.

Now, without these animals chewing and recycling all the different plants in different areas, you get a buildup of old dry material, that when it catches fire from a lightning strike or man, will burn so hot and so fierce it'll kill all the plants and their seeds. It takes years before anything grows there again. All the organics will be turned into blow ash, and the mineral soil is cooked in places, almost like brick.

The thing is, you need a great diversity of both plants and animals to keep everything fresh, healthy, and vibrant. Nature will find its own rhythm if left alone, but it often goes through a feast and famine cycle, taking years or generations to build up, and then you get a devastating collapse and it starts all over again.

This natural cycle includes everything, every living organism, plants, animals, bugs, bacteria, bees, birds, fish, trees, grass, viruses, predators, and man too.

Man is part of the natural environment of earth, and he prides himself on being its master—and he could be if he'd start paying attention and help things stay in balance, instead of taking too much of one thing, too fast, in a concentrated area, and then abandoning it to recover on its own. Now, that doesn't mean we shouldn't be helping ourselves to what we need, just like every other plant and animal does, and that is the natural way, but it's all got to be done with some thought, tempered with perceptions that ain't thought at all, but something more! Understanding ain't just about thinking; of course, you need that too, but it's got to be tempered by your heart. Our brains do not feel. They're only a recorder, like a computer, and they need guidance by something that feels, like a heart, if things are to make any sense at all!

The feast and famine scenario is about not interfering, not helping, or inconsiderate taking, letting things get so out of balance that they collapse and then start the slow process of rebuilding again, but it's totally unnecessary. If we used the brains and senses we are born with instead of pillaging and hoarding, we could help nature be productive and stable. Not boring and mundane, but vibrant and flowing. If we were half as human as we think we are, we could make everywhere we went a better place, rather than the mess we're making. Maybe it is like Here-n-There says: "We need to let our mind take a holiday once in a while and start letting some of our other senses have a say!"

It's not easy to set your opinions and all the things you think you know aside and really see what's going on around you, but it'd be a better place if we could do that once in a while, and we'd be well off for it. If we could just do that. Seems we're all scared somebody gonna take something before us and then we won't have access to it, so we better get it first or we would be missing out. That's sort of like the dog got his belly full of food already, so he pisses on what's left in his dish so no other dog wants to eat it. When that first dog gets hungry again he's gonna have to eat that food he pissed on, and maybe he gets sick from his own poison. You'd think our brain would be smarter than that, but maybe it's not our brain is the problem. Maybe we just can't see or feel and we need to give them other senses a chance to help our brain, our calculator, to make better decisions.

48. Diversity

I'm finally starting to understand the true value of diversity. I kind of had an idea before, but this is different. I'm not exactly sure why, but for some reason I'm beginning to see—or perhaps I mean feel—things on a depth that has been previously unknown to me. Maybe it has something to do with my biplane, or with the real-time satellite connection, or with the disk of Here-n-There's story that Melinda gave me, but my view is expanding. Not just visual, but my comprehension, understanding, my personal connection with this earth, is becoming more complete. I am beginning to understand, to feel its uniqueness, its complexities, and these things that I'm now understanding are the things that give this land, this planet, its greatness, its intrigue, its entertainment value, and its vibrant, intense beauty!

I imagine other planets, perhaps in our galaxy, that have organic life. Some of these planets... I'm imagining all this, but I think that planets are all made of different elements, the irreducible essence of something, and these elements are in all different combinations and quantities. Every planet unique, different from any other, and it is the elements—their type and abundance—that have allowed organisms to develop and become more than just ethereal energy. Maybe the ethereal energy has been around, somewhere, for unimaginable time, but it needs something to become attached to, to become an organism, an organization of elements that becomes flesh and blood. And I imagine that some planets, some globes in space, are made up of only a few elements and will therefore be limited in their differences of organisms, but earth, perhaps the most diverse of any planet, is made up of so many different elements that it is allowed, because of these many elements, to develop organisms in great and differing forms. This is truly diversity, these different organisms in such great quantities. In multitudes of shapes, sizes, colors, abilities, needs, wants, and time or age of togetherness.

All these almost unfathomable things are dependent, as organisms, on the abundance and diversity of the elements on each particular planet, and that this planet, Earth, is perhaps the most diverse of them all. Is that why I love this place so much? Is that why I've heard someone, somewhere, sometime, say, "This planet, planet Earth, is the jewel of the universe"? I'm not sure where I heard that, and I know at the time I heard it I didn't understand exactly what they meant, but I'm thinking it's beginning to make sense to me now.

Yes, I know I love this place. I love its diversity, and I want that diversity to remain and be enhanced, forever. I'm not thinking just about myself, my wants, needs, and pleasures, but about the pleasures, the happiness, the ability of the future to maintain this world's abundance and its diversity, for our kids, and their kids, and their kids after them. Who knows, maybe, in some shape or form, I'll be back here someday, long after I've left, and I want it to be as beautiful and as interesting then, as it could be now!

I've a job to do. I'm as driven now, with love, as I had been when I was a kid, but now I've a broader, more inclusive view, and I know I'll keep doing what I'm doing now until my end, and that I will do my best to love every minute of it. Even though some predator may be wanting to consume my elements or my ethereal energy, I'll do my best to enhance and maintain my appreciation of my own diversity.

49. Flying Machines

The airship is together and all the pilots, including Sarah and me, have been given lessons on its maintenance and control. It's tricky to fly in the wind.

The technician recommends, "If the wind gets up around twenty miles an hour, it's best to set down and cross anchor the ship."

We've picked out spots in the lay of the land that have calm places even when the wind is high. These can be used as safe ports to anchor down in the event that the ship gets caught out in unexpected weather. Most of the flying can be done on calm days, but safety is always a priority. In a side wind, the pilot angles the ship's nose more or less so the wind pushes it in the intended direction, similar to a canoeist or swimmer going across stream. The pilot Doug and Melinda picked out of the trainees for this job has claimed the ship as his own and is quite particular about who operates it in his absence. He likes a meticulous log kept of all flight hours, operators, and maintenance. He's the main pilot, but we agreed that all other pilots are to be taught by him any new tricks or quirks he learns in its operation, and that all pilots will keep their familiarity with the airship's flight, so they can operate it in the event he is unavailable.

The quadcopter's shine at short-range maneuverable flight, the winged drones can carry and recharge two copters for long-range work, and now we have the airship for lifting passengers or transporting heavy freight without roads or damage to sensitive ecosystems. All these air machines use lithium storage batteries to power their nearly silent electric motors, and work together to get almost any job done that BL needs doing. The airship is not fast like a winged plane, but it can hover motionless, set down almost anywhere, has its own cockpit console directly linked to BL's main control room, and can comfortably seat twenty-five passengers on its glassed-in observation deck. It easily loads and transports ten fully-grown bull bison per trip at harvest time.

Doug got a recharge station set up at the Green River Ranch and tells us that soon one will be needed at the new Elk Mountain Ranch that Sarah is now finalizing paper-work on. I flew with her there, and we made a good deal with the owners. The place stays in their boy's name, the family sold all their cows and will travel the world, while the present employees will remain on the ranch and be paid by BL.

A percentage of any of BL's future profits made on the place will be held in trust for the boy. BL holds a twenty-year extendable lease on all the facilities and land holdings of Elk Mountain Ranch. More bison are needed, and the wandering vets are notified to purchase every healthy bison they can get their hands on.

50. Melinda Finds a Story for Jim

When Melinda gathered Here-n-There's few possessions from the old ranch house, she found tattered notebooks scribbled in graphite.

They were difficult to decipher because their author had spent little of his youth in school. It did seem like a good story, of times gone by, and it was rooster-scratched by Here-n-There, from fireside memories of a time when he was a young man. Melinda, in between her many jobs and slack time in the evenings, with great care and meticulousness transcribed it, breaking it into linear chapters, correcting the many spelling mistakes, poor grammar, and slang.

When she finished, she handed a printed copy to me. She knew of my interest in any history that would help explain the circumstances instrumental in developing Here-n-There's unique character.

"Jim, if you'd been born in a different time and under different circumstances this could well have been your story," Melinda teased. "It will also help you to realize how privileged you are to have the support and guidance of your very special parents."

This is what I read...

Wishbone: the Boy, the Horse, the Majestic Mountains.

A. A Boy's Dream

An eastern flatlander ventures into the wild western mountains without knowing a damn thing about horses, this totally alien land, or its many wild creatures. No map, no compass. And for most of his trip, with no guide or companion other than a long-legged dapple-gray mare, the morning sunrise in the east, and at each day's end, the evening sunset in the west. With only a small bag of raw rolled oats, another of ground flour, a small tin pot, a little fire-blackened cast-iron frypan, a few fishhooks, a bit of line wrapped on a stick, and very little else, except for the unrestrained will and stubborn determination to proceed, in vague hopes of finding a place of his dreams. His wishes to seek a realm best described with one word: Shangri-La. This kid survives, coming close numerous times to meeting his maker, but always youthful luck, good fortune, and the will to live for another glorious day bring him back from the pitiless edge of death. For to die he would not see tomorrow, and tomorrow is what he looks for, because what he sees today is not satisfactory enough.

There have to be better ways to live than what his short years have shown him. There has to be more life, more peace, more acceptable excitement, and more things to appreciate. There have to be places, circumstances, and people around whom one can live with less heartache, less stress, less control of one's time and energy so the heart and mind can be filled with grand wonders. One just has to search, to leave behind the mundane known, to follow the dream, the ever-present subtle feelings that there is more. More of what? Even what clues he has are elusive. But to find fulfillment he is willing to give up all he has, because what he has is not nearly enough.

He is a boy who does not fear what he does not know. A boy who values his life so much that he is not willing to resign himself to the confining repetition that seems to be enough for most of those he knows.

Can a boy find what a boy seeks? What could amaze this youth enough to entice him to linger in appreciation, in awe and respect, in love and in longing of what is before him? For his attention to be held, perhaps he will need to stumble upon something that will so involve all his senses that he will forget who he is. He feels disconnected, empty, and he seeks life. Does this boy find his elusive dream?

B. Story Time

Where to begin? It's the second time I traverse, dumb-thumbed, across country, now almost fifteen years old. I'd been to the big West Coast metropolis the year before, giving a prairie wood tick a lift and a meal, before I discovered it, silently freaked, then ripped its engorged body from my chest, separating its body from its embedded head. I murdered it, leaving a festering, boil-like hole where it had fed. Now, a year after meeting that bloodthirsty tick, I get into the mountains and don't want to go closer to the rainy coast, so I head north. I know from the change in the trees this is far enough. I ask around town if there is any work.

Someone says, "About five miles out, there's a horse rancher looking for help."

Big place, he has a half-dozen mature studs and forty or fifty mares, along with all the colts, yearlings, and two-year-olds. Running quarter horses, real fancy stuff.

"If you cut your hair," he tells me, "I'll give you a job."

I think about it, but I'm not willing to give up my wavy locks. (I do work for him years later, but that's a different story.)

So up the road I goes.

A worker driving a road maintenance truck picks me up and says, "I know where you belong; there's some up the road who look just like you."

He drops me off an hour later at what he says used to be an old horse logging camp. Rustic, well-weathered log buildings with split-fir shake roofs, washed and dried horse-manure (fluffy, like gardener's peat moss) for insulation in their open-ended lofts.

Only one guy there introduces himself as Crazy Joe, saying, "Everybody else is in town getting groceries."

I haven't eaten in a while and am considerably hungry. Not a bite to eat in the cabin, but an old single-shot .22 rifle hangs high on the wall. I borrow it, go for a little walk, and bring back a nice wild rabbit. With Crazy Joe's help, we cook it on the wood-fired stove. It is finger-lickin', belly-fillin' good, for both of us.

Crazy Joe wants to keep the skin, so he nails it stretched on the woodshed door to dry. When the town crew comes home, the head honcho goes to get some split firewood for the cookstove. He sees this rabbit-fur skin, his face turns beet red, his big paws grab Crazy Joe by the throat and hoisting him against the wall, he screams, "*I'm going to kill you, you murdering son of a bitch!*"

Crazy Joe's face is turning purple, his tongue and eyes are popped out of his head, and I am wondering what the hell I've gotten myself into this time!

I am later to learn the honcho is a dodger from the war draft and a vegetarian needle-freak! Him and his girlfriend will shoot anything, including LSD or whiskey if nothing else is available. He doesn't believe in wasting good stuff on the stomach. I turn down his offer for 'a fix'. Crazy Joe will meet his match a few years later when he gets in a shootout with a narcotics officer. I don't stay here more than a few days, but get me some good connections for future adventures.

C. Characters

The macho honcho has a frizzy red afro. His girlfriend, Patti, is as skinny as a big city crackhead. He also has brothers who manage to avoid the draft with sports scholarships. He tells us how he listens to his brothers' professional games: He climbs to the top of a big old-growth Douglas fir tree, ties a bare chromed bicycle rim with spokes onto the tip of its highest branch, making an ingenious receiving aerial.

He then runs a wire down the tree, in through the kitchen window to an old 12-volt car radio and lead-acid battery he scrounged. With this, he listens to all the football games while he hollers, swears, and bangs his fist on the table like he is trying to scare the distant players. Sometimes I wonder if he realizes they can't hear him.

Crazy Joe, meanwhile, is a porker with long, stringy blond hair. Another guy, Freddy, intentionally cuts the top of his own foot with a chainsaw so he can get workers' compensation. You get the picture. These are a thrown-together crew of definite misfits. Their visiting friends (with the exception of yours truly) are the icing on a rancid nutty-fruitcake...

There's an old Native logger-hunter who has a piece of his rib surgically wedded to his neck vertebrae after a crashing tree 'got its revenge.' He can't turn his neck, so he has to turn his whole body if he wants to look in a different direction. This handicap is also complicated by the fact that his left leg and pelvis are also pinned and bolted together from other injuries. He later names me Lucky, 'cause I can find deer when everyone else gets skunks and track soup. You get plenty skinny living off track soup!

Then there's the other old Native cowboy who has a small, well-kept ranch a few miles by horse trail down the creek. He's a picture of the true old Western cowboy—jingling spurs, lots of silver, spade bit, red bandanna, leather batwing chaps, big Stetson hat, a ready laugh, and sparkling eyes. This, all in the trees, a half day's ride above the cactus-covered semi-desert of the Mighty River Valley. Many trails the old Natives draw pictures of with their descriptive words, and *thereby implant in my mind*, will become familiar to my feet and, later, to my mount's hooves. This story is *random bits of dreams, nightmares, and imagination…*

But that's not the interesting part.

D. The Set

I'm more than thirty miles from town on a narrow, crooked mountain road that was built not many years before by teams of hard-pullin', drippin'-wet-sweating, harnessed, heavy draft horses draggin' skoop-sloops—wooden-handled steel fresnos.

This land is beautiful limestone mountains with caves, cold-bubbling, fast-falling creeks, and lots of two- and four-legged wildlife. The place is an old fixed-up horse logging camp. Log barn with goat stanchions and chicken coup.

From within the kitchen house, I hear Patti holler.

"I hate that fucking billy goat!"

When she's at the kitchen counter, the billy gets on the little knoll, just outside of her sink window, twists his body so his penis is in his own mouth, then pisses. With piss dribblin' out both sides of his mouth, he looks her in the eye and grins. He never does that to anybody else, just her, and even though she is a committed vegetarian, she screeches, begs everybody, anybody, to "kill that fucking goat!"

Behind the kitchen house stands the bunkhouse, with rows of double bunks. Around each bunk are draped blankets for visual privacy, but they're not much for stopping the plentiful moans of bed sounds. Many characters come and go, all adding their particular quirks to the atmosphere. There's chunky Barbie, who makes it her mission to personally, intimately, get to know every man she meets. There's a handsome, although shameless, mixed-blood who, day or night, dismounts his horse, carbine in hand, and using it to push open the door, asks loudly enough to wake the sleeping, "Does anybody want a fuck today?"

He is often satisfied.

There's a couple who lives in a canvas teepee on the edge of a deer-stick-fenced garden. She with long wavy black hair, good-looking; him with a nine-inch bowie knife, which he always wears conspicuously in his belt sheath. This very knife would be used later by this couple to do an operation on my foot.

E. Where, O Where Did I Leave Off?

So the old Native with the buggered up neck tells me, "Sam, a guy across the Mighty River, plans to ride into yonder mountains for the summer."

I grab my chance to search for Shangri-la, and ask old Neil, "Tell me how to find Sam's camp."

"Cross the cable ferry, head upriver until you get to the second big creek, follow that creek upstream till you see an old dirt-roofed log cabin perched on a little flat way above and on the other side of creek," he says.

Easy, aye? Oh, but so wrong! Remember, I'm a flatlander, with no experience in country that goes up and down in places steep enough to scare a billy goat.

Before I embark, I decide I need a few survival supplies, so I get on a forest fire crew for a couple days to make a bit of cash. I work my ass off all night fighting this fire. Put it out, too! Never see a damn soul. Come daylight I'm going through the center of the burned-out area, just mopping up the little smokes, and come across about twenty guys sitting on a log, passing around a gallon of home brew rhubarb wine. They call me a dumb bastard for putting out their fire. Every once in a while, one of them starts up his chainsaw so the fire boss will be fooled into thinkin' they're working. The job pays five bucks an hour extra if you have a saw. No need, in these days, for hard hats, certificates, or identification.

"We'll have to go start another fire now for more work!" one of the wine jug sharers says. The fire suppression authorities, it takes them a few years to figure it out, but they learn if they don't hire any local crews, and instead bring in crews from other areas, new fires don't occur nearly as frequently.

I have a bit of money and a thin, slippery-nylon forestry sleeping bag, I buy a little Swede saw, an old double-barrel shotgun, cast-iron frypan, some fishhooks and a bit of line wrapped around a short stick, a tin pot, a small ax, a thin canvas tarp, and some rope. Someone abandoned a Welsh pony at the old stable. He bucks everybody off that tries to ride him, so Macho tells me, "Take him, he's just a pain in the ass."

So I have my outfit and a destination. Time to cross the river and see the mysterious mountain valleys yonder. But first I need to pack my stuff and convince this pony he wants to come with me. I'm barefoot—my own running shoes had been melted, ruined fightin' the fire—so Macho gives me a pair of worn-out oversize leather work boots.

"Just in case you run into too much cactus for your bare feet."

So I head out, on the way to the mysterious great beyond.

F. On The Way

It takes all of one day to get the pony and pack sorted out, so I take the shortcut, over the hill horse-trail, down toward the river, about fifteen miles. On the way I stop at old Neil's son's cabin, a mile or two above the Mighty River.

There are lots of Native people in this big, rustic log cabin. Many sharp broken rocks have fallen from the cliff face above and lie in their gravel front yard. Me, in my bare feet leading this pony. I use the slippery sleeping bag for a cushioning blanket between the pony's back and the wooden pack-saddle, lay the little sleeping tarp on it, set the worn-out wooden pack-saddle on top, put an old woven cinch under the pony's belly, and lash it all together with a bit of rope. I then tie my survival possessions on top.

For some unknown reason, this pony decides to put on a grunting, jolly good show for all the spectators on the porch as they bid me farewell. The little shit bucks till he loosens the pack. The whole outfit slips, unceremoniously, under his belly. Everything now hanging, pot and pan bang-clangin' together, where he can get a better kick at my valuables. He unloads everything while I try to anchor him with my bare feet in the sharp rocks. A half dozen people stand on the porch holding their stomachs, aching from laughing so hard. No one offers to help but they clap and hoot for me, immensely enjoyin' the performance like they's at a free rodeo. All that breaks is the handle off my cast-iron frypan and a bent (I'll have to aim sideways now) barrel on the shotgun. I'm glad the little Swede saw, being on top the pack, has come untied and flies off to the side, never encountering that active rebel's hooves. After he's had enough fun for one day, I repack him and head toward the river and the cable ferry crossing. The real test begins.

G. Mighty River

Finding the river is not difficult; it's a mighty big river! Crossing the cable ferry goes well, and looking up at these mountains from the riverbank is impressive. Not to be deterred, I proceed with the map old Neil has drawn in my head. To the first big creek is good, about six sagebrush miles. *These guys call that a creek!* It's thirty feet wide and well over my knees with cold, fast-traveling water. Its bottom is covered with round, polished rocks. So, through and over we go.

Neil said to follow the Mighty River, and that's exactly what we do. Neil forgot to mention, or assumed I had the sense, not to stay so close to the steep eroded gullies close along the river. These hard clay gullies are so steep and high the bases of them are littered with cow skeletons. The cows slip off the steep narrow trails when they venture to water, and over the years their bones accumulate in these ravine bottoms. Two days of up and down on skinny trails bring me to the second creek. Just as wide as the first, but much faster, with big boulders the water battles up against and rushes around. I follow the creek upstream, and the trail rises into high bunchgrass sidehills. Very colorful wild country, semi-open with big ponderosa pines.

A few miles upstream, I cross the creek as Sam's cabin was said to be on the other side. I'm heading up a trail that is one foot wide. It hugs a steep sidehill, but there's no problem until we come to a vertical bank a hundred feet from top to bottom. It's a warm day, so this wild-child wears only a pair of denim cutoff shorts. No shirt, no shoes. The trail goes straight across this eroded bank about fifty feet above the boiling water. Below, the water argues with rock boulders. So far, so good. I am leading the pony, and he's starting to enjoy this trip. He's probably thinkin', *This is better than bein' tied to the old barn.*

In the middle of this crossing, there's a six-foot gap where the trail has eroded, slipping away into the water below!

No room to swap ends here, methinks. *I can make the leap, it's not so far*!

I miscalculate and... straight down I go!

A small sagebrush temporarily saves me from my demise below. The pony with his pack sails overhead! He makes it to the trail beyond! I am relieved he made the leap rather than coming down on top of me. It dawns on me, much later, that I'm glad I let go of his lead shank, or I may well have pulled him with me. Now there's a scary thought. Perhaps old Neil should have named me Dumb-Luck.

My sagebrush, which I cling to while my bare toes scratch for a foothold, starts to come unrooted from the clay cliff. I can't end, broken by the rocks below while I blow my last bubbles in the freezing water! I scratch and claw my way to the other side without losing much more than a dozen-feet of elevation. Don't have much skin left on my knees, toes, or fingers, but I make it!

“Now, where’s that damn pony?”

He abandoned me to my fate. I find him a half-mile up the trail, happily munching good green bunchgrass in a little flat open spot. *We are both glad the other has survived.* I can tell by the way he looks at me. He’s probably been wonderin’ how he’s going to get his pack untied without human help.

So we find the cabin. Vacant. No one around. We have a bite, spend the night, and head back toward the ferry. This time we stay way above the steep eroded river gullies on the open benches a mile above the mighty water. Easy walking. Lots and lots of huge deer antlers litter the ground. Countless numbers of mule deer winter here, dropping their antlers in February. My feet are sore from the skinnin’ they took getting across the eroded trail, so I lace on the old work boots. They are two sizes too big, and the little rusty nails that hold the soles on are scratching my sockless, callused feet. Only scratches, so not so bad. We make it across the ferry and back to the old horse stable.

Oh, so extraordinary, very wrong. Two days later, I’ve red and purple veins running up the insides of both my legs, all the way from feet to crotch. I can’t walk, it’s even getting too painful to move, and I’m becoming delirious. It’s blood poisoning from rusty boot-nail scratches. The guy with the bowie knife convinces me that if he cuts into the core of the poison, it will drain and get better. I drink the only bottle of five percent alcohol beer for a painkiller, clamp my teeth on a rolled-up rag, and hold the hand of his girlfriend, while he opens up the bottom of my feet with his freshly sharpened bowie. I don’t remember squeezing her hand, but she shows it to me days later and it’s black and blue from bruising. I’ve incisions in both feet that nearly severed the main tendons—the ones stretched from the bottom of the big toes to the heels. The scars are, to this day, blatantly visible!

The blood poisoning is getting much worse: I can't talk or think, I'm soaking wet, chilled and feverishly hot, starting to shake. I'm dying. Someone will have to dig a shallow hole for me.

H. The Ride

I thank my lucky stars these guys are too lazy to drag me up the hill and cover me with rocks. They decide to lay me in the back of an old rusty truck and drop me off at the nearest outpost hospital, which is two hours' bumpy ride away. I've no money or medical card. I'm lucky again that the med cards in those days had no picture on them, so one of the guys graciously lends me his card.

I spend—not sure how many—days in the hospital, on antibiotics, with a different name. I'm confused when the doctor calls me someone else but soon clue in so as not to give myself away. When I can stand and walk a little, the doc writes a prescription for penicillin, says I'm well enough to leave, telling me they need the bed for someone else. There's no point in going to a pharmacy as I have no money, so I chuck the prescription in a garbage can and limp-hitch back up into the mountains.

This country is absolutely fascinating to me, and I want to know it better. The fellow I plan to ride with into the unknown has heard I'm looking for him (moccasin telegraph covers country fast). He's been out gatherin' shitters—cheap knothead horses that no one else wants—for his summer trek. He comes by the horse stable with a small but good-looking saddle horse and two big old nags for packhorses.

We head out, me leading this same pony—now happy to be away from the old stable—with my stuff on his back. On the second day we camp beside an old church at the first Native reserve we come to. One of the Indians wants my pony for his kids and swaps me for a real horse. Now I can ride instead of walking!

She's a dapple-gray mare, who I later name Wishbone because her back vertebrae stick up about four inches exactly in line with my tender tailbone. He conveniently forgets to mention (and I don't know enough to ask) she's unbroke! I lead her, me walkin', back to camp. After she bucks me off for the fourth time, I realize she doesn't like to be touched anywhere on the hindquarters. That makes me wonder what she's been subjected to. Anyhow, she decides I ain't so bad, and I'm too dumb and stubborn to give up, so after a few days of tryin', we become horse and rider.

I digress a little. This country is a haven for lost souls who, for very diverse reasons, don't mesh with society. Some of them remind me of the chicken who slipped and fell down the outhouse hole while trying to catch flies. Trapped, the rest of its days are spent waiting for someone to sit on the hole and recycle down some lunch. No one will reach down the six feet to rescue it, and it can't fly back up through the hole to freedom. Refugees all, giving themselves a chance to survive on the land, protected from ruthless masters by the rough bosom of solid rock mountains. But that ain't this story. So. Back to Wishbone and times ahead and how my feet got fixed.

I. So Sorry

Oh, I plumb forgot about Shorty, the less than four-foot-nothing real cowboy who rides the big Thoroughbred-Percheron cross horse that measures better than sixteen hands high.

I think, *He must climb halfway up a tree to mount this horse,* but then I notice a knotted rope hanging from the saddle horn he uses to shinny up with. How he gets the saddle on and off the horse's back I never learn, but he probably knows every rock and stump within forty miles that's high enough. He's a real-life old-dwarf who's rode this country since his birth on the family ranch around the other side of the mountain. (I'll bet he surprised his folks!)

I stayed at one of his line cabins for a night, on the way back from Lone Creek. A beautiful place nestled in a horseshoe-shaped flat, hidden high up on the side of a low mountain, two miles above the river. The dirt roof of his line cabin is piled, almost covered, with all kinds of antlers and horns from the many animals he's eaten over the years while attending his range cows. There's also many old tools about, all in good shape, that he uses to make everything from horseshoes to wagon wheels. It is his unlucky cows whose skeletons litter the bottom of the Mighty River ravines. It is also Shorty who informed my prospective partner of my wish to ride the mountain trails...

J. Sidetracked

Not to divert from this mountain adventure, but upon examining past interactions with this diverse earth and its inhabitants I've discovered it's best to be very open and fluid toward my surroundings, whatever they may be. Otherwise, my stubborn conditioned programming could very easily get me killed. There are many ways a person can die: on the highway, in a darkened back alley, on a sidehill, among a rowdy crowd, in a fancy restaurant with an unchewed fish bone lodged in your throat, or a half million other things. The point being, to enjoy and preserve your life you need to know and respect the rules of survival in any and every particular situation you may find yourself in, without allowing preconceived ideas to interfere with the truth at hand. There is much truth not pleasant but much that is, so you'd best be open to what you like, and you will recognize it when it's near!

K. About Wishbone

This dapple-gray mare grew up on the wild and partly open hills and mountainsides. Her dam and the rest of her herd ran free, looking after their own well-being. This includes avoiding hungry mountain lions, wolves, and the big bears who terrorize and feed on them! It also includes pawing through deep winter snows so they can get a bite of frozen brown grass, trying not to slip off icy or muddy clay and narrow trails, or even quicksand bog holes that will suck you in way above your ears. She is a good horse, a survivor, one who has learned from watching others of her own kind survive or succumb to their demise.

I doubt she ever tasted hay or grain. Such is the life of a wild-born horse. She could (with calm confidence) walk across a moving shale slide that would make an experienced mountain climber beg his imagined gods for another day of life!

She is four years old and at the beginning of the prime of her life. Her life turned out shorter than it should have been, not to negate my guilt, but that happened after she and I said our goodbyes. A sad story, not her fault, but the fault of a person who really should have known better. Looking back, I wish I'd known better too!

I still think of her more than fifty years later, and I thank her for the good times we had together this summer. I should have turned her loose to fulfill her destiny with her birth environment before I left the area, instead of leaving her at the old stable. When I later enquired of Wishbone's whereabouts, I learned that Sam had borrowed her to add to his pack string. In his care, she slipped off an icy trail and broke her neck when she hit the bottom. I once imagined what could have possibly caused a surefooted horse such as Wishbone to slip on a trail, but I now prefer to spend my thoughts on her generous gifts to me.

Let me thank her now by telling you of the sometimes crazy, often foolish, but always amazing things she and I did together, and of the devoted service she provided me.

"Wishbone, my friend, here's wishes to you. May we someday meet again, on a journey through the stars."

After Wishbone and I learn a few of each other's quirks upon our first short rides, I decide to figure out a way I can ride, along with my gear and food, without the convenience and luxury of a saddle. Using my bed blanket as the first layer on her back, I cover it with the light canvas tarp I wrap myself in for sleeping. I then strap this on her with a wide cinch under her belly and another over the coverings on her back. Where these two cinches join, I attach a pair of stirrups, one on each side, that I scrounge from a dilapidated saddle I discover abandoned in a cabin with a caved-in roof. Now we have a bareback pad with foot stirrups. The stirrups will allow me to transfer, through my legs, some of my weight onto my feet. This not only relieves some pressure off my butt, but also allows freer movement for Wishbone. The inside leg muscles that squeeze my knees onto Wishbone's ribs will develop in time. These muscles, that I as a non-rider use very little, gives a rider a pivot point at the knees, allowing contact, balance, and co-ordinated communication between horse and rider.

I tie my two small cloth sacks together at their tops, one half-filled with clothes, the other with a little food. These I drape over the pad so they hang and rest in front of where I sit. We are now as ready as can be for our summer ride.

Just one thing left to do before heading out. We must ride over the mountain to a little store that has a hitching rail out front and that supplies the locals with a few essentials. They also serve alcohol on the three wooden stools at the counter.

Local legend tells of a patron sat at the bar, ordering a shot of whiskey, no clothes on except for his batwing chaps and riding boots with dangling spurs. Bare-assed, his pecker straight out front, and his balls hangin visible below. I don't ask whether his girlfriend kicked him out of bed or whether he's in a hurry to get back to her! For all I know, he could have been out hunting for a sheep.

Another story the boys on this reserve like to tell was of a fellow who was castrated with the dull lid of a campfire-rusty tin can because he raped one of the girls. They hunted him, tracking him down as he tried to make his escape by hiding in the bush. Maybe they told this story to Sam and I so they could keep their women all to themselves. Basic natural animal propagation instincts; these guys do live very close to their nature!

I believe these stories because of different things I see with my own two eyes in the couple days I camp here.

This is a small village with its houses close together. While I'm talking to a guy standing on his house porch one sunny afternoon, he pulls out his oversize cock, and while shaking it, he hollers at the top of his lungs for all to hear, "*Does anybody want a fuck?*"

I hear no one volunteer, but I can imagine he gets at least one unfussy visitor after we have left. The point being, almost anything imaginable was not out of the ordinary for this time and place. Almost like a raunchy dance club, or even family TV today.

My feet are beginning to fester again from the blood poisoning not yet cured, and it is once more getting difficult to walk. An old healer lady heats an enameled pot of water on her wood cookstove, stirs in some leaves and Epsom salts, inviting me to soak my feet. That helps, and it may even have cured me if I'd kept at it for a few days, but I'm anxious to start the trek.

The pain from blood poisoning is excruciating. I am trying to ignore it, because I really want to explore these mountains. I still have the childish idea I will find Shangri-la in a distant hidden valley.

I do find a few of the keys there, to the door of Shangri-la, but I don't recognize them at this time!

We leave the two packhorses staked at the old church along with our gear and head up the trail over the mountain, to the grub stake store, about fifteen miles up, across, and down the other side. Sam on his good-lookin' little mare and me on Wishbone. A couple of Native boys want to ride with us to the store. In the valley bottom it's a sweltering hot day in July. The trail climbs three or four steep switchback miles up the side of this flat-topped mountain. We walk the horses slow, easy, so they don't overheat. When we reach the top, this trail levels off, and the air is much cooler and mountain-fresh sweet!

The whole ride up, we are subjected to the boys bragging about the speed and stamina of their mounts, so when on top one of them suggests we have a race to the store. Their challenge is on. The first one out of the race is Sam, when his horse blows straight through a sharp corner and off into the trees. In the background I can hear the crashing for a bit, but I have a race to win, so Sam is left to his tree-snapping fate, while I concentrate on the ride. I'm standing with my toes in the stirrups, jockeyin to give Wishbone unrestricted room to move under me. The clear wind whistles past and we leave the boys, on their fast horses, in Wishbone's cloud of dust. Wishbone and I have the whole trail to ourselves. We're loving it and never slow up till we hit the steep zigzag trail down, from high above the store. I leave her tied to the wooden hitching rail in front of the store. Halfway across the store yard, I realize I'm walking fine and my feet don't hurt anymore. Standing with my toes in the stirrups and working all the muscles in my feet and legs during the long race has broken the bowie knife holes open in the soles of both feet, and all the infecting poison has pumped out!

"Thank you, Wishbone. You ran faster than the wind, you made me proud and healthy. We outran the others by a very long shot!"

Once the stragglers arrive, we buy our cloth sack of rolled breakfast oats and a bag of bannock flour for the trek. The cotton sacks Sam dunks quickly in the irrigation water-ditch. I ask why, and he replies, "So they form an outer crust. A crust will prevent the flour from sifting out on the long jolting pack ahead."

We are now ready for the unknown, for the land of our dreams.

L. The Trek

With the packhorses we had left staked at the old church and all our gear, it's time to head into roadless country. The big bay gelding has a front leg swollen about twice the size it should be. He doesn't want to put any weight on it. Damn, with his big feet he stepped on a rusty nail in an old board that is lying beside the run-down church. We have to make forty miles today to our first camp, so Sam unloads all the bay's pack, transferring it among the other horses. With Sam dallied to the bay and me prodding him from behind with a stick, we strike out on the trail. It takes a lot of encouragement to keep him moving, but after many miles of tugging and prodding, a hole opens up on the inside of his leg and the thick yellow poison starts pumping out. With the pressure released on his leg, we make better time.

If we'd left him standing around, he would have surely died. It wasn't that we knew what we were doing, but more that we needed to cover ground, that saved his life, the same as mine had been saved by the race over the mountain the day before. Observing this has helped set in my mind that sometimes the old adage of "use it or lose it" applies in spades. I do not recommend this for broken bones, but I've often seen it work well for infections or bones that have slipped out of place. Movement is often a blessing not only to the body, but it also limbers the spirit!

After thirty miles of tough riding, I'm so tired I plumb go to sleep and wake up when I hit the ground after falling off Wishbone. We only have five more miles to go, so I climb back aboard and continue to the camp at Lone Creek. Next day I attempt to put shoes on my horse for the rough ground ahead. I know little of looking after a horse's feet, but like everything else I'm willing to learn the hard way.

Someone packed a wood cookstove into this old dirt-floored cabin, but it has long ago rusted out. The cast-iron top of the stove is all that's left of its former glory. Some enterprising soul replaced all its sides with stones, piling sand around them to keep the fire inside. The top of this stove is good, so it's fine to cook on. This is the last stove I see for the next six weeks!

M. Shoes for Wishbone

Back at the outpost store, I bought horseshoes of the proper size for Wishbone, one size bigger on her front feet than back, along with enough nails to hold them on. With a little shaping and bending they should fit her and save her feet from wearing thin on the many miles of trail ahead. If a horse is on a dirt trail there's no need of shoes, but we know not what lies ahead, so best to shoe. I never shod before, so I have much to learn. The front feet go okay; the back is a different matter. To hold the front feet, you stand beside the leg to be worked on, with your back toward the horse's head, and you bend your back and lift the hoof up so it can be held between your knees. Wishbone has never before been shod, but we've already spent time together, so we've developed a trust of each other. So, to work on the back feet, standing with your side against the wanted leg, your back still toward her head, you lift the hind leg up and over your thigh, resting it between your knees. The leg does not come from behind and between, like the front legs, through to your knees, but rather over the top of your thigh. This I don't know, but I am about to learn. The other major thing I am about to learn—and believe me, this is important—is that the pointy tip of the nail should be pre-bent a little, so when you drive them in through the preformed holes in the steel shoe and up into the hoof, the bend makes them curl and come out the side of the hard outer hoof rather than going straight up into the tender parts inside!

With the hind leg pulled up between my knees from behind, I proceed to drive the nail straight up into her foot. That nail going up into the tender parts must have been very painful for her, and because of the massive strength in a horse's hindquarters and my improper hold on her, she lifts and drives me, arms flapping birdlike, through the air!

After an instant of eternity, I land on my head twenty feet away. I always land on my head because gravity has more effect on it than on my lighter, softer parts. Wishbone's hoof pounds sense into me from bottom up; the ground knocks sense into me from top down. Both give me enough pause to figure out what I've done wrong. I thank my lucky stars again that I didn't get my leg ripped open from a sharp nail when I flew off the end of her hoof. There are large arteries on the insides of your legs that if opened up would bleed you out real quick.

We get all four shoes on without further mishap. Not a job a farrier would be proud of, but it'll work for now...

N. Onward

We have breakfast oats for morning porridge, flour and baking powder to make bannock, which some call fry bread. We've berry season in full swing, probably fish in the creeks, and we have the prospect of wild red meat to give us strength. As we ride along one afternoon, a momma grouse with half-grown chicks following crosses the trail in front of us. Sam pulls out his rifle to shoot her. I intervene on her behalf.

"You can't shoot; her babies will starve if you kill her."

Sam whines, "But I want the meat."

"We'll find something without young, farther up the trail," I assure him.

For the first week we follow old wagon trails that had been made in the dustbowl of the dirty thirties. A time when many people fled the starving cities and abandoned the abused, misunderstood, and eroded farmland. They traveled into still-intact wild country to make a living. Feeding their families with nature's game, building snug log cabins wherever there was water and enough good dirt to grow a garden, and if they were lucky, maybe a meadow with grass to feed a horse or milk-cow. A lot of these old trails and survival camps have not been used in many decades. The dirt-roofed log cabins have rotted back into the ground, and the trails are now grown thick with little trees. A few trails have been kept open by the passage of deer, elk, moose, and bear, along with many other critters. Most of these people, whose reminiscences of cabins we sometimes come across, left the wilderness life when the great war started, because there were many city jobs available working on products in the armament factories.

Because Wishbone's high backbone is in constant contact with my tender tailbone, an open sore develops where my skin has rubbed raw. Every day, sitting on the horse, the sore dries and hardens. The silver-dollar-size scab sticks to my blue jeans, and every day, as I lower my pants to have a dump, I have to peel them from the scabbed sore, reopening it. It takes weeks for the skin to harden and heal. Perhaps its healing has something to do with the fact I'm no longer sitting the horse like a sack of soft spuds. It takes a while to develop riding muscles, co-ordination, and balance to be one with the horse.

There are no creeks on our trail big enough to fish in, so after a couple weeks of nothing to eat except for bannock, oats, and a few berries, I'm craving meat. There's no deer to be found in this low country. I didn't know it at the time, but the deer are all up higher on the mountains at this season of the year, where there's more moisture and lusher, more succulent plants. We camp for the night on the edge of a big open grassy meadow. At one end of this meadow is a shallow reedy lake. I hear ducks quacking. This activates my digestive juices, and I decide that a duck will make a nice supper.

O. Horse Care

Before we get to supper, let me tell the greenhorns a little of how our horses are fed. A horse working hard needs good feed. They burn up a lot of energy on the trail. This energy needs replacing, or they soon get thin and weak. The wild horses often get so weak during a bad winter that they succumb to starvation. This affects the young and the old more than the strong ones of prime age, but just the same, it's a sad sight. Horse genetics developed in the warm, dry open country of Africa, Europe, and Asia and are not entirely suited to the harsher environment of the mountains of northwestern North America. They are hardy, adaptable animals, but this environment can be very detrimental to them. Most of these animals, with luck and perseverance, can and do survive without human help, but a horse that's working should and must be well cared for.

Our horses are not grained because you can't expect a horse to carry its food on its back, along with a rider and whatever other gear you might have, so we choose our campsites in places with good nutritious grass, running water and hopefully not too many bugs. The low, wet meadows are often so thick with biting mosquitoes that the horses are extremely agitated. The worst of these places are so bad that when you rub your hand down the horse's neck, blood drips off the ends of your fingers! It doesn't matter how much a horse drinks or eats; they cannot keep replenishing this horrendous blood loss and still stay in decent shape. When the bugs are bad, a horse likes to get up on the hillsides and ridges, where the wind blows the bugs away. A good horse will not stray too far from camp when not tied, but they are social animals and can be led off by roaming bands of wild horses, liking the company of their own kind. If the bugs are bad, an untethered horse will leave camp, soon putting many miles behind it in search of a bug-free area, leaving its master on foot to pack his own gear and himself. Horses can become very chummy, like a good dog, but especially in the summer they don't depend on humans for food, so they do not bond themselves to us with quite the same needs a dog might.

It is sometimes a compromise between a bug-free area and a good grass area free of obstructions. A staked horse can get entangled and hurt if the area is not chosen with horse's well-being in mind. If the bugs are not bad, and the grass is good, only one horse needs to be staked, with another one or two hobbled and the remainder let free. They stick around while a person attends camp or sleeps. We switch which ones are to be free each night, so as to give them all a chance to eat their fill. Often during a day's travel, we come upon an especially good grass area, so we take a break and let them belly up.

A horse is usually hobbled by tying its front feet together with just enough room so they can move around to eat as they choose. Still, the area must be chosen so the horse does not get hurt because of its restraints. Another method to keep a horse around camp is to stake them in a good grass area with a rope twenty or thirty feet long. This gives the horse a large circle to feed in and should be sufficient for the night if the grass is abundant. Again, entanglement can be a problem, so a person must be cautious and alert to all possible mishaps. A burn from the rope becoming entangled on a horse's leg or from improper hobbles can seriously impair or ruin a good horse, or any horse for that matter.

Some folks stake their horses with a long rope tied to the halter, but as the horse eats it's always stepping on the rope. They learn not to tangle their feet with it, but neither the rope nor the halter last long with four feet stepping and pulling on it. Wishbone is a smart horse. It doesn't take long to teach her how to hobble or to tether on a hind foot. Hobbles can be made with either a leather belt-like strap in the shape of a figure eight, or a soft thick rope. The leather hobbles are one more thing to carry, so I use a soft rope, but either way you must be careful the leg does not get rubbed raw. The hind foot tether is the best way to stake as it gives the horse easy movement and is not hard on the rope, but the horse must first be trained for it.

Of course, the horse must be well broke, quiet in nature, and understanding of the rope before an attempt should be made at foot staking. The process of teaching a horse does not take long, but must be done with patience so the horse understands the concept and becomes accepting of it.

You have its halter on with a short lead shank, and then you tie another rope to the horse's front foot. You lead the horse with its halter shank, and when it starts a step forward you pull its foot rope. Gradually, the horse will learn to lead by pulling on the foot rope only. When it accepts being led by one front foot, you transfer the rope to the other front foot. After it understands and accepts being led by either of its front feet, you do the same with both hind feet. The big advantage of a hind foot stake is, when the horse is grazing it's dragging the rope behind, not stepping on it with all four feet, and it has free head movement. Before leaving any horse staked or tied, one must be sure the horse understands the rope, or a major wreck can and likely will occur.

Never use a slipknot to tie a horse. As the rope tightens, it can leave a nasty rope burn or if it's around the neck can soon asphyxiate a horse. A horse has a very fast metabolism, and if its air is cut off it will be dead in seconds, whereas it takes minutes for the same to affect a human. Always use the bowline knot, as it will not tighten on itself and is very easy to untie whenever you like. It's a challenge to learn this knot but is really quite simple once you get the knack of it.

Before I leave the subject of horse care, I should mention one more thing: you must be well aware of any sores that may develop from an improper pack, rope burns, or any other trail injuries that occur. A horse must be well cared for. A fat horse is no good for the trail as they're too soft and sore easily, but a skinny horse is a shame on its master. A horse must be given time to eat to stay in decent shape, but they can cover a lot of ground, carrying you and your survival gear across miles of country. I look after Wishbone as best I can with luck and the little knowledge I have. She teaches me many things as we travel together.

I'm so glad she was able to run free as a young horse as she's learned many survival techniques that save us more than once. A naive pen- or pasture-raised horse would have freaked and took me with her in some of the situations Wishbone and I find ourselves in.

She's a calm, collected, willing, strong, and independent horse. She's not real pretty except for her dapple-gray color, but she is indeed a very fine horse! At first I use a soft rubber bit in Wishbone's mouth, but it's not long before no bit at all is necessary as she responds quite willingly to subtle cues from simple things, like the way I shift my weight, balance, leg pressure, or verbal command. When we come to a good patch of grass and it's time for a break, it is much easier for her to eat with a free mouth. She never takes advantage of this, as I see some horses do, by only eating when I give my okay.

I do however use soft rope reins attached to either side of her halter, just to keep a good connection to her, mostly for my own sense of security.

Back to duck supper. And can you believe it? The dog wouldn't eat meat.

P. No Quack for Me

It's afternoon when we come upon this meadow. The grass is almost knee high, thick, and there's plenty of water; it'd been an old homestead. Even though all the buildings have long since returned to the ground, there are interesting artifacts. One thing I discover, whoever lived here long ago had a wagon and horse team. A part of this meadow that is particularly spongy soft has a corduroy road across it. This looks somewhat like an upside-down train track. First, they laid eight-inch trees in two parallel lines about six feet apart. They placed more logs, about eight-feet long, side by side, crosswise on top of these parallel under pieces. The end result is a road a half-mile long, floating on top of the soft boggy ground that the horses and wagon can travel across without sinking. All these road-trees still show marks of being cut by hand, with an ax and a crosscut saw. There was no such thing as a chainsaw in those days, at least none available this far into no-man's-land. These men and the few women who accompanied them were a tough bunch.

They were hard as nails and as resilient as rubber. It seems their lives were often short as they worked themselves beyond human endurance, but they were free, and to them that was a necessary part of living. They were the trailblazers, the ones who went first into the wild unknown, discovering things that would make life easier for those who followed. Some of them died young in their journeys, but they lived the way they chose and were scared of little. They were the artists of their day, bringing visions of an unknown country to their fellow humankind. I admire their grit and self-determination.

We'd been covering a lot of ground lately, so a good rest and feed are in order for the horses. Just wish the bugs weren't so bad.

Damned if I can remember where that shotgun got to, but I wish I'd had it this day. These ducks are them little small buggers, not the nice big mallards I was hoping for. I am using an old and very rusty single-shot .22, which Sam has been carrying on his packhorse. He sawed the stock off to make it easier to pack, but that makes it very difficult to steady on a target because, without the shoulder piece, it wobbles all over the place. These ducks look mighty small sitting way out on the water, and I can't keep the sights of this wobbly piece on them. Rather than risk scaring them with a near miss, I decide to sneak around a small hill to get closer.

This little hill is covered in trees except for a flat opening on top. When I come into the opening, I see a deer lying down, soaking up the last warmth of the day's sun. This deer is looking at me from thirty feet away. I think it will jump and run, but I guess it never seen a human before, so it has no fear.

Q. Food

Over the next few weeks I learn how unafraid these deer are, but right now I am just hungry. We have been eating nothing for weeks other than porridge oats and bannock for breakfast, a few berries throughout the day, then for supper we have bannock and more oats. That gets monotonous. A person starts to crave such things as sweets and protein: the body's way of saying it's not getting enough of what it needs. If I was to do this trip again, I would make sure to include a sack of dry beans and something sweet in the food pack.

I remember hearing once that chocolate-covered ants are a delicacy. I'm not sure why anyone would want to waste good chocolate by covering an ant, but maybe they know something I don't.

When we cook our oats in the little pot on the campfire we set them aside, waiting for the bannock to finish. The pot has no lid, so often the ants get in it before we're ready to eat. It takes a while to pick the ants out with a twig. One particular day I'm very hungry and too tired for this tedious task, so I just stir them up and begin eating. The ants are crunchy and very sweet. I like them, as I'd been having cravings. After that, I intentionally set the pot so it'll get lots of ants in it, stir them into the oats, and yum-yum. That sure smartens them oats up.

I done a little hunting as a kid for small game and was raised around many animals on the farm, so it's instinct for me to know that to keep an animal calm you have to make sure to stay calm yourself.

I do not want to spook this deer, so I sit down in an easy, fluid motion. Even moving with exaggerated slowness can alert an animal to your intentions. Do not look in their eyes, as that lets them know you are a predator and puts fear or challenge into their hearts. The trick is to pretend, without exaggeration, that you do not see them. I put a shell in the old gun. To keep that stockless contraption from wobbling all over so I can make a clean one-shot kill, I lay down with as much body-to-ground contact as I can get. I center the sights for a brain shot and squeeze the trigger.

Click is a very loud sound when you're expecting a sharp *crack*. What? Something's wrong! Is the shell no good, or is it the gun? Don't look at the deer! Don't let it know you're worried and nervous! Keep calm. Sit up slow and ease the shell out of the gun. The shell looks good. There's no corrosion on it. There is also no firing pin indent on the back of this shell. Is the firing pin broke or is it the pin spring? Take the bolt out of the gun and examine. There's so much crud and dirt on the bolt face that the firing pin cannot extend far enough to reach the shell. Find something to clean it with. A pine needle is not stiff enough. A small piece of broken stick might work. Carefully clean the bolt face. Looks okay now. Insert the bolt back in the gun, feed the shell in. The deer has been watching me this whole time. It hasn't moved. It's still calm! Try again. Very careful aim. Squeeze trigger. The quiet is shattered by a loud *crack!* Instant death. We got food. Now the work begins!

I'd like to tell you it was a buck deer, but that would be a lie. It was the first deer I'd seen in weeks, and I thought I might not see another. I was hungry and naive! It was a female deer, but that's not the worst. I'd like to not tell you of this and be able to forget it happened, but it did, and it shames me still. It wasn't just that it was a female deer. Too late to worry about that—must get her processed before this warm weather ruins the meat.

R. The Task

It's a half-mile back to camp. I walk fast and get Sam to come and help me. We tie her legs together with a pole between them and lift her onto our shoulders. She's heavy, but we carry her back to camp. I use my knife to remove her innards by opening up her belly. That's when I discover the fawn inside! Of course, it's dead from lack of oxygen. What a heartbreak! It's a real shame to have done that, but to survive you have to eat, and sometimes that means doing things you wish you hadn't done. I didn't know it at this time, but I would soon see many nice buck deer. It's not a shame to kill a male deer when there are lots, as not many males are needed to keep the species going. One male deer can breed many does. If there are too many bucks they fight each other, often to the death. It takes a female deer to raise a fawn, and to kill one is to kill many. The nasty deed is done, so let's make the best of it and not waste the life I've so foolishly taken. To waste her now would be more than shameful. It would be a difficult to forgive crime!

I learn later there are many adult hunters, even to this day, who profess to be keepers of the land yet feel no shame in killing females. Some have so little respect for our wildlife that they kill and wound many more animals than can be replaced by birth. These killers are much worse, with their modern tools, than ruthless wolves. They feel no remorse for what they do, and their lack of respect gives them a strange sort of entitlement to devastate the future of our already challenged wildlife. They are adamant in demanding it is their traditional right, but modern tools have changed abilities, and morals have not correspondingly evolved. If this devastation were traditional, we would have starved ourselves long ago. It's a terrible state. As I write this, the killing goes on, even worse than ever before.

In all of my previous years, I had been encouraged to respect the life of others, so I was saddened by the taking of this female and her young, but what is done cannot be changed. It is only something to remember so it's not repeated.

This deer, now gutted, needs to be skinned, the meat cut up into thin strips and dried for preservation. All simple things to do if one knows how, but without any kind of experience or guidance they can be challenging tasks. The skinning and cutting up goes well, as I'd handled many smaller animals for our dinner table as a youngster, but I'd never had to dry meat before. This sounds like a simple task, but there are many subtle tricks, learned later, that I would have liked to have known at the time. In the warm season, if you just hang the meat it will soon be covered in flies, which can contaminate the meat with their eggs, soon turning into maggots. Maggots are nutritious in themselves, but are repulsive and not good for preservation. Smoke is needed to keep the flies away. The meat all cut up in strips, it needs to be hung in a way that it can be bathed in smoke as it dries.

In a scrap pile from the old homestead is an old-fashioned wire-steel bedspring that will do the job. We could have made small pole racks to hang the meat strips on, but this spring is handy and will save us a lot of work. We tie the bedspring on all four corners with rope so it hangs between trees, flat with the ground and high enough so a low, smoky fire can be built underneath. We don't want to cook the meat, just dry it slow with enough smoke to keep the flies off and help preserve it. We lay all the meat strips on the wire bed frame, gather small branches from the pine trees that are close around, and build our wide and smoky fire. It takes three days to dry the meat. It turns black from the tarry pitch of the pine branches and has a very strong smoke flavor. I learn later that willow or some of the sweet-juiced deciduous trees make fine meat-smoking material, but one should never use anything with tarry pitch or strong flavors. I do get used to eating it, and it keeps me alive, but it has so much pitch from the pine smoke that I am pooping coal black. Live and learn. It seems some of us learn the hard way.

S. On Our Own

A little back history of my riding partner seems in order. I knew nothing about Sam when I started riding with him and know little of him now. We share a quiet, peaceful co-existence on the trail and around camp, occasionally exchanging necessary words. I don't know how it is for him because, like I say, we never talk, but for me I feel no need for talk. I just enjoy the movement and mesmerism of this wild, majestic land.

I learn he'd been a vegetarian from the big cities of the east coast when I offer his dog a piece of deer meat and the dog refuses it. This dog has eaten nothing its whole life except for cooked grains, vegetables, and beans. I'd never met a dog that wouldn't eat meat with gusto, so it is a surprise when the dog turns his nose up at the meat and walks away, but a bigger surprise is yet to shock me.

Now, I should probably say that perhaps I was trained, some, to be politically incorrect. I do remember hearing such things as "Politicians flutter in the wind," and "War is a rich man's game, paid for with the sweat and blood of peons," but I was never trained to be homophobic. It just seems natural not to be sexually attracted to my own gender. To me, guys being sexually intimate with each other is about as repulsive as bestiality. A story an aunt told about one of my uncles seals this deal. He was surprised, in the barn, pants down, standing in a wheelbarrow he'd pushed up behind a big Holstein cow. He claimed the cow had consented and that she'd enjoyed it. For years after, every time a cow was due to calve they'd rush to the barn to see if the new calf looked like uncle.

On another note, same song, one of my grandmother's sows gave birth to a piglet who had both male and female organs, so to me it is understandable there is sometimes genetic gender variance, all the way from one side of the spectrum to its opposite and every shade of gray between. I can see females sometimes being affectionate with one another because they got a special deep motherly gentleness that they like to share, but males are aggressively domineering and that just don't seem to me to be anything but brute animal instincts, and I like to think I'm a little more evolved than that. I hear tell that some four-legged male critters practice homosexuality, but as far as I've ever seen that only happens with caged critters that haven't been raised in a free natural setting. The exception being those that are genetically mixed. I just happen to have been solidly born on the strictly heterosexual side, and I plan to stay that way.

No one has a right to torture another with condemnation just because of the way they are born. I once heard that human society is becoming bisexual, and in the future we'll become trisexual (meaning it will become acceptable for us to try anything). There has to be much more to healthy interaction than our extreme focus on getting our rocks off. I do try to remain neutral on the subject of personal interaction because I'm a firm believer in free will. But I do see there's much unhealthy physical and emotional domination even in so-called normal relationships

On this trek, our custom after a meal is to roll a smoke and have a cowboy coffee. Just coarse coffee grounds thrown in a pot and boiled till black. No sugar, no milk, but it's a treat just the same. Sam says he likes coffee because it keeps him regular.

This evening, after our coffee, I rest with my head propped against an old log, relaxed, stretched out, and enjoying the fire. Sam moseys over and, standing full frontal, he pulls out his dink, shakes it a bit, intentionally exposing himself, then proceeds to piss close beside me. Now the custom is to walk away from camp a ways and relieve yourself in at least a semblance of sanitary privacy, so this is more than a little strange. Many a time I've witnessed dogs, with a leg lifted, proclaim their authority of ownership. *What am I being marked for?* I was given a lot of freedom in early childhood, encouraged to think and do for myself, taught never to accept force or coercion. It seems I am being hustled, and I don't enjoy it one bit.

As I said, I wasn't raised to be homophobic; that's just something that comes natural to me. I'm no expert when it comes to girls, but him and his dink is not something I want any part of. A person has to draw the line somewhere and he'd crossed mine. I, of course, being quiet and noncombative whenever that's an option, ignore his indiscretion and pretend I've not been offended. I take my one blanket, which also serves as part of Wishbone's bareback pad, and my small thin tarp away from camp and over closer to where the horses graze, curl up, and go to sleep. In the morning I arise early, split the sack of dry deer meat, leave half for Sam, get Wishbone ready, and ride off, leaving Sam with his three horses, his dog, all the rolled oats and flour, pots, pans, gun, the whole outfit. I'm heading farther west, traveling light, but I am free—no guilt, no bullshit, and for damn sure, no dink in my face.

T. Wishbone and Lonesome Me

I have little idea where I am, except in some very wild country, enclosed within the rugged western mountains. We've come through a lot of diverse areas since leaving the river—all of it roadless, most of it rough, some without even a small game trail to follow. I know which way west is because of the sun. I also know the coast is a hundred and more crow-flight miles in that direction. I have no idea what lies ahead, but I'm young, independent, stubborn, and strong. One of the things about being naive, which is both a blessing and a curse, is that there's nothing to fear because there's nothing known. How can you be afraid of something if you don't even know it exists? That does get one into trouble, but it also opens many doors if you survive the trouble.

I have a damn fine horse. I don't know how good she is till many years later, after I've ridden scores of other horses. Few of them could compare to Wishbone's talents of survival or even her many other pleasant attributes. I may well have left my bones in those hills if it wasn't for her calmness in the face of death, and her determination to live even when the chances seemed slim.

So west we proceed; no rush, but every day we travel. Nothing for me to eat but smoked-black deer meat and a few berries I sometimes come across. Wishbone eats grass while I sleep, and she also gets some nice feed along the trail in special spots we stop. There's lots of small, clear, cold streams coming down from the mountain peaks. We steadily climb higher each day as we make our way into the heart of these majestic and massive mountains. This is incredible country for someone as young as I, who has no previous experience with this type of rugged, untamed land. Some of the mountainsides are beginning to open up into sidehill meadows with decent grass and many flowers. We're seeing lots of deer, most of them with large velvet-covered antlers. Thinking back, the does were probably hiding, in seclusion, nursing their newborns. The bucks lift their heads from grazing as we ride by within a few feet. Looking at us with mild curiosity, without showing the slightest fear. We are often almost close enough to reach out and touch them. They have obviously never been spooked by human contact. I wish it could be one of these fat bucks in my cloth sack, rather than the one that is.

One particularly beautiful, sunny afternoon I find myself sitting on a big open mountainside surrounded by a dense and colorful profusion of diverse, vibrant wildflowers. The colors and shapes of their blooms are astonishing! I am amazed and overwhelmed, soaking in their beauty! As I sit in awe, tears well in my eyes, blurring them to the life surrounding me. As half-inch tears roll down my cheeks, I realize I am so sad because there is no one here for me to share this beauty with. No sound escapes my lips, but my heart aches for human companionship. It is time for me to be with people again!

It is many miles and weeks from where we've come, and the chances of finding our back trail are slim. If I'd have let Wishbone have the lead she would have taken us straight home, but at this time I have no idea of a horse's homing ability. At any rate, I'm not one to quit on an idea, so we continue west and up. Every day we are higher in elevation. We're getting near the top of high and rocky peaks. There are few trees up this high and it's cold at night, even in August. Not much for Wishbone to eat except rock and, even though the sights are grand, we both wish for more hospitable, lower ground.

I see two peaks not far above us and think, *That would be a wondrous place to watch the western sunset from.* On the way up this pass, between two solid granite peaks, there are a few inches of snow with many smallish rocks protruding. This kind of going is very hard on a horse's feet, so I walk, leading Wishbone, giving her back and her feet a rest, as I often do in our travels. I like to walk, and I'm sure she enjoys the reprieve of having no load other than two small bags—one with dry meat, the other with a few clothes. In this pass, a slight hollow between peaks that are not much higher, critter tracks are imprinted in the shallow snow. The wild animals in this vicinity also cross here. There are big buck tracks, as well as cougar, bear, wild sheep or goats, and many smaller unidentifiable ones. It's a much-used pass from one mountain valley to the next.

We watch the sunset and then head down the western side to find a level enough spot to camp the night. There's maybe six inches of snow on the ground, so it's not a concern until Wishbone breaks through, just her ears sticking up! I've unwittingly led her out over a snow-covered cliff! This is a huge winter drift that remains all summer. The top of it melts during warm afternoons and then forms a solid crust, allowing me to walk without sinking in. Because of the few inches we encountered earlier, I assume this snow is the same depth. Wishbone, being much heavier than I, breaks through, and we are in major trouble. I lay down on my belly to spread my weight out and not break through, ending up in the same predicament as her. I have no idea how deep this snow is, but it could well be thirty feet or more—enough to put an end to both our adventures. I have a hold of Wishbone's lead rope so she knows I'm with her. We are on a slight downhill incline. She doesn't freak out. If she'd started struggling she may have gone down so deep there would have been no chance of extricating her.

I talk to her, and maybe this is part of her calmness, but she's seen bad situations before, and she keeps her wits. Slowly, she raises one foot at a time, getting a little more of the dense snow under her each time. The fact we are going slightly downhill I'm sure helps. It takes a while, but we make it out of this cliff drift, then go a ways farther until we find a flat enough spot that'll do for the night. There's no grass here, but we can travel no farther in the dark. It is too risky on this mountaintop, not knowing if another cliff awaits us.

Years later, upon telling this mishap to a big game guide who sometimes used this pass, I am informed that any time they take horses through here they always make sure they have at least one shovel with them, to dig their horses out. We get lucky and survive, but it could have been worse!

Since there is nothing to tie her to on this open, sloped rock, I hobble Wishbone's front feet, roll up in my tarp, and wait for daylight.

I feel a weight on me when I awake. Emerging from heavy covers, I discover it has snowed hard this night. A good thing we stopped when we did because it has been a whiteout. In the very few hours I slept, we got over four inches, maybe six, of heavy, wet snow. I can hardly see Wishbone standing forty-feet from me. She has a thick layer of snow on her back. That and her dapple-gray color blend with the rest of the landscape. I shake the snow off my bed-pack, get Wishbone ready, and we head down the west side of this beautiful, cold, challenging mountain.

We go a few hundred yards and there in the snow is the biggest grizzly bear track I've ever seen. A monster! His front paw is bigger than a large dinner plate. He didn't smell us when he passed because it had been snowing so hard and the wind must have been in our favor. The little snow in his tracks says he passed just before the storm quit. He would have killed my hobbled horse with one swat of his huge paw and then swallowed me for dessert. I look at his track long enough to see which way his four-inch claws point, and we head the other way.

U. Into Lower Country

Enough of high Rocky Mountain peaks for this boy and his captive horse!

I hope that monster bear stays up on the mountain. And no more deep snow for us. I doubt a horse would ever venture up into this high rocky country on its own, and I'm sure she is as happy as I am that we're over the hump and heading downhill. It isn't all down, but we are back into vegetation. It's warmer the farther down we go and everything is green again. Not much to eat on a rock top, and that wind sure blows cold way up there. Sunny one minute and whiteout the next. Very volatile and incredibly, unpredictably beautiful!

You could say without exaggeration that if you stayed in one place for a single day you could expect to get sunburned, soaked in rain, hail, or snow, frozen by the wind, and then thawed out again by the strong sun. You'd have to be very alive, prepared, and strong to live for long at this altitude. We'd put on hard miles with little to eat, so we are not tough enough to stay here long!

Still heading almost due west. No back trails for us. West has been the plan, so unless something better presents itself, or we hit something impassable, we'll continue on. No telling what is down this side of the mountain, but we'd just as soon not have to climb that high again. Nothing to see but more mountains and wild expanses. We'll try to stay in the valley bottoms where it's warmer and there's green feed for Wishbone.

I'm spending more time now leading Wishbone and walking. This steady traveling is hard on her on the rough ground with little to eat at our night camps. We're both very relaxed as we slowly make our way along. We see big trees now. This west-facing side of the mountains must receive more moisture than the east side that we'd traveled up. The trees are tall and close together. There's still some opens that make traveling easier, but they're in the lower flat areas between high peaks. Some of these areas are soft and spongy with small, scattered clumps of dwarf spruce trees. We're always searching out the easiest, most open passage in the general direction of where we want to go. It's a little like tacking with a sailboat into the wind. Sometimes you have to go sideways to go ahead, 'cause straight ahead is impossible. We run out of easy going while skirting along the base of one mountain.

There's a big semi-open flat between this mountain and the next. It looks like it might be more open and better traveling on the other side. This open has a lot of dead trees, many of them fallen and laying flat on the ground, some of them partly submerged into the soft, moss-covered earth. We have to cross this area or cut our way through large dense trees ahead of us. That would take weeks if we had a saw or ax, which we don't, so across this open is our trail. The ground's soft, but it seems stiff enough to me. Fools are sometimes blessed with luck, and that's our fate this day.

Wishbone would have followed me into a raging fire if I'd asked her to. She never balks or pulls back from any of my directives. She is not a stupid animal, just dedicated to her service, to one who has no way of knowing how fragile life can be. No way of knowing how easy it is for the earth to take back her own. Mother earth gives so willingly, but she demands payment. She collects her dues in respect and allows you to live, or she takes her price with your life!

She let us go this day, but she has a hold on us, up to our belly buttons, before we pay her demand with respect.

As we walk across this soft, open meadow I am wondering why so many trees have died and fallen over. The ground feels spongy soft, but it seems firm. I walk along, leading Wishbone, while I admire the scenery. I'm looking at the mountain on the other side of this meadow when Wishbone sinks! She breaks through the top moss-covered crust that seems like firm ground to me. The top layer of this meadow is a dense mat of vegetation, which gives way under the concentrated pressure of Wishbone's four feet. A human foot has very little weight per square inch compared to a horse's feet. They are heavy in body and their feet are small. She punches through this thin surface and is stuck. The only thing holding her from sinking in farther is the small crisscrossed logs that lay on top the ground, now under her belly...

Oh my. We seem to be experts at jumping out of the frypan and straight into the fire!

Once again, Wishbone shows her mettle by remaining calm. I am at the far end of her lead shank, which is about six feet long, so I'm still on unbroken surface. That's quicksand under her, and the bottom could be twenty feet deep—who knows, maybe more? We sure don't want to find out the depth of this sucking hole by testing its grip with a struggle. The small logs under her are holding her up for now, but they will also make it difficult to get out. She'll have to lift her back legs up and over them. This will be a delicate undertaking. If she struggles, the rotten logs could break and down she would go, or a sharp broken branch could tear the thin skin of her belly open. Then I'd have to help her die with my pocketknife.

Oh my, what a mess we have gotten ourselves into. Wishbone's eyes show no fear, just the recognition of the trouble we're in.

I don't know if I could have made it out of that country without her, but I don't think twice about finding out. I'm with her, all the way, and she trusts me. What to do? I have no long rope I can run to the nearest tree to help pull on her. I couldn't budge her eleven hundred pounds anyhow, even if I had a good rope. I must stay calm. Take our medicine and succumb to our fate, whatever that may be.

Many years later, I watch a wild stud-horse intentionally cross an area similar to this. He lay on his belly with his back legs up under him and his front legs stretched out in front. He made it across a sixty-foot bog hole by crawling an inch at a time. The rest of his small band stood and watched till he was on the other side, and then they followed him, doing what he had done. To my amazement they all made it. I do not expect you to believe this, but I do, as I seen it with my own eyes. Perhaps Wishbone had learned in a similar fashion. I have no way of knowing, but what I do know is that without my help, except for my admiration of her, she proceeds in a similar fashion.

The belly logs make it difficult for her, but slowly she shifts her weight to one side, allowing her to lift one hind leg up and over the deadfall; she then shifts her weight by rolling slightly to the other side, lifting the other leg over as she had done the first. She takes her time doing this, carefully and with determination. She's a thinker, and she seems to know exactly what's needed. She pays her dues this day with respect. Respect for the Earth and the Earth lets her go! Her manner guides me to this day, for on that day she solidified in me what it takes to live through a situation such as this. I'm amazed and admire her calmness. What I seen is akin to a firing squad victim looking into the eyes of his assassins, knowing he is at peace with his maker, and without fear or flinching, accepting his fate. We make it across this sinkhole to more hospitable ground and never look back. We are both in need of a rest.

V. More Trail on Solid Ground

We're still a long ways from anywhere we might want to stay, and we are both homesick for our own kind. Nothing to do but keep getting on. We can cover a lot of miles in a day if the going is open or we have some sort of trail to follow. Wishbone has a fast walk that clicks the miles behind us. I often walk and lead her, giving us both a break. During our travels, I appreciate the feel of the ground underfoot, and it saves her energy for the times when we need it most. On the soft open trails I ride, as that is easy for her, but where it's rough or rocky she follows me.

One day as we walk, I notice a lynx ahead of us on the dirt game trail we follow. It's paying attention to something just off the side of the trail and hasn't noticed us. We walk toward it. I'm sure it must have heard Wishbone's hooves on the ground, but most wild animals show no fear of a horse or the sound of its feet. Not like they fear a man. I do believe man is the most feared animal on this planet. We've educated most things to run for their lives when in our presence. This long-haired cat ignores us, and I can only assume that it's because of a combination of the quietness of my campfire-made moccasins, the mesmeric sound of Wishbone's feet, and whatever is holding its attention trail-side. As we get within twenty feet, it sits on its haunches and stays focused on the hidden rodent it wants for dinner. We stop and admire its splendid coat of luxurious fur. What an incredibly beautiful animal in all its wild, vibrant glory. We must have disturbed its hunt, for after a while it arises and floats off, as if it had been a ghost.

We continue on. In a few days, still high in these mountains, we come upon a large and well set up canvas wall tent. It is complete with a wood heater, propane cook top, and a well-stocked larder of food. There is no one around. It has been recently set up and looks to me like a guide outfitter's camp. They must have packed all this stuff in with a team and wagon, or maybe a small 4x4 pickup or jeep, on the narrow dirt track that ends at this camp. They probably set it all up ahead of time and are now out picking up a client. It could also be a prospector's camp, but this is excellent big game country, and it looks like a hunt camp to me.

I wait for hours for someone to return, but no one shows. I've been craving sweets and a jar of corn syrup beckons me from a shelf. I've also been out of tobacco for weeks and here teases a full unopened can. They have a truckload of food and supplies, so I figure they can get along without the syrup, but I sure feel guilty about taking this can of tobacco and a book of rolling papers. I hope that when they return they bring some extra smokes with them, or there will be a grumpy guide someone will have to cope with. The syrup is tasty good when I dip my smoky meat in it. I would really like to have been able to pay, in some way, for the tobacco and syrup, as stealing is not my way, but I done took it. I've paid my debt for that crime, but not to that individual. I hope I didn't cause too much grief.

We now have a dirt two-track to follow, and we head down this seldom-used trail.

In a few days the trail turns north. We would have followed it no matter its direction because we'd had enough of majestic beauty and seek the familiarity of our own kind. I know this is not the trail to Shangri-la—rather, it leads back to familiar things I've known already, but so be it. Wishbone and I have had enough. We are still a long ways from the river, but we'll find our way there somehow.

It is a few more days before we see recent signs of man in the form of a pole cattle guard across the dirt track. A Russell fence stretches each side from the cattle guard. A wooden slip-pole gate lets us continue along the rutted two-track. Another half mile brings us to a log-fenced meadow that grazes a few head of saddle horses. Wishbone can't resist expressing her joy and longing. She lets out a loud and prolonged whinny. The other horses run toward us out of their open meadow. It's getting late in the day and this is a good place to spend the night.

We backtrack to the other side of the cattle guard we'd just come across. I don't want to camp with these horses on the other side of the fence because their visiting may cause a wreck with entanglement. I can't turn Wishbone in with them because I have no right to disturb someone else's stock, so we camp alone, with some distance and a pole cattle guard between us. This cattle guard is made with six-inch pine poles laid across the road. The road has been dug out a few feet deep before the poles were laid. There is a four or five-inch gap between each pole. The idea being that any cow or horse will not attempt to cross this, as they're afraid their feet will slip through the openings and they'll be stuck.

For safety, I hobble Wishbone before I turn in for the night. I am having a peaceful sleep when I'm awakened by a strange clunking noise. It takes a few minutes for me to realize what this sound is. It's pitch-black this night, and I have no light, but I know the only thing it could be is my talented horse. Her front feet are tied close together but she's determined to go for a visit. With her nose feeling the way, she places both front feet on a slippery pole, then one at a time she brings her back feet ahead onto another pole. She then has to lift both closely hobbled front feet, at the same time, onto the next pole. In this way, she's almost fully across the cattle guard before I apprehend her. She must be disappointed when I lead her back through the pole gate onto my side. I can't be mad at her when she's so talented! She's also smart enough to resign herself to my company for the rest of the night. The grass is very good where we're camped, and I hope a bellyful will help calm her frustration. Tomorrow's road lays north, and that's where we will go.

W. Where Are We Going?

Our two-track is heading almost due north, but it must also be heading back to some form of our so-called civilization. Old habits are hard to part with, even when they're not pleasant. They are familiar, and that is a longed-for aspect of our being. Even when we know we want something different, the old familiarity keeps calling us. It takes a lot of self-control to proceed on a new way, and I just don't have it at this time.

One afternoon, as we ride past a large open meadow, I notice a wolf pack skirting the far side. They're on the hunt for whatever they can tear apart. When they see us, they hide in the trees. Someone has for sure educated them on the distance of a rifle shot.

In a few days, this trail starts swinging east, and I now have the feeling we are making a very large circle. This will have to bring us close to where we started two months earlier. Wishbone must know where we are because her normal fast walk now picks up into a ground-eating shuffle.

We pass a small ranch, and I think about stopping to unburden my guilt of the tobacco theft, but I'd have to work to pay it off and that would take time. Both Wishbone and I are determined to get back to familiar places, so on we go. After another couple days the good dirt-truck-trail turns again and starts heading southeast. It won't be long before we're dropping in elevation down toward the warm benches of the Mighty River.

We can smell home, and this encourages us to proceed with little rest. I think Wishbone is in more of a hurry than I am; she seems to walk faster the closer we get. We are now above the Mighty River on open bunchgrass sidehills. This is very nutritious round grass, and it doesn't take much of it to keep a horse going. For the last eight miles or so, the trail drops down close to the river to get around some steep impassable rock cliffs. The wild goats live on these cliffs, so the mountain lions—or cougars, as they're called some places—have a time getting to them. A little lower, where we are, is the domain of bighorn sheep and mule deer.

When we come to the last big creek that needs to be crossed on our home stretch to the ferry, a good-looking lady who has been bathing in the cold water encourages us to take it easy. She stands before me in her freshly bathed nakedness as she takes in the intense but shy, mysterious wildness in our eyes, our extra lean physique, and smiling, she softly proclaims, "You ought to slow down a little and rest awhile."

My surprise at seeing anyone at all here is exagerated by the fact she is a beautiful naked woman, a few years older than I, and has a very attractive but unsettling aura of perceptive self-confidence. I, of course, am speechless, and my only outward response is to give Wishbone her okay to proceed for home. I would respond different if this same scenario presented itself today, and we'd not have the same story, but so be it—onward we travel.

I later learn that as many as forty people call a hidden valley behind those rock cliffs home, but that is a story for another time. This day we proceed toward the ferry crossing and familiar territory. It's nearing dark when we finally come into view of the steel cables strung high across the river.

I'm determined this wide and wild river will not keep us on our side. We are blessed with another stroke of good fortune. Even though it is long past the ferryman's work hours, he brings the deck over and saves us a cold and dangerous swim.

XYZ. Back Across the Ferry

I'm sure Wishbone could have made the crossing on her own. With me hanging on to her, it would have made it difficult at best. If I'd have let go my grip on her in a river such as this, I'd have lived my last day! Thanks to the ferryman, we crossed safely. We must have been quite a sight after being on the trail for two months, but we get no comment as we cross, so perhaps our sight is not so much out of the ordinary for him.

There is a steep switchback horse trail that climbs up to the first bench a half-mile or so straight above the river. On this bench is an alfalfa field belonging to a big beef-cattle ranch. This field has aluminum water lines running brass sprinklers. When we break over the edge of the hill in the dark, the sprinklers sound to me a lot like hissing snakes. I'm not sure if it is this sound or the aroma filling the air from the alfalfa that sets her off, but Wishbone comes unglued and goes straight up in the air. When she comes back down, the huge set of mule deer antlers I had picked up off the ground on the other side of the river, and have draped across our saddle pad, jab her in her bony ribs and up she goes again! Now she's bucking hard and off I go. Perhaps this is her way of expressing joy at being closer to her native home. She doesn't go far on her own, and I soon catch her up. She has a little munch, but I can't let her eat much of this rich feed. Her system is not used to it, and there's a real possibility of her bloating after being on dry feed for so long.

We camp this night on a grass flat above the hayfield. Tomorrow, we'll climb another steep five-mile switchback horse trail and then another ten miles on a slow incline to the crazy place at the old horse camp. What's left of our trail is not much compared to what we've been through, and it goes by quick. When we arrive at the old horse camp, I stake Wishbone on an open hill with lots of grass and do a little visiting.

The lady whose hand I bruised when her boyfriend operated on my feet offers to brush my tangled hair. It hasn't seen any attention since the ride started and is a knotted mess. She's very patient getting me back to a semi-civilized state, and I lose track of time propped against her knees. When she's done we make sweet love. It seems a fitting end to a very long and lonesome ride. The next day I'm informed her boyfriend is looking for me with his nine-inch bowie!

That's the stimulation for me to do what I now long for—to hitch the 3,000-miles back to my flat homeland, to see my dysfunctional family and old familiar friends. I make arrangements to have Wishbone taken care of, say my goodbyes to her, thinking I will soon return for more of her company. Little do I know we will not see each other again.

Wishbone, I should have thanked you better for your devoted service. I do think of you often, and I keep you in my heart. May you never be led by a fool again.

One venture ends...

From memories of youth.

Here-n-There

51. Bison Leap's Harvest

The floating airship is a thrill for the school children, tourists, our employees, investors, and business associates. It clocked many hours of airtime this summer, observing the bison, other wildlife, and the landscape, but it has other important jobs to do.

The fall harvest goes well. A crew is brought in to help process the 400 heavy critters that need to be culled. Here-n-There had educated Melinda on which animals to select, so it was her job over the summer to identify and record the chip code of the ones destined for harvest. First, she checked the DNA computer records of any that were not needed for their genetics, and then she flew to get video confirmation. That completed, she observed the herd and one by one she selected the others until we had the right bull-to-cow ratio. There were a few cows that also needed to go, but not many.

We used the airbus to transport the Lights-Out copter and its pilot. A government food inspector rode with the pilot and another stayed on-site to inspect the carcasses. The inspector riding in the ship noted a bull acting strange, as if there was something wrong with it, so he noted its chip and relayed a message back to the inspector on-site to separate its carcass from the others and give it a thorough inspection. The bull was healthy except for an old neck vertebra fracture, probably received from a fight. This would in no way affect the quality of meat. We were pleased that all our meat graded 100 percent, health-wise. Only the very good carcasses go for human consumption. The rest makes pet and scavenger food, unless, of course, it was toxic, but with our health protocol we did not expect to find any sick critters.

As the airbus hovers high above the herd, the triggerman sends his copter out to any microchip on the hit list.

"Excellent job, not a single animal suffered," the pilot said.

With an animal identified, the triggerman comes in from behind and, while passing over the animal, activates Pinion's mesmerizing sound while he lowers in front. The animal is totally calm while the air gun is aimed with visual and centered with sonar. From only a few feet away, the needlelike detonator puts the animal to sleep. It drops to its knees as if it just decided to take a nap. Ten in a close area are done in a few minutes, and then the airbus hovers low without landing; in no time at all the pilot and triggerman have the animals hoisted on board. They are hung and bled in the ship, and the blood collects in a reservoir to later be added to the compost pit. That makes the best nitrogen-rich fertilizer for the hayfields. The critters are quickly transported to the cooled hanging shed, and then the airbus heads out for another load. Once hung, the bison are skinned and cut up, hides stacked and salted, choicest cuts of the tenderest meat frozen, the rest sliced thin and dried.

A refrigerator truck transports the meat to our big warehouse in town. Samantha had overseen its setup. This year she's volunteered to stay in town till she is confident the new recruits are properly trained and competent at their jobs. 120,000-pounds of first-class pemmican, along with the choice cuts, were made this year, and much more will be made in following years. A market is being developed for it in most countries around the globe, and the preliminary feedback is outstanding. The income from these sales will give the bison the right to proliferate and spread across the prairies. It is even noticed that some vegetarians are buying Samantha's pemmican. They have heard of Bison Leap's business practices and of our desire to transform the prairies back to their natural sustainable state. They are in support. Besides, it has a lot of other healthy, nutritious fair-trade ingredients, is quick and easy to use, and it tastes "Oh so, yummy."

Doug envisions the day when our flying machines are much more automated, guided by satellite. I assert that for now it will be better that everyone involved has a hands-on feel, as much as possible, without upsetting the critters. This is personal and needs to be kept that way. Our people are not cold, unfeeling killers; they are lovers of the animals they transform into meat so their offspring can survive and propagate as nature intended. To ensure that a respectful personal connection to nature remains, it is best that people see the living animal and not just meat on a plate. We will not automate any more than is absolutely beneficial or necessary.

Jake is talking with the airbus pilot, wondering if we can figure out a way to transport hay to isolated parts of the range for supplemental feed in times of winter need.

"It won't be difficult," he says. "We just need to drop the observation basket and hang a different hookup to self-load and unload the bulky hay."

That way, the bison never need to be brought back to the fields and will be allowed to choose their own wintering grounds, without fear of them getting trapped in deep crusted snow and starving. These air machines are handy tools, and even though at first they seemed to be an expensive investment, they're showing their value. The more the bison are left to do what they know best, the cheaper it will be to keep them contented and healthy. They just need a little help from their small, hairless relatives with the big brains and kind hearts, and the bison will give back in return.

Doug and his engineers are designing an electrical system for Elk Mountain Ranch. The irrigation company drafted up a proposal to convert all the hayfields into computer-controlled pivot moves; they're suggesting there are a few hundred more acres that have never before been irrigated that could also be watered. We plan to build a harvest building there, which will be similar to BL's building, except it will need to be larger. It will also be necessary to build better housing for the many EMR employees.

I've been remembering how Pinion's teachers set up their camp circle, and I'm intrigued with a modification of their idea. The pasture the horse herd is in has a large and very flat area only a half-mile slightly above and beyond the present, original buildings. A cold, sweet spring flows out of the rocks above this flat, making its way down a treed draw toward the river. I tasted and tested it. It's low-mineral, cold, clear, pure water. I believe this flat will be an excellent site to build a small village on and vow to talk to architects about my village idea.

Sarah is still finding suitable ranches for our future expansion and is processing many requests for bison seed stock. BL doesn't want to let too many animals go until our herd numbers are built up more, but it's a good idea to send a few, just to get that side of the business going. Ged's manufacturers are ready to build huge numbers of the sound-tower fences. We tried a few miles of this fence at the Green River Ranch, around the hayfields, and Pinion's sounds are everything she first claimed them to be. Everyone's looking forward to a large crop of cute, playful calves next spring–early summer. BL has more land available when we have the numbers to populate new places.

The copter and control-monitor system for the Wyoming biologists is almost complete. Doug's engineers test it as they go along, and it's looking like it'll be a better system than the one we set up at BL. Doug is, in his words, "a wee bit jealous," but he knows he can update our old system, and perhaps he should be satisfied for now with building a nice one at the EMR. Doug and the engineers—in their dreams—are thinking of a main monitor center to set up at the head office in Denver, or better yet, Boulder.

52. Elk Mountain Ranch

Elk Mountain is a productive ranch, very easy to work, and BL is more than a little pleased with our luck. We now have many sections of land under our management and have only had to purchase outright a small portion of it. This new place needs money spent on it, but again, Sarah made an excellent win-win deal with its owners.

BL will pay, from our own company, any expenses for regular upkeep and maintenance on the whole place, including the existing buildings.

In twenty years this place will be in at least as good a condition as it was in before BL took possession. Any upgrade expenses will come out of the profit share that is set up for the hereditary son, so if BL builds buildings, we will lay out the cash first, but we will be reimbursed. Half of all profits made at Elk Mountain will be held in the boy's trust. Because the buildings will remain and are owned by the land, the funds that BL initially lays out for building construction will be reimbursed to BL from the share of ranch profits deposited in the lad's trust. Of course, all the maintenance and upkeep of these same buildings will be paid for directly from BL's share of profits.

The ranch house is to be maintained and kept clean and vacant for the owners to visit as they like. In twenty years, all the buildings will become the property of the boy. He can, at that time, decide whether or not to extend or renegotiate BL's lease.

The boy's dad made a promise to *his* dad that the place would never be sold, but would be passed from father to son or daughter for eternity. Sarah now understands why he followed those cows around long after he didn't want to. It seems that most folks born of the land pride themselves in sticking not only to their word but also to their commitment to the soil from whence they've come.

I talk to architects about village plans, and we decide to go with a modification of the circle camp that had been set up at BL. We didn't want to build a bunch of separated houses in the standard archaic square-grid pattern—with their own yards and all that unused wasted space—that dominates present social culture. Everyone owning their own riding lawnmower is not something we want to encourage or perpetuate. Nor do we want to build ugly row houses that keep residents in their own boxes and disconnect them from each other and from the earth.

We acknowledge that every individual needs private space—a space you have to be invited into before you can enter—but we want more than just that. We want to build a real community, a place where it is easy for people to interact without stepping on each other's toes, and to foster a natural earth connection, a place conducive to the evolution of the community's social consciousness.

BL will instigate the modern equivalent of some of the old indigenous villages that prevailed on the planet since human time began. The old villages were built this way, not just for protection from their enemies, but also to foster co-operation and a sense of belonging. These are very good things, in our eyes, and we want to give them a chance again to help man get back in tune, in harmony, with his neighbors.

We will lay out a pattern, a dodecagon, like a big circle with twelve straight sides. Twenty-four cabins will be built around the perimeter, two on each of the twelve sides, with a roadway around the outside of them. In the center of this flat-sided circle is a gathering space, a water fountain pool for the kids on hot summer days, shade trees and gardens, picnic tables and barbecues, fire pits, and a games area. This is a safe place for the little ones to play. No vehicles are allowed in the inner circle.

The houses face toward the center, so it's easy to look out and see that all things are okay. All windows have one-way glass, both thermal and vision. There is no need of curtains except for heat retention on cold winter nights. These windows are the latest version of one-way mirrors. You can look out without restriction but no one can see in, allowing you a clear view of the outdoor central area while still retaining your privacy.

The cabins each have two bedrooms, with a kitchen-living room and bathroom. Well-built, solid, and warm. They have turquoise tin roofs and sand dune stucco siding with simple troweled-in designs. Each cabin has a small private outdoor sitting area, both front and back. The cabins have fireplaces for aesthetics, but their main heat is electric, generated by a turbine installed in one of the creeks falling from high in the hills. In the very center of the common yard is a large hardwood-floored gazebo with a stage, a fully equipped kitchen, and moveable tables for social gatherings.

A bigger hangar was built just off the side of the airstrip, a cell tower goes up on one of those rocky crags, and an air traffic control house and computer-communications complex goes on the knoll just above the new village. A dozen (or more if needed) small four-wheel drive electric pickup vehicles were ordered for workers to get around in. These give four hours of continuous use in hilly country. They carry passengers and light loads, but are mostly used from the village to the shop and hayfields. Doug will see that charging stations are set up strategically throughout the ranch for convenience.

New pivot system irrigators were installed and a large bison harvesting building is also needed. The workshop already on the place gets plenty of use to keep the haying equipment in good repair. BL built a new drive shed to park all the farm equipment in out of the weather when not in use.

We did not need to build or repair any fences. Pinion's miniature sound towers take care of that. Some sound towers are set up at the water springs and along the creeks to keep the hoofed critters from making a mess of the fresh surface water. Gravity-fed water troughs are installed for them to drink out of. Where gravity is not an option, small solar-powered pumps are used. Through buried lines, the critter water is piped out onto flat areas, away from its source. Small, shallow cement drinking tanks, installed at half-mile intervals, allow full utilization of the grazing land. Water flows into the high end of a tank and out the low end, back into another buried line and onward to the next tank. This keeps the tank water fresh and clean. There's no spill around the tanks, so the surrounding ground stays dry and firm. If an area around any particular tank becomes overgrazed, that tank can be turned off, encouraging the critters to seek a different area.

In the past, vast areas, especially around towns and cities, had been fenced off to keep the grazers away. Understandably, people didn't appreciate them making a mess. This has kept the critters away, alright, but it also allowed the plants, especially the grass, trees, and bushes, to build up with years of dry, dead organic matter. This sometimes catches fire and burns with an uncontrollable intensity, often consuming the outer parts of these same settlements. Even when the fire does not burn houses, it devastates the outer peripheries, causing an unsightly mess, creating erosion problems that, among other things, fill the watercourses with mud and ash. BL knows the grazers are a necessary part of every ecosystem. They just need a little encouragement to do their part in an acceptable, compatible manner.

Because they sometimes get time between their many other jobs, I ask the farm crew to take down the wire fences. The wire is sent back to town to be recycled into a less intrusive product.

BL spent a sizable chunk of money on all these new additions, but it will pay for itself soon enough. There is a nearby fellow with a small logging company who has his own portable sawmill. He is hired to harvest enough of these tall, straight beauties way up the hill to build the houses. He and his crew are also decent carpenters, so they not only selectively harvested the trees, but also milled them, turning them into the buildings needed.

We didn't want roads cut in all over the hillsides. I made sure that the timber harvesters understood what we meant by selective logging.

"You do not select the best and to hell with the rest. You must first identify the best trees, vibrant and healthy, and those are to be unharmed, protected for their genetics. These are future seed producers. You then thin out the poorer trees around them to give new young saplings a chance to grow. The same way a farmer does with his livestock or plants. Always keep the best alive as future generators."

We ordered another leased airship to ferry the logs down to the building site. BL needs a floating ship here once we start bison harvest, so we might as well get it now. This one has a custom-made quick detach system, so it's versatile. The cockpit is a permanent fixture, but the glassed-in basket that's used to transport people can be disconnected, and in its place other implements can easily be attached. One is needed to haul hay, another for bison harvest, and yet another for lifting logs. In the future, if other tools are needed they can be manufactured to use the same hookups. The original ship at BL Ranch is retrofitted the same. The money we will save by using our own trees goes a long ways toward the down payment of the airbus, so the bookkeepers are content. These airships are not cheap, but they've proven their worth at BL already. They are a part of the big picture now.

53. Sound Posts

In future years, BL will make loads of money from our sound posts. Once they are proven effective for bison, then everywhere fences are needed, people want them. The cost is less than a third of a conventional fence: no muss, no fuss. You can set them out by hand and then move them somewhere else without giving it much thought. With the appropriate sounds the birds are not affected, as they are often observed building their nests near the protection of the posts.

A country in Africa requested test samples to be set around village gardens to keep plundering elephants out. This would save the elephants' lives if effective. I thought that some types of angry music would probably be effective as a fence, but I was happy to concede that Pinion's silent sounds were much better. BL donated the first thousand towers free for this trial. If it works, BL will ask Pinion and her family if they'd like to visit Africa with the audio engineers to fine-tune the sounds specifically for that continent's unique critters.

The research and development team is working on a pocket sound pen to replace bulky cans of predator pepper spray and heavy firearms in certain circumstances. The pens are safe, cheap, and handy for millions of people to use, and no harm needs to be done to the animal. In fact, if they are used properly they can actually bring animals and people closer together. People need not be afraid of the animals, and the animals learn they can only get so close but need not fear humans if they maintain the comfort zone.

A note of caution will be stamped on the pens: "These pens are useless against deaf animals." Other than this caution, it will be near utopian for humans and the large, formerly dangerous animals to not have to fear each other anymore. That will be educational for all species, two- and four-legged alike.

54. Newsletter

- Sound fence now installed at BL Ranch. No more need to harass elk. Wire fence around hayfield remains as visual boundary for new pilot training—Melinda and Doug
- Airship arrived at EMR. Begin logging soon. Pivots operational. Water turbine working... estimate two hundred mule deer on hillsides, forty bighorn sheep up higher, small flock of fifteen mountain goats, no count on whitetails or moose yet, many blue grouse, female cougar with three young seen yesterday—EMR management
- Four hundred bison ready to load in Utah next week. Plan to unload at EMR this Friday—wandering vets
- Sound posts effective in Africa, Brazil wants sample load of ten thousand, the proceeds will purchase many bison—Ged
- Wyoming biologists impressed with new flight system. Will need to locate and train more pilots and control center office staff—Denver PR

- Pemmican warehouse almost completed with this year's produce, all product spoken for and receiving orders for next year, staff excellent, will not need me next year and that's okay—Samantha
- PS. My Linda is having my baby... Yahoo! Dad says he's going to set a date for us to ring the church bells. Doug's the only man for Melinda!

55. Jim's Smoking Gears

I am very interested in the Wyoming biologists and their future program. I do have a habit, sometimes, of getting tangled up in my own thoughts. It's all very complicated, but if we are going to get the wildlife and wildlands valued and enhanced the way we think they should be, then we need an easily acceptable way for them to become valuable in the eyes of the general public.

We have to make it obvious that this is much more than self-interest. Bison Leap is becoming a profitable company, but profit is a small part of our goals. We want this idea of enhanced nature to outlive us, and for that to happen it will have to become everybody's business. Otherwise, it will never have the strength to sustain itself for future generations.

From what I've seen and understand, all humans need to provide themselves with the necessities of life. First there's food and shelter, then comforts and entertainment. If these necessities are not met easily, people start doing things they normally wouldn't consider doing to satisfy these needs. If that means bulldozing a forest to plant another few acres of saleable crop or building a faster highway across pristine landscapes, then that will be done.

What we are working on is how to get that natural life to become more valuable in its supportive sustenance to the general public than what they will get out of it if they convert the land into roads, factories, and fields. One of the big problems is, even though most folks claim they value natural public resources, they will feel justified in flattening them if they think they need to. If people assume they can get more of something from an area than it can give if left be to do its own thing, its life will be in jeopardy. I understand this, but I cannot accept it as the best or only way.

As I understand it, the natural ecosystems have spent eons of time figuring out how to maximize the production on any given area. This often goes through a feast-and-famine scenario, which is not exactly reassuring, but it is not nearly as disheartening as seeing what humankind is doing. Before the industrial age, we simply didn't have the tools or knowledge to change the landscape in any significant way. Now, with vast data banks of facts (confusingly disguised as knowledge) and self-propelled machines, things can be changed in a hurry.

The preindustrial societies were hunter-gatherers and farmers who took whatever they needed without much thought as to ever running out. That was the way then, and it worked because man was not capable of taking too much at once. People's mechanical abilities have developed at a faster rate than their moral values, and this needs to be addressed.

Sure, there were always some who saw beauty and knew restraint, but mostly people never took too much, simply because they couldn't. Unbeknown to preindustrial humans, some of the big restraints were germs and viruses. There were sharp-toothed predators and much intertribal warfare, and all of these things kept the human population in check, contributing to our inability to destroy the environment that so willingly gave its sustenance. What I am seeing now is that we have developed an amazing amount of mechanical knowledge of how to manipulate our environment, but our ability to understand and therefore appreciate the intricate rejuvenating life of this environment has not kept pace. This is the disconnect, and if nothing's done to change it around, to give it a new direction, then not only will the natural environment be destroyed, but humanity will eventually be forced to succumb too.

Now, at this late stage of the game, we have to make that natural environment worth money. That will be the only thing that will give our fellow man pause for long enough that the human race will have the time needed to come to its senses and start appreciating what is in fact our true sustenance.

Other than with nuclear fission, humankind really has no way of destroying the basic elements, but we sure have the power in our hands now to completely destroy all the organisms, and this is exactly what seems to be happening. Turning them into photo opportunities won't be enough to save these organisms. They'll have to be much more valuable than that if they are to survive. We have to make these animals—not just the bison, but all the other diverse organisms—so valuable that their monetary value alone will prevent anyone from abusing them. If we can hold off the genocide for just a few more years, the true heart and mind of humanity will wake from its mad euphoric rush to control, gather, and hoard, and then we can truly lay claim to being masters of the earth.

This mastery will have nothing to do with coercion or the disappearance of species. It will have everything to do with the fluid enhancement of all planetary life and its appreciation. We only need to get the human species to pause long enough to observe the beauty before them. That will be enough, because they are good people, and they are fully capable of not only surviving, but of learning how to live in a state of appreciation, of love, of admiration, and of connectedness.

56. Cougar Kittens

I was concerned when I was told about the cougar and her kittens. I like these big cats, and they have as much right to be here as I have, but they could throw a screw into our plans if we don't handle them properly. A single big, hungry long-tailed cat could not do much damage to BL's ability to make wildlife valuable, but how many of them are there? An adult cougar will kill and eat a full-grown deer or young bison every week. Not much as simple math goes, but when you figure out how many deer that is per year, and then how many offspring those fifty deer would have had, it's a huge impact over the life span of a cougar. A cougar, wolf, or bear has a very limited monetary value—mostly as a trophy hanging on a wall, or perhaps a few dollars as a photo in a scrapbook—but all the deer a predator kills could be food for people, which would make them valuable and therefore worth protecting. A predator, under natural conditions uninfluenced by man, can take a sick or genetically inferior animal out of circulation and will help protect the herd from disease or malfunction. We do have this in mind for the future, but right now we need to get the herd numbers built up so we can show people their value. Then, the herds and their environment will be protected.

The flight crew can take a sick or unfit critter out of the herd without killing a hundred healthy reproductive ones. We vaccinate them, supplement their feed in times of need, keep their numbers in balance with the plant life, and fill people's bellies with their fine flesh. This, as with the bison plan, gives people a great appreciation for them, and this is also good for the four-legged predators. As the herd numbers climb and their range expands, then so will the numbers and range of the predators. A little different thinking than the present accepted norm, but if you follow it through, in the end there is no other way to enhance the total diversity of the natural environment.

Some may think this way of raising wild meat is no better than the commercial way domestic animals are raised, but there are many differences. The wildlife evolved here before we took their environment; they utilize that environment a lot more efficiently than any of the plants or animals man has replaced them with; there are aspects of this natural environment that we may have totally overlooked. If we destroy all or parts of it that will someday bite us on the ass so bad we'll be back to a feast-and-famine scenario before we realize what we've done.

It's obvious that humans are stuck in endeavors to recreate and control. Humans, at one time, figured we knew how to master all aspects of planetary life, but it is starting to be understood that we have made major blunders. People are not happy. They're not fulfilled or living in any appreciative state; they're no longer able to feel, and in their grief of loneliness, they fill their days with mechanical activities as a distraction. This only compounds our lack of connection with the simple pleasures that bring us to what we seek. It's like a dog chasing his own tail because he's looking for his supper. Better to slow down a little and feel the depth of life.

The answers are here, right in front of us. We need to stop branding, stop trying to own and possess things. Put that same energy into enhancing all these things around us, and there will be plenty for everybody. We'll then re-connect back to our state of appreciation, our sense of belonging, our feelings of fulfillment, and our life of energized happiness. We can be as free as angels, but even better, because we can still have our flesh and blood and all the wondrous senses, sensations, and abilities that allows. The bodies of all beasts, including ours, are able to sense and interact with the environment in astounding depth, simply because bodies are made up of this same elemental and complex organic environment.

It's all so simple, so fluid, so interactive, and we want to make controllable robotic machines, bank accounts, and possessions of everything. There was even a guy who claimed ownership—under man's legal, international planetary law—of the moon and was attempting to sell pieces of it. Can you imagine someone—a person or business—owning the moon? What's next, someone claiming sovereignty of the stars because they've filed a claim on the World Wide Web, and they deem that to be as valid as someone from the past planting a flag on a so-called previously undiscovered continent? I have to laugh at the absurdity of it all, but really, it's not funny, and I do have other things I could be doing.

57. Original Grand Plan

Sarah's and my original 'grand plan' is not just about bringing the bison back, but about enhancing all the animals, birds, bees, flowers, and all the other thousands of organisms that make up our vibrant diversity. We want to bring them back, not just for themselves, but for humanity too, as it was originally intended long before we ever had an inkling that there was such a thing as an intention.

"Shit, there are some people who have the gall," I say to Sarah, "perhaps because they do not know who else to blame, that all this mess we're in is God's fault. They don't know the human word *God* was originally meant to be representative of the combination of all the elements, the organic organisms, and all the ethereal things that one can never quite put one's finger on, all these things put together, and their interactions with each other. That is the meaning of the word. The word God is, among other things, a verb of interaction, not an unchanging noun of personal solidity. Of course, there are some of these things that, no matter how aware we become, will always be just out of our comprehension range, but there is much within our range that, in our occupational busyness, we overlook."

"I'll get you a podium if you keep this up," Sarah teased, but I continued anyhow.

"One of the big problems is that some enterprising souls, a long time ago, had set themselves up to be the go-between, between the touchable things, the ethereal things, and their very complicated interactions with each other. These guys demanded homage, and still do, and as if that weren't bad enough, they gave everybody an out, a way of pretending they had no say in the outcome of these interactions, and therefore what will be, will be."

On and on I rant. I have to let it out; I've been feeling the blues today, and I just can't stop myself.

"People are becoming disillusioned, depressed with all this foolishness and confusion, but they've been doing it this way for so long now they've forgotten how things could be. They've forgotten how to appreciate and interact with their environment, and all about the energy that makes it beautiful in a way that's enhancing, not just to this environment but to themselves. They are disconnected from the source of their life and they are lost, condemned to suffer because of their own blindness, their fixation on made-up facts, and their belief that the go-between has made reservations for them in some better place. As long as they keep their homage bill paid, their seat on the getaway plane will be held in their name, so no need to worry, as long as the reservation is held."

Sarah groaned. "I wish I had a set of earplugs." But today she was my captive audience, and she knew I was almost out of stale air, so she heard me out.

"You can plunder this place, and when you're done you can go to a better place. Do they really have no idea that this place that they plunder is the best place, the jewel of the universe? My God, they have beauty all around them, but they shit on it because some morbid organized jackasses have told them there is something better somewhere else, and they believed them. Because if they didn't, those jackasses would have stuck a sword in them or tortured them with fire until they submitted to the will of these same power-hungry jackasses. Heaven and hell are not places; they are states of being. Simply, they are just fluid descriptions of the depth of our interactions with our surroundings at any given time."

I sighed. Sarah understood and was sympathetic, but all the same she was glad my rant was done.

It's a mess, alright, but we can't give up, we can't lose hope, we have to have faith that we can make it better; we love our elements, ourselves, and this place too much to abandon it, and besides, we know our brethren among our own species are fully capable of understanding, knowing, and feeling all these things that make all life, everywhere, grand. We just need to keep working on our prairie painting, BL's sculpture, so that all can see it, become an integral part of it, and live in awe.

It's like vandals have entered your house and knocked everything about, breaking things and mixing others up. When you come home, you don't just abandon the mess and move into your neighbor's place—you grab a broom and maybe some tools and you fix and clean it back up. I feel like this, with this planet, this prairie, these mountain foothills, and I will do what I know best and make it a better place for the kids, for their kids, and for their kids' kids too.

58. Guides of Wyoming

The head biologists in Wyoming understand BL; in fact, they feel the same way about most things. They have never made sense of it all, not quite in the same way as we have, but then they never had the upbringing or the opportunities that Sarah and I have been blessed with. The biologists have love in their hearts, they have understanding and education, and they're organized into a mutually supportive conglomerate that has public respect and power. They have a government mandate to get their will implemented on the land with only a few stipulations: They have to pay their own way by bringing in enough money so any opposition can be satisfied with education and alternative support, they need to bring in dollars, and they need to find ways to satisfy all the conflicting concerned groups that what they have in mind is also something that will satisfy these groups' needs and wants in a more fulfilling way than what's available now.

BL has laid the groundwork, and it's now time to bring it out into the public domain and work out the quirks and bugs of our system. BL has the prototype well started and will help guide these biologists. It is much bigger now than can be handled by BL in a direct fashion, so we will act as consultants only. We have no authority, but our words of advice are much sought-after. BL looks forward to witnessing the effects of our words in the change to the landscape of the whole state of Wyoming.

This will not happen in a big hurry, but progressively, subtly, over the coming years. It will happen in the way Sarah and I and all the other members of BL have planned. We've worked hard at what we know best and now it's payday. Not just in money, but in the joy of seeing our world start to live again. This is the big payoff, and that is all we've ever hoped and strived for.

59. Samantha and Jake's Guesthouse

Samantha very much enjoys company. All the inquisitive and supportive visitors showing up at BL gave her an idea. She likes to stick around home. She and Jake have traveled a bit, mostly to visit us kids when we were off to school, but they've also been across the big waters and have seen some sights. Her heart is in this land, and that's where she wants to be, but she does enjoy the stimulation of others, especially those interested in this area and in particular those interested in BL's doings.

She and Jake talked it over and agreed it would be nice if they could spend a little more time with these folks. A guest cabin would help satisfy not just Samantha and Jake's needs but also the needs of any who stayed there. Jake formed the cement and rock foundation up the creek a short walk from their small house. This will be a cabin like no other.

Jake admires the hair on the bison hides stacked flat in BL's cool shed.

"This will be just about the warmest insulation anyone could ask for," he says, "and it's free. No coal needs to be burned to make it, and no land needs to be disturbed to mine it. It's a natural by-product of an organic beast, and I like it."

He built the guesthouse with two separate walls: an inner and an outer one. The inside of these walls are hollow and open to the attic. He filled the wall space and attic, too, with bison hair, before the roof was covered in.

He clipped these flat hides with a modified hedge trimmer, put the hair in a big tub of warm water, added a bit of natural soap and disinfectant herbs, agitated it with a circulation pump, then spread it out on screens in an empty roofed shed, and let the breeze dry it.

It is fluffy, so warm, and it smells like a summer breeze. He forked it into the hay baler so it'd be easy to haul down to the guesthouse, and now it's time to finish the cabin. They sand-stuccoed the outside and tinned the roof, put in nice thermal windows, a hardwood floor, custom kitchen cupboards, a big bathroom, and handmade rustic furniture, and it is ready for its first inhabitants.

Samantha and Jake spent their third honeymoon there before they made it available to guests, and it is warm, quiet, and peaceful.

Samantha whispers, "I can hear the heartbeat of the bison and it's the same as the heartbeat of this grand flowing land..."

"Maybe we should keep living here and let the guests stay in our old house," Jake suggests.

"But I want to stay closer to my garden and all my familiar things," Samantha tells Jake. "Maybe someday you can tear our old house down and build one just like this cabin in that exact same spot, under my favorite cottonwood with the lilac bushes, saskatoons, blackberries, and pines that we planted so long ago."

I'm wishing we'd designed the houses at EMR with this same insulation in mind, but those houses are almost finished now. Maybe we'll get to build more houses someday, and if we do we'll make use of this warm bison wool. In the meantime, BL will find and encourage someone to start another by-product business.

60. Colorado

Elk Mountain Ranch straddles a state border. Most of the ranch lays on the Colorado side, with the remainder in Wyoming. The Colorado government biologists are keeping an eye on what's happening in Wyoming. They are cautious but intrigued by the possibilities. The mountains of Colorado are an international destination for well-heeled tourists. The biologists and especially the state tourism bureau do not need or want any controversial publicity. Colorado knows BL has a very good reputation, but just the same we are changing things, and as is always the case with change, there can be unforeseen consequences.

Colorado put a lot of effort and money into pursuing their international tourist trade, and will allow nothing to jeopardize that. They are, of course, open to anything that will enhance this trade, but they must be sure before they commit to anything new. They are not about to get themselves into hot water by jumping in with both feet, but they would like to test it a little. The state instructed their biologists to "give BL pilots the go-ahead to vaccinate and microchip all the big game, including that momma cougar and her kittens that are in the immediate area of EMR." The monitoring and info collection will all be done by BL's system, but all data needs to be transmitted to the biologists' office for scrutiny. This is good news. The Elk Mountain system is not fully operational yet, but it soon will be. BL looks forward to working with the Colorado game department and the tourism bureau.

61. Wilberts

Our head office in Denver received a call from Wilberts, a well-known multinational company, asking if they could send a representative to BL to observe our operations and possibly talk of investments that may be in both companies' interests. BL is and has always been open to all possibilities of advancing our ideas, so we welcomed their visit. We had a few days to prepare, so we did a little research. This huge company has been in business for over seventy years and is the largest retailer on earth. They started small, with one store in a little U.S. town, but now have stores in over forty different countries.

We asked ourselves, "What do they want with BL?"

BL prepared as best we could with the knowledge we had of this interested company. Our most experienced PR reps will meet the Wilberts reps at the airport in Denver. They'll all have lunch at a prestigious Japanese restaurant and see what is needed from there.

Good Japanese food is always a treat, with its interesting flavors and fresh, wholesome tastes. It's a good way to spend time with friends or, in this case, new business prospects. The Wilberts reps are cautious about giving away too much of what they have in mind. They'll need a better look at all aspects of BL's operation and are especially interested in meeting as many of BL's personnel as possible in the few days they plan to be around.

BL administration directed the PR people to "cater to every whim of the Wilberts reps." After all, BL has nothing to hide from anyone, and our company became what it is by being totally transparent with all our associates. Perhaps something good will come of this meeting. Even if all Wilberts want is to get free ideas from our company, then that's okay with us. We will give willingly.

At first, it appears to our PR guides that Wilberts might be looking for new recruits for their own company because of the way they're so personal with everyone in BL's head office. We spent a few hours there that afternoon and the next day visit Elk Mountain Ranch, then on to our original Bison Leap Ranch and the Green River Ranch. We land at the airstrip in the village near BL because the ranch strip is not long enough for the plane size needed to carry everyone. BL's airship meets us and gives everyone a bird's-eye view of the country. This is a first for Wilberts, and they are delighted.

At EMR, the Wilberts people seemed more interested in our personnel than they were with the actual business, so a PR spokesperson asked why.

The Wilberts reps explain that their company grew from one little store into the business it is now by treating every business partner with personal respect.

"Every associate is important to our company, and all must feel as if the company is an important part of their lives."

In this way their company has grown and prospered—not because there had been a few ruthless, super-smart people at the top directing things, but because every one of their associates, and there are thousands, have a personal attachment and commitment to their company. Wilberts wants to be sure all BL personnel feel the same about their own company. They've clearly done their homework. They know BL's business inside out and have also investigated, as much as privacy ethics allow, every BL employee. They want to meet each one in person before they proceed with putting their proposal forward.

In two days, a courier delivers a package to Bison Leap's head office. Inside is a list of Wilberts's ranch land holdings, complete with maps, water licenses, financial statements, and employee records. Their summation in part asks: "Would Bison Leap be interested in taking over the management of these lands for the mutual benefit of Bison Leap and the Wilberts corporation?"

This is incredible! Bigger than anything BL has ever had anything to do with. Bigger even than anything Ged's family company has ever been involved with. A meeting is called, and all BL investors, administrators, employees, and associates who are available to attend are encouraged to do so. This is not a decision to be made lightly, as it will involve all aspects of BL; every person in our company will be affected.

It soon becomes obvious that Wilberts have been investing in a lot more than retail stores. For the last forty years, they have been quietly buying very large ranches in many countries, mostly in North America, but on other continents as well. Rather than paying corporate tax, they've been putting money into large beef cattle ranches, among other things. These acreages they selected are some of the largest, most productive anywhere. Wilberts is not a ranch company per se, so they do not have the expertise in personnel for all the intricacies of this type of business. They found that even though their initial investment is safe, the ranches are not doing as well as expected, and they feel a more hands-on management approach by someone who really knows the business will be more appropriate.

They are especially impressed with BL's bison and our pemmican approach to marketing. In light of some of the negative public opinions of cattle ranching, BL's specific marketing approach makes much more sense from a business point of view. Public opinion is changing, and the Wilberts executives pride themselves on always being in the right place when the waves come. They see a big wave coming with wild free-range bison.

BL's public openness to scrutiny, its perceptive abilities and vision, and its goal of implementing and enhancing sustainable planetary life is a business that Wilberts most definitely want their company name to be associated with. This association not only makes immediate money-counting business sense, but it will also help Wilberts overcome some major public image blunders they've made in the past.

62. Bison Leap's Big Step

Does BL want the job of managing all these ranches, eventually converting them to bison, and marketing the products?

After very little deliberation, the answer is yes. We only pause slightly because even though Sarah and I have been planning this since we were kids, we had no idea it would happen so fast. Are we ready for something as grand as this? It's a huge responsibility. Is our company, Bison Leap, ready? Wilberts have offered us millions of acres of the best ranchland in parcels scattered all the way from the northern Canadian prairies through the central plains of the United States and on into northern Mexico.

Some are in the foothills of the mountains, some on the wide-open flat country. Most places have a small percentage of their total acreage in good irrigated land for hayfields, but it is grassland and foothills for the most part. A few places are deep in the mountains with open valley bottoms. Most of the places have plenty of clean water, some having big rivers, creeks, springs, and even small lakes.

Wilberts chose these ranches with the same diligence they used to choose locations for the thousands of retail stores they have scattered across the globe.

Mostly these ranches are capable of being very productive, with a minimum of machine work or human labor. Some parcels are very large, with two or three—and even five in one case—original ranches all joined together into one. That particular place would take a good rider on a strong, fast horse ten days to get from one side to the other.

These are self-sufficient places, exactly what Bison Leap has been dreaming of, but it will take a lot of teamwork, juggling of personnel responsibilities, and finding new people to fill needed roles. It can't be done quickly. Wilberts have given us plenty of time to decide, and even more time to fully implement the takeover. It is a rare opportunity, and opportunities such as this don't come around twice, so BL would be fools to turn their offer down. We really have no choice, even though we are already stretched as to our abilities.

At our stakeholders' meeting, the unanimous decision is that BL will take on the project under cautious conditions, one of them that we be given six months to look over all the properties and meet individually with the resident help on these places before we give our final decision.

BL discusses that "there may be certain places that might not be compatible with our plans, and those, if any, we would like to take out of the package." This all seems acceptable to the Wilberts company, so a formal meeting is planned to finalize the obligations, timeline, and basic interests of each party.

Ged, Sarah, Doug's dad, Dave, members of the Public Relations Team, along with the Legal and Accounting Teams, and I will all fly to Kansas City next week to sign a stack of pending obligation papers. Ged chartered a plane for our trip. We all meet at the Denver airport and land in Kansas an hour later. A private bus delivers us to a hotel downtown, only a half block from where the meeting is to take place in a Wilberts conference room. Oddly enough, not one of us, except for Dave, has ever been to Kansas City, so in more ways than one this trip will be an adventure.

We have the rest of today to relax and wander the city; tomorrow, at 10 a.m. sharp, we all meet in the Wilberts building lobby, proceeding from there to the conference room on the seventh floor. What a view that turns out to be, especially for me. The office tower looks out over the area where the Missouri and Kansas Rivers meet—green, relaxing, inspirational, but always in motion. A perfect setting for accomplishing what needs to be achieved today.

63. The Boardroom

We are greeted warmly and escorted to the boardroom. The Wilberts reps are already present, some mingling in conversation, others seated at a long bird's-eye-maple table.

Introductions are made and a stunningly attractive woman, about Sarah's and my age, introduces herself as Tasha.

She reaches out to me and says, "I've been instructed, if that is agreeable to you, to personally introduce you to every resident on every one of these ranches."

I've lost my ability to speak, but I can *see* every day of the rest of my life with her by my side. When I look into her eyes, I *see* the stars on a clear desert night, and the blue-green Earth lit with a full moon twinkling on a rippled sea, and *there is our unborn son, floating across time to greet us.*

Her lips part ever so slightly, she smiles, and I hear a fluttering breeze through summer aspen leaves, conversing with a clear mountain stream, bubbling over moss-covered rocks. Then I hear her laugh, and I think, *I've made a fool of myself*, but she's not laughing at me, she's "just happy we've finally met."

I'm no help with the paperwork; my thoughts and feelings are lost to this time. Sarah and Ged are fully capable, so they get all the agreements signed while I memorize scenes from my future with Tasha.

My voice comes back at the end of our meeting, just in time to tell Tasha, "Yes, I will be delighted if you will guide me to all these places and introduce me to the people who are to be my friends from this day forward."

We part, with a smiling Tasha saying, "I'll call you in a few days."

I'm pretty much useless as far as getting any work done, but I do manage to ask the office staff if they will make a map overlay of all Wilberts's ranch properties, starting with Wyoming and Colorado, then going north–south and east–west from there. I request that they all be GPS'd so I can study them with satellite before I physically travel to any of them. I want to get an idea of where these places are situated and how they can be made to interact with each other. I'm hoping they are clumped together and not individually isolated from each other. I think that most likely, knowing what we do of the Wilberts Corporation, these ranches will be lovely places and situated in clumps, and that will be perfect for what lies ahead.

"If possible, I would like an estimated cattle-carrying capacity, the approximate acreage, the number of employees, and the normal tonnage of feed put up each year on each place," I ask.

This will give us an idea of what to plan for, but of course we will actually have to get a close look at each place to really know how to proceed. This is going to take some time, and I'm glad all our people know their jobs well and can get along without me for a while.

It doesn't take the office long to learn that Wilberts have purchased, within the last year, many ranches in the vicinity of Bison Leap and the Green River and also many near the Elk Mountain Ranch. There are, in some places, other privately owned ranches between these places, but this is surprising and very interesting news.

After studying the map overlay, I realize these places are all situated in the same vast area as my porch dream. I learn later that Wilberts have other land in areas that are not rangeland but rather cropland. They have not forwarded those to us. They have silently sat in on some of BL's public meetings and have submitted land they are quite sure will be of interest to BL for our bison project. Wilberts have done their homework. They've intentionally made it easy for BL to say yes.

To build the bison herds up to the numbers needed to fill the carrying capacity of all this acreage will take twenty, maybe thirty years. A lifelong task, but I can think of nothing I'd rather be doing, as long as Tasha is willing to help. She phones on the third day and asks me if I can get away from BL to see some of these places, and could I meet her tomorrow at the Denver airport? I'll need to bring luggage for a week's travel. It will be a whirlwind tour, but if I like what I see we can do it in more detail at a later date.

I manage to say goodbye to Jake and Samantha, to Doug and Melinda, and to Sarah and Ged, and then I spent the rest of the day checking and rechecking my bags. I'm at the airport three hours before Tasha's plane is due to land. I wouldn't miss this even if the oceans rise forty feet and all the mountains crumble to the ground. This is my time, and I will enjoy it to the fullest. I'm twenty-nine years old and now know I've never felt complete before meeting Tasha. This is so very special, and I do look forward to our coming week.

I need to walk outside a little, on the treed grass, so my heart will calm down and stop beating so loudly in my ears! I don't want everybody in the airport to hear it thumping. There's time and years ahead of us, so I breathe deep, bring my strength back, and calmly watch the clouds and river roll by. I don't hear her approach from behind, but I know it is her hands that reach up and cover my eyes; when I turn she pokes me lightly in the ribs and laughs when I wrap her in a bear hug.

Tasha's plane waits for us on the runway, two pilots in the cabin, and a lounge set in place of the normal rows of seats. Tasha explains that this is one of many of Wilberts' planes and they have made it available to her for as long as we have need of it.

64. Tasha and Jim's Flight

After we settle into the airplane's lounge, Tasha explains that she grew up on a large family ranch near the junctions of the North and South Platte Rivers in Nebraska. She received degrees from the University of Texas in Agribusiness and then returned to help the family ranch. Shortly thereafter, the Wilberts Corporation made her folks an offer they couldn't refuse. She had then reluctantly gone to work for Wilberts in their Kansas City office. Tasha knew the ranch business, and it wasn't long before she was given the opportunity to oversee all Wilberts ranch holdings, and, for the last four years, that had been her job.

"I have personally visited most of these ranches, and it was on my recommendation that Bison Leap was investigated," she tells me, adding, "I am quite familiar with BL's business practices and am impressed and very hopeful for the future of ranching if BL can implement its dreams. I'll dedicate myself to that dream if BL so wishes."

This is music to my ears—a symphony playing to the wind on the ridges and the birdsong in the creek bottoms. I hold her close and cannot help myself. I confess my love of her, describe things I've heard, felt, and seen from the moment I stepped into that boardroom. There is silence as we bask in each other's warmth, sitting side by side on a comfy leather couch at ten thousand feet.

We will land in Billings, Montana, soon and get a look at the first of many ranches. Tasha states that many of the places had airstrips when Wilberts purchased them, and "they extended the length of some runways and built new landing strips on others." On some, the runways are still short, so we will need to leave this plane behind and fly a smaller two-seater into them. Those will be short flights from a domestic airport, out to the ranch. There are a few places she thinks I will like to see first before we get into too much detail. I've a good idea of which places she refers to, and look forward to every minute of it.

I'm thinking of the times Tasha and I will share, of the first horse I will find for our son; perhaps a daughter's presence will want to honor us too. I'll let Tasha pick out the ranch where we will live, and I'll build her a bison-wool-warm house. It will matter little to me if we live on a ridge top or a valley bottom, as long as she is there. Woodsmoke will rise from our fireplace chimney, even if it is just to let everyone know that warmth lives here. Guess I'd better get her views on all this before I make too many plans, but I have no doubts Tasha will be delighted.

65. Wilberts's Plan

After we land in Billings and order lunch, I ask Tasha about the land Wilberts have purchased near BL's holdings.

Tasha explains that Wilberts has no intention of making BL's expansion difficult. Because of their preliminary investigations, they know they want to be in a position to be affiliated with Bison Leap. Wilberts's intentions are to maintain ownership of this land, and if BL decides to partner with them then BL can retain ownership of the bison and all bison products. Wilberts will help BL market the products, but BL will be under no obligation to sell to them and can retail or wholesale to anyone BL wishes to. If BL decides to take over the management of these places, BL will need to cover all operating costs. For that, BL receives fifty percent of the profits made on each and every ranch, but at the same time BL will also be obligated to cover any losses. The ranches are now complete with farm machinery and fully stocked with cattle. Wilberts retains ownership of these cattle, but

BL will market the calves, and most years that will allow the ranches to show a profit. The cow herd needs to be kept up to date with replacements from the calves, but BL can, at our discretion, sell the cows and replace them with BL's own bison. Of course, if or when the cows are sold the sale proceeds of those cows will be retained by Wilberts. They are also in a position to and are willing to help BL in any way they can.

This all sounds like a win-win situation to me, and I realize this had probably been in the papers at the board meeting, but I missed it.

Tasha also states, "Wilberts would like to help with any bison purchases, but as far as we know BL has already got a preferential obligation from anyone in a position to sell. We believe it will be in everyone's best interests if BL retains ownership of all bison under their care, at least for the immediate future."

"Is there anything you don't know about BL or me?" I ask her.

She smiles. "Yes, there's lots for me to learn, but I've a feeling all will be revealed soon. I hope I won't have to send you out for lessons."

I chuckle. "I'll be your lion and your wolf, your teddy bear and your puppy dog, but if I need to know more, I'd rather be taught by you than anyone else. And please don't threaten me like that again."

Tasha has a small two-seat plane rented for our afternoon flight to the ranch, and while the Wilberts pilots wait in town, Tasha and I will spend the night in the management house out on the ranch and are back in Billings early morning for another flight to Great Falls. Tasha's general plan is to hop-skip along the eastern side of the Rocky Mountains, north to the Peace River country of northern Alberta, then turn east and south from there.

"We won't see all of the Wilberts ranches north of Denver on this trip," she says. "We will try to see only the biggest and best of them."

On the next trip we'll head south, down into northern Mexico, Utah, Arizona, New Mexico, Texas, and then north again through Oklahoma, Kansas, and Nebraska, stopping at Kansas City before returning to Denver.

"Maybe you'd like to show me your cabin at BL," Tasha coos. "I would like to meet your family and take a ride on the airship."

Maybe Doug or Melinda will give her a lesson on the quadcopters, and she's also interested in the electric planes Sarah and I have. Tasha has an electric car she keeps in Kansas, but she's never been in the air with a silent plane.

"It'd be nice to fly without the raging noise of a petroleum engine," she tells me. "I've been flying since I was fourteen. Maybe you'll let me teach you how to do dives and rolls in your biplane."

"I'll likely pass on that one," I respond, thinking she can teach me dives, rolls, and acrobatic wiggles in a softer setting any time she likes. I'd also let her fly my biplane first chance we get...

When we see the size of the Billings ranch, I realize BL's bison herd will need help in building their numbers up. I recall that most of the State and Provincial Park herds have their numbers reduced almost every year to prevent overgrazing of their confined space, and most of these animals go for pet food. I know there is much public opposition to that way of handling the excess, but long-term contracts are held by the pet industry. I ask Tasha if Wilberts will buy out these pet food contracts. That would give BL access to many more animals.

Tasha calls the office in Kansas to ask them to look into that possibility. If this can be accomplished it will cut the time down from twenty-five to more like ten years that these Wilberts places can be fully stocked with BL bison. It'll keep us hoping to get the infrastructure in place to look after and process that many big shaggy beasts, in that time frame. *So many things to think about.* I will enjoy this trip, my time with Tasha, and the ranch decisions can wait until we've seen them all and my mind is more focused on business. For now, I have other, more pulsating things directing my attention.

This story is not about intruding on our private time together, but one of the pilots is later overheard saying, "If there ever was two people that should have been born Siamese, joined at the eyes, lips, arms, and hips, it would have been these two."

We travel north without much time to linger anywhere, but at every ranch we visit, we are welcomed with friendly hospitality. Each place is well-kept, and the employees seem genuinely contented. I like the feel of these places, and they are all productive. None of them have been overgrazed, the cattle are healthy and content, but what impresses me the most is the openness of the residents. Most of them have been on the places for many years and seem to be more than satisfied with their individual responsibilities and duties. This will help make BL's work easy. I have met so many people, it will take me a while to get their names straight, but I look forward to it.

Tasha and I are two peas grown in the same garden. We think alike, not just on the small things, but on most everything. We share our hopes and dreams, and we complement, understand, and inspire each other. By the time we get to the Peace River Country we both know we want much more of each other. We know now why we waited and had not compromised or committed to anything less. We feel lucky, we laugh and tease, we are in awe and admiration of each other. We are in love.

From the Peace River we fly southeast into Saskatchewan, then south again into North Dakota, South Dakota, and Nebraska before turning west for Denver. It is a fast trip. We've seen a lot of country and landed on some outstandingly beautiful ranches. I am committed without even seeing the more southerly places, and it is not just Tasha I am committed to. The whole layout of the ranches could not be better. These are vast acreages, some of them not adjacent to each other, but we can work on that. The bison will love the roaming room. A few of the places have crown or state land between them and that will involve public politics to allow the bison to roam there, but the good news is that most bison are classed the same as cattle and not classed like publicly owned wildlife, so this will make it easier to obtain the grazing licenses required for the public land portions.

The laws are such that wild critters like deer can be owned privately and kept behind a high fence, but as soon as they step onto public land they are deemed to be owned by the public. It is different with domestic cattle and bison, in that you can, as long as the public agrees, obtain grazing permits to occupy public land while paying for its usage. These grazers need to be identifiable, and the usual way is for them to be branded. I assume we can get the microchips accepted in lieu of a brand...

We share a fuzzy, warm, sweet kiss goodbye, because Tasha has some office work to take care of in Kansas. She tells me she'll be back in Denver soon to show me the southern places.

66. Time for Explanations

It is time for us at Bison Leap to explain ourselves. There are still many issues that need to be addressed, many different points of view, and many different human needs that must be satisfied. The public relations firm has their hands full with all the requests from different interest groups asking, "What are BL's intentions?" They all want to know how BL's business is going to affect them. We want and need all these people to understand, accept, and support this project. It will have to be that way for us to proceed much further.

After all, this is not just business; this is about a new way of life, a co-operation between man and the natural environment!

Nothing good ever came from one group or individual forcing their opinion and ways on others. This whole undertaking is about understanding and co-operation; that is the only way it will ever work. The only way man and nature could form a mutually beneficial relationship is if man, being the one with the big brain and capable heart, can set his possessive conditioned needs aside and start sharing the resources. This will not be an easy thing to do because of humanity's many generations of egotistically programed hoarding habits, but we could change if given a reason to.

There is nothing that will change the old ways of being other than a demonstrated better way of being. A phrase deserves repeating: "It is not easy for any critter, including man, to change its ways; old habits are familiar, and even though there are new and better ways they are unfamiliar, so the old ways keep beckoning, drawing one back to the familiar, even though that may be known to be detrimental in the long run..."

The big challenge will be for BL to explain our new way to all the varying opinionated groups in such a way that it will interest them and hold their attention long enough so this new way can become familiar and therefore understood and accepted. This all needs to be written in an easily read publicly accessible newsletter. The documentary film is definitely a big help, but a hands-on experience is needed to seal the deal. There needs to be easy ways for anybody interested to interact with BL and get personal benefit from that interaction. After all, interaction is really what this is all about—the positive interaction between people and their natural environment in a mutually supportive manner.

These are not new ideas to BL or our PR firm, but to have the ideas and to put them into practice are two different matters. It will take some work, some well-thought-out steps on how to proceed, and some dedicated sacrifices to implement these ideas in order to bring them into being.

Talk drifts away on the wind like a forgotten dream, but BL's intention is not just to dream about better ways but to actually start living these better ways, not only for ourselves but for all humankind and our natural environmental support system. This dream of bringing humans and nature back together is more than a fantasy to us. It is a necessity; something we really have no choice in.

We have to do what we were born to do. We have to live with the full capacity of our understanding. We have to share that understanding, that way of life, with all and everything we interact with. And we do have to interact. We have no more choice in the matter than we have in our ability to understand this whole affair. It is definitely an unusual affair—not a temporary entertaining diversion from the truth, but a lifelong commitment. Our commitment is to live in the best possible way, in a way that is sustainable, uplifting, and supportive, not just for our individual selves. That would be pointless, unfulfilling, and oh so very lonesome. We want to live in an inspiring setting, fluidly interacting with our complete world, the way we know it is possible to be.

To be fluid and interactive is about the opposite of being possessive, but truly, why would anyone desire to be possessive, especially if they know they have a fulfilling alternative? BL will present a choice and give people a chance to get used to it. This will not be, one day you're a dedicated slave and the next day you have angel wings. It will take time and effort, but it can be done. In fact, it is really the only thing worthwhile. Anything else is just putting in time and taking up space. BL will do our best to help make this earth a better place for all the diverse life-forms that call it home.

We know there will always be room for improvements, in understanding and in interaction, to be made even after we are long gone, but while we exist here we will put every effort we can behind our convictions. In this we have no choice, this is acquiescence, and we are content, happy, and energized with that.

The Bison Leap associates are pleased to hear of my impressions of the ranches I've seen. For us to take over the management of these far-flung places we need our own plane. It will have to be fast to cover the distances, but not too big so it can land on short runways. A four-seater is about right, but we need to upgrade our pilots' licenses to fly at night with instruments only and at high elevation. Ged is our only pilot with that kind of experience, and he is asked to do some research to find the best plane for this job. The business deal is not carved in stone with Wilberts yet, but BL will be prepared when the time comes.

67. Melinda's Post

Melinda posted in the previous newsletter a story she had given me, where Here-n-There talks of "*seeing* the trees," and in this one she posted another, except this time she did a little editing to make it easier to read.

Here-n-There starts by asking her if she remembers the one he told her of the trees' light, and then he proceeds... "Well, all organic beings have a light, and I will tell you a little of the human light..."

The ethereal body of humans (he begins) has been referred to by words in many different languages and cultures, but the words I prefer are *luminous body*, because it describes this part of us in very simple terms. Some may not *see* it as luminous but rather as a feeling of powerful energy. Either way is fine, and informative, but the beauty of its luminous brilliance is an enjoyable pleasure, so this story is a description of *sight*. So as not to confuse this issue, it need be understood that the *sight* of this luminosity is not done with the eyes, but rather with the *luminous body* of the perceiver. The prerequisite for *seeing* this, as in some other endeavors, is to have a still mind. This stillness of mind frees the energy of awareness, allowing it to recognize other perceptions not normally in our so-called conscious world.

After much investigation and deliberation, I've come to the conclusion that the mind is much too easy to condition. The mind was meant to record the input from our other senses. It was never meant to interact with that input but only to keep it in memory for instant access. For many strange reasons, we have put our mind in a position of leadership, much to our detriment. Now that we've relegated our mind to a position way past its abilities, we've also had to redirect most of our finitely available energy to hold it on its focus. This has starved our other senses into a state where they are no longer able to help us make sense of our world. These other senses, or aspects of ourselves, have atrophied to the point whereby they are unrecognizable to our overworked mind. If we still our mind, giving it a chance to rest, the freed energy can now wake up our other senses, giving them their chance to interact with our world in a direct uninterpreted manner. This freedom of our senses now gives us a true world, one never before acknowledged.

Of course, at first the mind rebels, for fear it will lose its authority and even its sanity, but as soon as it recognizes all these new, wondrous inputs it is satisfied, contented, and helpful in its originally intended job. The world now becomes mysterious, wondrous, vibrant, beautiful, and oh so much more than ever before. Now, all our other attributes, including our recorder (the mind) work together, enhancing each other, and we become human again. We are much more than robotic fact-carriers fighting a predatory world. We are organic awarenesses, and we need our senses alive, interacting with our world, so we must give them a chance.

What happened to still my mind enough to stop my known world in order for me to perceive the luminous body of another? This is a two-part story because it is about two separate instances of this phenomenon. A big part of each story is about the setting in hopes the description of the setting may bring some understanding of what it takes to partake of this beauty.

This first story I will call "Business," because that is what instigated it...

There was a time I was a single parent with a lovely young daughter to look after. With my duties as a parent, I could not work at a full-time job outside the home, so we had very little money. We grew a nice garden for most of our summer food, but we still needed cash to buy essentials to survive the long, cold winter. We had plenty of dry firewood all split and stacked and a small, not so warm cabin to keep the weather out when the cold and snow came. We used kerosene fuel in our glass lamps and carried our water from a nearby creek that also supplied us with a few small but very tasty trout for supper.

I had a unique painting that I could part with for our winter money supply. This was my only nonessential possession of value, so it was important I not pass up any presented opportunity to sell it, but I could not take a chance on losing it. It had a very limited market, as it was not something many people could appreciate or afford. I had informed a few people of my intentions. It so happened that a person I did not know came from a great distance to visit one of those I had told. This visitor wanted to look at my painting, and he fell instantly in love with it. This, I knew, may well be the only opportunity to sell for a good long time, so I was anxious to make the trade, but the man had no money. He wanted to take the painting with him and told me once he arrived home he would immediately send me the funds. I really could not afford to lose this painting to a stranger, especially to one who lived such a long distance away.

He and I were standing outside in the early darkness of evening, talking. I was considering telling him it was impossible for me to let him take the painting without getting paid first, but at the same time I needed to sell it. So I listened intently, searching for a decision. He was talking calmly, trying to convince me I would receive my much-needed money.

When I am really listening to someone I often lower my head and tilt it to one side, paying more attention to the feelings invoked rather than to sight and words. I was doing this as he talked. I was not looking at him, but I was listening to every nuance of his voice, trying to feel if I could trust him. He stated that his word was his bond, and that his word was the most important aspect of himself. He then stated that to him his word meant so much that to lie would mean he did not believe in himself. As he talked, his physical outline disappeared from my side vision and I *saw* his luminosity as zillions of spider-like filaments, radiant with vibrant light about twice the size of his flesh body. It appeared to me I was looking directly at his luminosity, even though with my eyes I was not.

I took this vision as a special sign that I could trust this stranger. I gave him the painting, and he left with it in his possession on his distant journey. The next time I ventured to town to check my mail, I received a stamped envelope enclosing payment in the full amount, including his thank-you note. I now had enough cash to get my daughter and myself through the winter.

I did not at that time analyze what I had *seen*, but after years have gone by I conclude, as with all such phenomena, all that is necessary to partake of these perceptive aspects of ourselves is we set our judgments and preconceived ideas aside long enough to let our *true selves* take over. We do this in full consciousness but without selfish possession. A simple wondrous trick, the effort of admission being minor compared to the wonders of the *view.*

This second story I call "Natell," because she was the instigator.

This is a time I lived alone. I was sorting out personal issues and studying dream analysis. I facilitated a dream workshop for a group of people and afterward attended the after-party gathering. A gorgeous, energetic, and, may I say, sexually coy, young lady who had missed the workshop presented herself to me as I was about to leave. It seemed she needed something from me. She used all her resources to delay my departure. As I stood by the door listening to her talk, her body disappeared from my sight and, as with the previous businessman, I *saw* her luminous body. What an incredibly beautiful sight. I gave her my full attention after *seeing* this, as I thought it also must be special.

I have since learned all organisms have luminosity, but few humans know of its existence. In this case, the thing that was special is that my attention was heightened while at the same time I allowed her to trap the attention of my mind to the extent it was lulled into relaxing enough so my other subtle senses could take over. I thank her.

I've been informed that our luminous body at all times *sees* the luminous bodies of others, but we are not conscious of this because our attention is fixated on the chatter of our minds. This leaves no energy for more fulfilling endeavors. Usually when the mind stops chattering we fall asleep. The trick is to stop the chatter but stay conscious. When that happens many very *wonderful* things are possible...

Transcribed from the recorded voice of Here-n-There.
There is still Here–Melinda.

When I read this, I decided the Bison Leap newsletter should now be sent to the residents on all the Wilberts ranches that had been offered to BL. It was also considered whether the newsletter should be made available to any interested party. This would need to be a unanimous agreement, so I asked everyone to submit their vote on this matter to Melinda.

68. Business Details

Wilberts's Kansas office arranged for BL to buy out the bison, pet food contracts in both Canada and the U.S., with the condition that these same pet food companies have first option to purchase all or part (at their discretion) of BL's dry bison pet food by-products in the future. Another win-win situation for all involved, including the bison. The more money these beasts are worth the more of them will get to procreate, and that will be good for the land and all other species as well. Even the bugs and bees will benefit because the bison, if well managed, help keep all the plants fresh and vibrant.

BL discussed all these ranches and the infrastructure we need to put in place to convert them, from the commercial cow-calf operations that they are now, into the bison producers they will become. There will need to be many new buildings built, airships to lease, more copters and pilots to train; we need to purchase and transport every bison available.

Would Wilberts consider putting up the funds necessary to build needed buildings? If so, BL would be able to pay for inside finishing and any tools specifically related to the bison works. The buildings will belong to the land, so they should be built and owned by Wilberts, but the tools are portable so they should be in BL's possession, same as the bison. If this is agreeable, then BL is ready to commit to the management of all these places.

It is not long before the Kansas office gets back to us stating, "Whatever BL needs to proceed is agreeable, and Wilberts looks forward to a long and fruitful association."

BL estimates we need upward of one hundred quadcopter and airship pilots in the next five years for our own operation. We are asked by the Wyoming biologists to train pilots for the state program. Perhaps Colorado will soon put in the same request, and maybe some of the Canadian provinces are interested too.

Would Doug and Melinda consider moving to either Elk Mountain or Green River to set up a training school? If they are agreeable, BL will build a building to their recommendations, and a notice will be sent to all Wilberts ranch residents, to give them first option on the pilot course. The majority of the pilots need large animal experience. There will also be pilot positions for people without animal skills. BL needs electricians, computer programmers, clerical staff, butchers, and food prep specialists. Ged will get a shipload of Pinion's sound posts made, and the communications people will have to make sure all the places have fast internet service.

We will have to decide which places will be developed first. We will take it one ranch at a time as the bison herds build their population numbers. Next spring, BL is expecting over two thousand of our own bison calves; half of them will be heifers, so the herd will increase fast. We have to stay ahead of the bison with the ranch infrastructure. BL asks Wilberts ranch residents to make the trip as their time permits to one of the established BL ranches to get an idea of what to plan for in the future. This is a paid excursion for them. It's a good company morale-booster along with being educational for everyone. The four-seat plane will get many air hours on it. Perhaps a pilot or two should be found who would like to make it their second home.

69. Public Relations

The public relations people completed a list of parties interested in BL's business and some ideas on how they can each be satisfied. If done properly, this will be good PR for BL and will bring us much valuable understanding and support. It will be very rewarding to have everyone behind our project and is much cheaper and more productive than trying to explain ourselves later. There is one common theme that would help with all these interested parties, and that is to give each and every one of them guided tours of BL's properties. Tours will build a connection to the land, a bridge to understanding and fulfillment.

We will not attempt to trick or force the public into allowing BL to develop our dreams, as that would not have the desired effect. BL needs people to understand, accept, and support this project in full awareness, so even though these guided tours will take up a fair amount of BL's time and also be expensive, it will be money and time well spent. There are people with specific needs that demand a little more than just a guided tour and these will also be addressed.

For hunters and sport fishermen, the guided tours and use of BL's facilities will satisfy most of their needs to be in the wild and interact with nature, but it will help if they can take some wild food home with them. The fishermen will be given access to the waters on BL's lands and will be allowed to catch a limited amount for personal consumption. Torture of fish with the old catch and release licenses of the past will be discouraged, but fishers can feel proud to eat what they are allowed to catch. The hunters will be encouraged to participate at harvest time, and for their help they can take home meat that is tender and nutritious, guaranteed healthy, and killed humanely.

To help emphasize BL's reasoning behind our desires to abandon what are, to us, archaic practices of catch and release, Melinda posted another of Here-n-There's stories in the newsletter.

"The Baby Jackrabbit, No Cage for Him"

As a kid, I was energetic, inquisitive. Spending every day in the outdoors, mostly playing, investigating all the nooks and crannies of the woods, creeks, and gardens. One sunny day, at the back end of our huge raspberry patch, just before the creeks and woods start, I notice a very young jackrabbit, sitting and nibbling his salad. He is alone, as momma rabbits tell their young to go fend for themselves as soon as they're old enough to find their own food. His whole body is about the same size as his head will be when he is fully grown, so he's quite young and could fit into my hands. A multi-wire fence runs between the garden and the woods. This fence is grown in with a plant we call goldenrod. It grows about up to my shoulders and has nice bushy yellow flowers on top. The stems of this plant are like straight sticks about the same size around as your little finger. It grows very close together in some places, and along this fence it grows so thick your hand would not fit between the stems. This little rabbit is sitting on the raspberry side of this grown-in fence, munching on a succulent dandelion leaf. He looks very soft and cuddly, so I want him for my pet. I try to pick him up, but of course he is wild, so he runs. I chase to catch him.

He tries to get through the fence and back to the woods where he was born, but he can't get through the thick goldenrods that have woven themselves up through the fence. He gets stuck and I catch him. He doesn't scratch or bite me. He just gets small, like he is trying to hide in my hands. I carry him carefully, so as not to hurt him, up to the barn where I have a nice wire cage to put him in. This, I think, will be a good home for him for a while, at least until he gets used to me and I can call him my tame pet.

I pick some old dry grass to put in one end of the cage so he has a comfy soft bed. Then I pick some very tender dandelion leaves and a few other soft yummy plants I know he will like to eat. Finally, I get a small dish of water for him to drink and carefully set it in his cage. I leave him to get used to his new home and go to the house to get myself something to eat. I've had a very busy morning and am hungry. A few hours later I visit my little wild rabbit. He's lying on his side with his head in the water dish, trying to drown himself! He's almost dead!

He's given up on life because he's in a cage, and he desperately wants to be free. I gently pick him up and take him outside to a burdock plant. Burdock plants have broad flat leaves—something like rhubarb leaves except burdock grows higher than your head with big leaves from top to bottom. I put this sad, almost dead little rabbit under the big burdock leaves in the shade. He is hidden and it's quiet, cool, and nurturing for his spirit. I leave him, so he can decide for himself what he wants to do.

In an hour I go back to check on him. To my delight, he's sitting up and again looks like the happy little rabbit I first seen along the fence at the end of the raspberry patch! I do not disturb him, as I don't want to scare him into running again. I leave him sitting there to see what will happen. An hour later, I again check on him and he's gone. I decide then, *sometimes living things should be left alone to choose their own lives; it is not our right to take a beautiful free life and put it in confinement for our own pleasure or amusement.* Sometimes we get lonesome and would like a friend to keep us company, but there are far better ways to make friends than to confine what we love. To a born-wild critter, simple confinement is unendurable torture. Their free spirit leads them, and if their confined body cannot follow, then their spirit and body separate, leading to their demise.

—Here-n-There

The farmers' and ranchers' main interest is not hunting or fishing, but they are very interested in what BL is planning with the land, water, and wildlife. How will this affect their ability to make a living?

We assure them that BL will do everything possible to keep the wildlife off of their cultivated lands and help to keep the water flowing pure and clear. We offer Pinion's sound posts anywhere a problem might show up. We also encourage farmers, on the marginally productive parts of their land, to adopt BL's system of natural plant and animal production. BL helps educate, support, and guide them in this endeavor. We will also help them harvest and market any of the natural products they produce. Another win-win situation.

The tour operators are given access to BL's lands, facilities, and flying machines, for a token fee, just enough to cover BL's costs, and far cheaper than these tour operators can find this same service anywhere else. We encourage them to pass this savings on to their clients, and this is very good for the tour operator businesses. The tours are busy in all but the nastiest weather. This also relieves pressure from demand on BL's time.

Public school children, along with their teachers and guardians, are given absolutely free tours and educational talks. These need to be scheduled well in advance, but the schools can take advantage of this service as often as they wish. The airships prove to be a big draw for students, and the proximity to natural lands and wildlife in a safe setting is much appreciated by school officials and parents alike.

The Native Bands are also given educational tours, and BL representatives are sent to their lands to talk of ways these Bands can improve their participation in the project. They are offered the same support services the farmers have been offered and are supplied with bison seed stock if they wish to participate.

Environmentalists, animal rights activists, hikers and campers, photographers, and lovers of the land are all treated with fairness and respect. They are given access to BL's services and facilities for a nominal fee, or redirected to the tour operators. BL spends much time listening to their individual needs and concerns, explaining ourselves and demonstrating the intricacies of this business to help build a mutual understanding. This, we dream, will evolve into a supportive system that will last for eons into the future.

The consumers of BL's products are met with openness and transparency; nothing is hidden at BL. Consumers are assured they can trust BL's products to be wholesome, nutritious, and grown and harvested in ways not only good for the land but good for the consumer and the long-term enhancement and sustainability of Earth's diverse environment. All of these aspects of BL's business are open for public scrutiny. BL is soon known to be eager to hear suggestions and input for better ways to obtain these goals.

All investors of either their time or funds are considered family and are given free rein to participate in any and every BL activity as their hearts desire, but, of course, there is safety and certain procedures that need to be learned.

Those of BL that are already familiar with these aspects are willing to share their experiences and knowledge with any who wish to learn. This is an open business, and that is the way it was meant to be from its conception. BL encourages this in all ways possible.

There will never be No Trespassing signs on any of BL's properties or businesses. We install motion-activated talking signs encouraging interested people to seek assistance for guidance and educational services offered by BL.

BL participates with all government departments, and we are open to any suggestions or concerns they may have. BL also contributes to local needs in many ways. This has been demonstrated with BL's help, to health institutions, schools, and some charities but is also extended to road maintenance and other public works infrastructures.

Not that they should be singled out more than any other institution, but insurance and financial institutions are not needed because of their interest and inflation policies, but any that are more inclined to be socially helpful we welcome for their expert input. The mathematicians of BL explain that interest and inflation is a private business that was set up centuries ago by tricky financiers to accumulate power for themselves. It is one of the most detrimental demons ever unleashed upon our planet, and it is now affecting every earth organism.

One of the office mathematicians writes a little of what he calls poetry, and he says this is supposed to be humorous, but it seems more than that. He posted it for all to read.

Today's newsletter in part reads;

Something to think about?

MONEY IS NOT THE ROOT OF EVIL!

INTEREST AND INFLATION IS!

REVISED DICTIONARY:

MONEY - a portable recognition of services or goods rendered. Nice...

INTEREST - if you perceive yourself to be or are in need, I will serve you if you agree to pay back not only my service but extra. Shame on us.

INFLATION - to manipulate money (i.e., service rendered) so that the service to be paid back is now more than the original service given. Of course, the interest still applies on the whole lot. This is the smoke and mirrors of modern slavery...

Conclusion: We need to work within our present monetary system, but that does not mean we cannot influence this system whereby tokens of services rendered can be exchanged, with the mutual agreement that these tokens are not influenced by inflation, interest, or time.

Not all mathematicians just count beans...

Translation Of Previous Paragraph:

As a simple token of services rendered, there are many positive conveniences attributable to money. Problems arose when a few very intelligent, but socially irresponsible, and ruthless people convinced others, who at the time were in need, that these elite computationally intelligent few would help those in need, on the condition that the needy would pay back more than the token given.

This, over time, eventually became standard protected practice and allowed the ruthless few to accumulate so much that they have now positioned themselves into mastery over the masses. The masters are so adept at counting and flaunting their power that they no longer have an inclination or obligation to feel.

The masses are forced to do their masters' bidding, and the masses now have little time to think or feel or the energy to rebel. They have resigned themselves to numb slavery, while their masters ruthlessly feed off their energy and plunder the planet's natural resources. The present monetary system has become a new planetary religion, to the detriment of all, but it is so ingrained and hidden behind smoke and mirrors that few understand it, and so we plod along toward our demise. The few who manage to get off this treadmill and get a clear view of the problem are often tricked, whipped, and forced back onto this black hole trajectory!

The common people will know which institutions are becoming socially responsible because these institutions' interest rates will be slightly lower than the rate of inflation. This policy will eventually have the effect of making inflation disappear. When inflation disappears, then interest will also be history. People will then be exchanging one token of service for another of the same valued service. No interest and no inflation. No masters and no slaves. It will be a difficult treadmill to get off of because it is intentionally designed to perpetuate itself, but it can be done.

The challenge is: "The intelligent masters will need to slowly but surely instigate and bring about this change. It is becoming increasingly obvious that the alternatives are indeed bleak. BL's business practices have made it obvious to even the present power hungry that the rewards for change are well worth investigating!"

Many of the lawmakers, politicians, and policymakers are encouraged to fully participate. They'll be kept well informed of all BL's proceedings and objectives. It is important that these leaders understand all of the many aspects of BL's business because, after all, they are the ones who have the most experience and expertise in helping to keep all of society running in a somewhat compatible and smooth fashion.

The public relations firm will maintain an openness toward any new social aspects that develop. These will be addressed as they come up. Our dream is about an evolution of human consciousness. There will undoubtedly be unforeseen challenges and understandings showing up in the future. BL welcomes them with an open heart and mind. This is BL's mandate, presented to you, the public, to encourage your input and participation.

Compiled by the Denver Accounting Staff

70. BL's Intentions

The combined bison-producing land area of BL and Wilberts is now approximately one acre out of every two hundred of the North American bison's old-time range. Even though some of BL's land is not the most productive of the bison's former territory, it is now looked after by science and consideration, so it outproduces even the best of the previous rangeland.

BL's intention has never been to restock the bison to their full former glory. Some places where the bison once roamed are now used by cities, and some is very valuable cropland. There still remains room for expansion into areas of once-productive grassland that really is too dry to be farmed and should never have been cultivated. These drier areas can be reseeded to natural grass as they once were. All BL needs to prove is that we can produce more dollars on these acres by grazing bison than what is now being produced there with the marginal grain crops being grown. Some of this cultivation is supported by slight of hand business and subsidized interference and that will need to be addressed, but as understanding develops these issues will work themselves out.

Some areas have no surface water for a critter or bird to drink. BL can fix this with small drilled wells powered by wind and solar. These can be installed at approximately one mile intervals, and even though not much water will be consumed this will allow the land to be utilized to its sustainable potential. In the near past, these areas have been cultivated with much detriment to the environment. In the even more distant past, these same dry areas had grown an accumulation of plant matter, but because of the lack of drinking water, it was not utilized by the critters, so it had built up to be a fire hazard, often with disastrous results. BL will help these places come to life for the benefit of many organisms, plants, insects, birds, and animals, big and small.

71. Jake's Bison Wool

Jake has noticed the heavy blanket of wool the bison shed every spring. It is being rubbed off on trees and big rocks the bison use as scratching posts. Jake wants this wool and hair for the house insulation business, and now the fine, soft under-wool is in high demand for woven and knitted clothing products. Jake tried a few different designs of rubbing posts for collecting these sheddings and is impressed with a steel tripod affair that has many fingerlike projections on it. The bison love to rub on it and leave many pounds of their sheddings for collection. Jake recruited the fabricators to build a bunch of these scratch posts. They are stackable for transport, and the airship can set them out near wherever the bison happen to be in the spring shedding season.

Many years ago, government agricultural departments mapped all the grazing areas for mineral content of the soil and water, so the farmers and ranchers would have a vague idea of what fertilizers to use or types of supplements to feed in each particular area. Some areas have a natural toxic overabundance of one particular mineral; others have deficiencies. For the health of an animal or plant, a specific balance of many different minerals is needed.

The free-roaming wild animals at one time traveled many miles to locate or avoid specific elements at certain seasons of the year. Their bodies could sense which particular area to avoid or which plant to eat to get the needed element. Even though BL gives them as much wandering space as we can, it's no longer possible for these critters to wander the many miles they once did in search of specific nutrients or medicinal plants and minerals.

Our office staff have the government agricultural maps of these mineral abundances or deficiencies and are now giving the different areas specific numbers and relating these to BL's bison pastures. The veterinarians and nutritionists are working together to formulate the proper ratio'd mineral block for the bison to lick in each different area. These lick blocks are set out near Jake's scratch posts to help keep the bison healthy.

We must be careful not to put the bison blocks that have too much copper in areas the wild sheep frequent. The sheep would be poisoned with the same amount of copper it takes to keep a bison healthy. Different animals need different minerals at different times of the year, according to what is available in their diet (food and water) and what stage of the process their body happens to be in at that specific time.

Pregnant females, for example, need an abundance of specific elements to be able to give birth to a healthy newborn. All organic cell division (including plants and animals) requires a specific quantity and ratio of vitamins and minerals according to the complicated makeup of that individual organism. This ratio varies at certain times in each organism's life depending on what development stage they are at. Every organism has the ability (to a limited extent) to take up, expel, or repel certain elements, but if the elements are very much out of balance in the organism's environment, a toxicity or deficiency will develop, impairing the organism's ability to cell divide. Depending on the extent of the imbalance, this can lead to stunted growth, sickness, cell distortion, or, in extreme cases, death of the organism. When an organism eats, drinks, or absorbs its environment (as it must, especially in the case of cultivated plants or confined animals), it has little choice in the matter of its intake.

Confinement, domestication, and the lack of free will can lead to a necessary numbing of senses, whereas wildness and freedom necessitate choices, which demand awakened senses.

Health can get technically complicated, and because an animal is no longer free to follow its age-old sensory instincts, science has to help by supplementing them with what they need. With study, it is easy enough to do. The right balance of minerals helps keep an animal (or plant) robust with a healthy immune system, and this shows up in their liveliness and production, which is the bottom line for survival of the BL concept. In certain areas, the bison also need controls for certain internal and external parasites. This control is administered through the scratch posts after the wool is collected. These are healthy bison and are well looked after. They're allowed as much free will as possible according to the restrictions now placed upon them. In a few years, the natural diversity of nutritional and medicinal plants will re-establish itself, sometimes with the help of botanists and herbalists who have educated themselves on past naturally healthy landscapes.

A re-established natural diversity of plants (both nutritional and medicinal) will help reawaken an animal's senses of choice, encouraging them to reemploy the old unrestrained depth of bodily knowledge necessary for their physical health, quality of life, and longevity.

72. Southern Flight

Tasha calls to see if I am "ready to visit some of the southern properties."

"It would be better if we had our own small, fast plane," I tell her. I am always trying to think ahead. I figure a four-seater would be about right.

"That can be arranged," Tasha replied, "but we agree, for this trip that we'll take the Wilberts pilots along."

More investigation is needed to find the best plane for this particular job. Ged has been researching this, and we are content he will find a good one for us.

I meet Tasha again at the airport in Denver. A group of tourists, assuming we are a master-carved statue because we haven't moved for so long, take photos of us in our standing embrace. The pilots smile and chuckle to themselves and are happy with the diversion. South we will fly in a big oblong circle before coming back to Denver.

There is a state-of-the-art communications system installed on this plane, so keeping in touch with business matters will not be a problem. Tasha and I will extend this trip a little longer than the last one and not worry about getting behind in our work. After all, this is important business.

The first ranch we set down on is in southern Colorado, just north of the New Mexico border. It has a lot of high country with scattered trees and is a little shy on water, but it extends east out onto miles of open grasslands. A north–south interstate highway bisects the eastern part of this grassland. I don't appreciate the highway, but it's a big place. The highway has a few underpasses for livestock to travel from one side to the other. I'm not sure how the bison will respond to these, but there's room, with a few improvements in water, for many thousands of bison to graze.

They can migrate from the low grassland country to the high mesas as the seasons change, so that is a bonus. Perhaps in the future something can be done about the bisecting roadway. The plane takes us on into Arizona and southern New Mexico, and on to more big places, but again the land, for the most part, is on the dry side. It will take many more acres here to keep a critter fed than it does in wetter areas, but these are vast places. The bison are built for travel, so they will do well with some improvements in surface-water distribution. Western Texas and northern Mexico is the same. The river and creek bottoms are lush and green, but there are long stretches in between the watercourses with not a drop to drink.

BL will need to invest in a small, portable water drill that can be set down in likely spots with an airship. We need water tanks installed at a minimum of every mile to make proper use of these acreages. These water holes will be an oasis for all critters. They'll need to be built strong so the bison can't wreck them with their rubbing. They also need to be built so birds, bugs, and little critters can get a drink without fear of being trapped and drowned in smooth-sided tanks.

I am really starting to appreciate the country where Sarah and I grew up, with its abundance of water and green plants. The bison, at one time, did well in this dry country, so BL will help them do that again. Central and eastern Texas does not have high majestic mountains, but it's pretty country and receives enough moisture to allow decent plant growth. The bison will have an easy life here. Western Oklahoma and northern Texas is where the grazing potential is impressive. This is grass country. Wilberts selected ranches here with rolling hills and plenty of small creeks and little lakes. This area is the most productive of the southern ranches we've seen so far. They do not grow quite as well as the northern places, but they have short easy winters so the bison will not have to grow their coats as thick or eat as much to keep warm in the harsh winds of the bitter-cold winter storms.

There is plenty of diversity from the far north country to the far south, and BL will try to select bison that are most suited to these different areas. They are adaptable animals, but we will try to make it easy for them in any way we can.

Tasha and I are pleased with each other's company and very much looking forward to the day we will live side by side in the same house. Neither of us is quite sure yet where that house will be. We still have many places to see, and there's no rush to decide. For now, we are content to be nomads, as long as we're together.

In the days of old, the best grassland was in the east central plains with its just-right amount of moisture. A lot of this area is now split up into small intensely cultivated farms. The Wilberts bought places here, where there is rough country not so good for tractors because of its up and down nature. These will keep a high concentration of bison happy, but in general I prefer the areas a little further west. Sarah and I grew up with a view of the mountains, and that feels to us like we are held in the protective arms of Mother Earth. The other lands are good too, but the rough country feels more like home to me.

Familiar things are inviting, and I am no exception to this rule; if I have a choice, I will stay close to my birthplace, but of course Tasha is a much more inviting view to me than any mountain or river, so I will be wherever she chooses to be. She awakens my senses as they've never been awakened before, and I know that like Samantha and Jake, and like Sarah and Ged, this will be for as long as the sun shines and the grass grows. Quite possibly long after that.

73. Elk at Bison Leap

The six elk originally at the old homestead have done well. Each cow has raised a nice calf every year. Jake feeds them with the bison when the snows get deep, and they are healthy and contented. Every spring they disappear, heading northwest up into the high mountains, following the greening grass. BL has never kept track of how far they go, although we could have with the implanted chips and the copters. The pilots have many other things to do, so we let them go, assuming they'll be back again once the weather turns nasty high in the mountains. That has been the elks' pattern and this year will be no different... except it is!

When the pilots saw them congregating outside the perimeter sound fence, they turned a few towers off to let them enter. Few people know for sure how wild animals communicate, or how much information they share, but this early winter these few familiar elk came back to BL ranch, with sixty friends following close behind. They've all settled in like they belong.

Melinda checked and none of the new ones have been microchipped, so she calls the government biologists and asks for their permission to chip, vaccinate, and take blood samples of the bunch.

The biologists give their go ahead, but express surprise at the numbers.

There have not been many elk in this area for more than fifty years. No one knows where these new ones have come from, but they seem content to spend the winter with BL's bison and enjoy the supplemental hay when the snows pile up. Melinda is training new pilots, and they get these elk all tested, chipped, and vaccinated. Blood tests indicate they do have some internal parasites, but other than that they are clean. Jake's scratch posts will take care of the bugs, and Melinda's computer records keep account of the elks' movements. The Wyoming biologists are working on getting all the state elk tested, chipped, and vaccinated, but it will take them a few more years.

Before the days of highways, farming, and fences, the elk migrated, sometimes for hundreds of miles, stimulated by the weather and food resources. In the early spring, they would be in the low river bottoms and on the south-facing sidehills where the plants start to grow first with the warming sun. As the land warmed up, they followed the new green growth as it climbed in elevation toward the peaks. They stayed in the open meadows of the high country until the cold and deep snows told them to head back down to the lower elevations where they would spend the winter. They had patterns established from many generations of learning. Their young would repeat and continue them. Once the fences had been built, these patterns were disrupted, and as the country became settled in the river bottoms with roads, houses, and dogs, the elk could no longer make use of the low country, and it was hard on them.

They were often forced to winter in the cold high country with the deep snows and little to eat. The young and old often succumbed to prolonged starvation at these altitudes, and the herd numbers were reduced drastically from their former days. Only the very strong survive when times are tough and these times are tough on the elk, the same as for most wildlife.

BL likes to see these majestic elk and view them as another of the Earth's gifts, but even so, the bills need to get paid. BL can afford to feed eighty elk for a few months every winter, but what if this bunch brings back an even bigger herd next year? And these ones will also have young; their numbers are bound to grow.

What usually happens when the population starts showing up around residential, ranch, or farmland is that the state wildlife officers get complaints, so the hunting season is then extended to reduce the elk numbers. Those that survive are again forced to hide out in the high country.

BL does not want to see this scenario repeated, but like any business we have monetary obligations, and if those obligations are not met we will be forced to go out of business.

Can the state and BL work out some arrangement to everybody's benefit, including the interests of these elk? BL and the Wyoming biologists have been doing very good things together and have developed a mutual trust and respect. With BL's chip and computer monitoring system, we can easily keep records of the amount and dollar value of the feed the elk and other state-owned wildlife are consuming while on BL's property. By vaccinating and supplementing the diet of this wildlife, BL is decreasing the mortality of these species, and from past experience this has shown to enhance the population, so yes, BL can be compensated for our efforts and expense.

BL keeps meticulous records of the arrival dates not only of the elk but also the deer, sheep, moose, and wild goat populations on our lands. We monitor their health, and vaccinate and supplement them in times of need. For these services, BL is allowed to cull from the herd animals that are surplus. BL will receive payment in meat by taking the old, the injured, and extra males with the same criteria we use to enhance our bison herds. BL will do this cull, under state supervision, throughout the winter and early spring after the supplemental feed has brought the condition of the animals up to a healthy standard. The herds will leave BL for their spring migration healthy and in much greater numbers than if they'd had to fend for themselves in the deep snows of the mountains.

Even with BL's share of the animals, the herds will increase. This compensation payment BL worked out will be extended, by the state, to all private properties as long as those properties have a monitoring and record-keeping system in place. BL will make our already developed services available to any property owner in the state of Wyoming. Hunters are still allowed to buy tickets for harvests on state property, but with less than half the cost of a state hunt, they can help in BL's harvest, be guaranteed satisfaction, take healthy meat home, and there is no stress of the chase on the animals. The herds are monitored closely, so they do not exceed the carrying capacity of the land. In a few years, there will be a lot of majestic, independently free animals walking around. This will be good for the wild herds, good for the land, and fulfilling for the bellies of all those who want to eat them.

This is a huge step forward in wildlife management for the whole state. The big challenge now will be how to keep these animals off the highways and out of cultivated fields. BL can also be of assistance there with Pinion's sound posts.

In certain areas where the animals need to cross the roadways on their migration routes, overpasses (greened-in walkways) will need to be built, but the state will wait and let the animals tell us where these are needed.

Colorado is beginning to implement some of the wildlife management procedures that BL and Wyoming have worked out. Colorado will hang back a bit and let Wyoming blaze the trail before they get too involved. This all takes time, and no one is in a real big rush because no one wants to make hard-to-correct mistakes, but we are making progress and everyone, including the natural landscape, is benefiting.

74. Doug and Melinda's Choice

Melinda and Doug travel back and forth from BL's old homestead to Green River and over to Elk Mountain with the new electric plane BL purchased for them. Jake uses my biplane to keep track of things at Bison Leap. He made a short airstrip not far from Samantha's garden, and with the little plane he gets almost anywhere he needs to go in a few minutes. Doug installed a charging station in Jake's biplane hangar, so he travels back and forth without the worry of running out of juice.

Melinda chooses to stay around BL, and Doug agrees with her. They enjoy the diversity in this area and decide this is their home.

Once it becomes local knowledge that BL plans to build a pilot training school, the small nearby village offers to donate a two-hundred-acre parcel they own. This is on the village edge, is relatively flat, has the runway nearby, and nice old cottonwood trees shade the creek running along one side. BL can have the deed for this land if we would like to build our school here. The village will be more than compensated by spin-off business and taxation after the school is complete.

Bison Leap, as with most everything else we do, will build a school like no other!

I submit a rough pencil sketch to BL's stockholders of what I would like to see built. Input ideas are requested before the plans are sent to architects and engineers. It takes a while to go through the process, but what a complex it will be.

This isn't just a bunch of square boxes; this is a masterpiece. A village BL is proud of, and a tourist attraction; when complete, it will be the envy of and inspiration to millions!

First, we widen and extend the length of the old village airstrip. We build a good-sized hangar off to one side, near the windward end of the strip. Beside the hangar we erect a tower, similar to an air traffic control tower. It functions as that when needed, but its main purpose is as part of the training classroom for quadcopter, air-bus, and drone pilots. On the opposite side of the tower from the runway is another landing area—circular, for airships and copters. In the hangar itself is a classroom for preliminary instruction.

One of the Wilberts ranches borders this two-hundred-acre piece and is handy for finalizing the training of pilots who will be working directly with the wild critters.

A short walk from the hangar is BL's village. We call it "Wagon Wheel," and it is special. Built to live in, to be inspired by, and to be socially evolutionary, this village is a separate extension of the original village. All our services are open to the public.

Wagon Wheel has a welcoming gatekeeper, whose function is to inform and direct new arrivals to all the many services that Wagon Wheel provides. It's patterned similar to what we built at the Elk Mountain Ranch, but is much more sophisticated and houses many more people, along with varied services. We started with a twelve-sided central common building. This houses food services, a children's school, doctors' offices, art and craft stores, and many others. These change as needs evolve. The second story of this central building is open inside with a hardwood floor, moveable seats, and a stage. It's used for dances, community gatherings, and public talks.

Radiating out from this central common building are twelve glass-covered walkways, similar to spokes of a wooden wagon wheel. These spokes have planter boxes and comfortable sitting benches. The walkways lead to the living apartments that encircle the village perimeter. Each apartment has a small private outdoor area, front and back, two floors. The upper floor has three rooms, a complete bathroom, and two bedrooms. One bedroom can be used for a personal office if desired. The ground floor is an open kitchen-living-room combination with a small two-piece washroom. These apartments wrap around the village in the same twelve-sided circular pattern. The buildings are all constructed and insulated with Jake's hollow-wall, bison-wool insulation method, so they're cozy, warm, and quiet. Inside and out, these buildings are designed with fireproof materials.

Each unit is supplied with services from underneath, through the full-circle service basement. It is constructed this way because we might receive better ideas in the future, and we do not want to have to dig everything up again to install new products or fix existing ones. Communication cables, electric power, water, heat, and a drain system are all hung through this circular basement then fed up into the apartments. All the apartment and grounds services are simple to access and easy to repair.

The drainage line feeds to a community microbial digester and water purifier. Two drain systems are required, one for easy-to-compost natural organic waste, the other for anyone using persistent pharmaceuticals. The toxic drain leads to a special cleanser for processing.

The organic digester has a clean-water outlet, which feeds into the nearby pasture for irrigation. No harsh cleansers, pharmaceuticals, or toxic chemicals are allowed to be flushed into the organic system, so the integrity of our environment is maintained in a supportive manner.

The whole village takes up very little space and uses a minimum of resources but is very easy to get around in while still maintaining maximum individual privacy. Anything your heart or mind desires is at your fingertips. It's easy for residents and visitors alike to mingle in an unobtrusive manner. Yet you can still be as private as you like.

There is a common salad garden in one of the open-air spaces between the walkways. Another space has a solarium-garden sitting area. A larger field-garden area is just outside the village circle. In the individual private spaces at each residence you can, if you like, have your own small sanctuary. This whole village is a sanctuary, but some people like to have more private quiet time than others, so that is accommodated.

Wagon Wheel is powered by wind, solar, and geothermal, but everyone is expecting the new fusion generators will be available soon.

In between the remaining covered walkways are trees, green spaces, sitting places, water fountains, gardens, and play areas. The apartments are joined at their ends, and in this village there is room to house 150 resident families along with guest accommodations.

BL has many pilots to train for our own use on all the land we caretake, plus we will be training the Wyoming biologist pilots, and we are now getting interest from other states, provinces, and countries.

All Wagon Wheel services are open to the public, and who knows in the future how expansive BL's wildlife services will be? We are already much in demand, but this village is big enough for now. We could build another someplace else if the demand grows. This one will help us plan an even better complex if that is what the future wants. Tasha and I reserve an apartment here for ourselves. Our Wagon Wheel village is centrally located to BL's land management duties, and with the extended runway it makes a convenient home base.

The way our business is set up is a bit frustrating at times, dealing with people's lack of knowledge and/or stubbornness. No one, not even if they have a particularly good idea, can proceed without first getting one hundred percent approval from everybody. This does at times seem to slow down or even impede our progress, and that is the frustrating aspect of our organization, but the good part of that—and this is why we originally set it up this way—is that no one gets to assert their authority to make a detrimental or uncorrectable mistake. Any time a mistake is made, everybody and everything suffers for it, so keeping this in mind it is reasonable that everyone should first have an equal say in any intended action.

This simply means you must present your well-conceived and well-intended idea to all concerned to get their understanding and approval before proceeding. This makes it necessary for you to develop a clear understanding of your project, and it also makes it necessary for you to develop your benevolent communication skills, rather than (as in customary business) your tools to force compliance toward your personal will.

It's important to keep in mind that even though you may well understand your own projects and be proficient at communicating them to others, there are others who may have legitimate ideas but may not be capable of thinking them through clearly or be as proficient as yourself at communicating. It is therefore paramount that we put as much (or more) effort into listening to others as we put into having others listen to us.

The system of approvals BL has set for ourselves is the only way any project can be truly beneficial and sustainable, so BL's way of doing things more than compensates for the frustration of going through our people-approval process in every personal attempt to accomplish a specific goal. Oftentimes, when an intended project is explained to someone who has no previous experience or understanding of the presented concept, unexpected insights surface that make it necessary to change or improve the project, or at other times make it clear the project should be abandoned altogether.

Communicating can be a very complicated art, but the rewards of having yourself understood, along with being able to understand others, is the ultimate evolution of ourselves as humans. Developing and enhancing our senses brings us into states of being that enliven and energize us, as only the contrast of doldrums and deprivation can explain.

All these projected and receptive arts of communication not only apply between humans, but also apply between humans and our natural environment. The earth and all its inhabitants share a common life. None can be fulfilled or complete without the others.

One cannot fear or appreciate something without first having knowledge of its existence. Similarly, one cannot know that one misses something if one has no knowledge it existed in the first place. Extinction cannot in any way be life-enhancing because it is a part of us gone forever. Even though that part may have been mysterious or even unknown, at some point in our future development it is most likely that our evolution will be slowed or arrested because of the unavailability of the missing, extinct parts.

If a whole species existed without any memory or description of a thing such as simple sound, how could they know what they miss? Let us maintain and enhance our diversity!

75. Cougars

The pilots at Elk Mountain Ranch are keeping a close eye on the momma cougar and her three kittens. The kittens are growing fast and their mom is a good provider. She's now killing a deer every couple days to keep her kittens fed. The microchips of the deer attest to this, even when the pilots do not observe the kill. She often takes another before her last one is cleaned up, and the pilots assume she's killing in order to teach her kittens the fine art of the stalk. The basic harshness of nature, at times, is difficult to understand.

A big tom cougar passed through the valley. He killed and ate two of the kittens. When he tried to get the third, the momma cat took out one of his eyes with a clawed swipe down the side of his face. This convinced him to seek quieter territories and he disappeared, not to be seen again for quite some time.

One pilot wants to teach the kitten to kill only the sick or injured deer and to leave the young and healthy alone, but it is difficult because the old momma cat has her own tricks. She takes every opportunity to bring down a new meal and often kills the young and newborn. BL would like to change her habits, but that's the way she's been doing it for her many years of life, so it seems she will continue till the day she dies.

The kitten is different. She's young enough that the pilots think they have a chance of teaching her what is wanted. The momma is devastating the deer population. She also takes many mountain sheep lambs, and this is the major cause of the wild sheep flock's low numbers. One evening the momma cougar jumped a big healthy buck deer and broke its neck, but she didn't jump clear soon enough, and when they crashed to the ground a sharp-pointed tine from the buck's antler ripped open an artery in her neck.

The big buck and momma cougar were found entwined and both dead. An autopsy reveals their story. The pilots leave them where they lie, and it's not long before small scavengers clean them up. There's only the lone kitten left now, and she's not big or experienced enough to hunt on her own. If she is to survive she will need help.

The pilots talk of whether they should intervene on her behalf or not. Some say, "Let her be and let nature take its course," but one pilot has developed an affection for this kitten.

He takes it upon himself to look after her. There are a few decrepit old deer, and some that have injuries from mishaps. Whenever this pilot sees the kitten near one of these, and that she is hungry, he puts the deer down for her with the Lights-Out on his quadcopter, but whenever he sees her approach a healthy fawn he harasses the kitten. This seems to be working, as he soon notices the kitten will sneak by a fawn and its mother, without disturbing them. She seeks out the sick, the injured, and the very old. She's learning these will be her next meal. She'll need help in the hunt for a while yet, but she is growing and she is trainable.

She will be a great asset to BL's plans for the future, and the pilot is praised for his foresight, compassion, and determination. With "Miss Tigress's" constant watch on the herds and her trained ability to take out the sick and injured while leaving alone the young and healthy, she will help BL in our efforts to keep the herds in fine shape. Oftentimes, the sick or injured critters isolate themselves from the herd and are hard to locate with the quadcopters, but Miss Tigress can find them with her keen senses and end their suffering. This is breaking news: a big wild mountain cat living an independent life while helping man to enhance the wildlife populations.

This pilot is given a unique job. He will train predators, and as BL expands he will train other pilots in this newly developing knowledge. There will be times when we meet untrainable predators, and these the pilots will be obliged to deal harshly with, but on the whole it will be rewarding work. There'll be bears, wolves, coyotes, and even eagles and ravens to train, but the pilots and the predators will learn as they go. It will be a different world when all the wild animals and man work together to help in each other's goals. There will be some difficult sad times ahead too, but there'll also be glorious celebrations when unexpected things work out for the benefit of all.

It is observed and noted that the old one-eyed tom came back for a few days when Miss Tigress matured and they made kittens. Two cute, fuzzy little ones. As the kittens grow, Miss Tigress teaches them what she has been taught by the pilots, and other than for a few pilot interventions, this hunting technique is passed on to future generations.

76. Natural Business

The whole world is now paying attention to Bison Leap. Well, not exactly the whole world, but the better part of it. Or at least all those who are concerned with making this planet, our home, a better place. Those who have often thought the naturalness of Earth worth preserving and enhancing now have a chance of implementing their visions.

We at BL knew from the start that we'd need to get ourselves into the visible spotlight of the general population's consciousness in order to attain the support needed to get this feeling to grow. We certainly have had a good start...

In general there has been a high percentage of the human population who seemed to be just biding their time, waiting for something better to happen.

Of course, some are still hoarding and building walls around themselves for protection against their own kind and against the numerous natural planetary forces. They have lots of reasons and excuses to justify their actions, but it's much better now, this new direction things are heading.

BL believes the old ways can be changed, and people will help us if they can see a safe and reasonable way to do just that. Now people know, and BL has helped make it obvious, that there are other possible ways to live. People are trusting BL's business practices because we are open, honest, and fair. BL is clearly not accumulating and hoarding so as to position itself into places of power. We share everything we have. We do have a lot of power and influence, but it's obviously different from what most people have been accustomed to.

In fact, for those who've not yet had personal dealings with BL, there is still some mistrust of our company's motives. People have been trained to be very cautious of business because it seems it was acceptable practice to fool and take advantage of people's good nature. "Buyer beware" was a legally protected and accepted norm. In those circles, anyone who was not wary was considered to be a fool, and it was standard procedure to take advantage of them. This had gone on for so long that even the lowest people on the rung of this structure were in agreement. They had gotten used to it, and that was the way it was, so people adapted and accepted it as a normal standard. In general, everyone outwardly complied. Even those who knew better eventually succumbed because the pressure to comply was intentionally overwhelming.

These were the customs BL had been up against, but we knew this way was all upside down and backward, and our mission was, still is, to change this around, to give people a chance to make things right. Not to repent and ask forgiveness for sins because that is not what this is about, but to actually start appreciating and respecting all planetary life so natural forces can and do start to work together again.

There is opposition, there are struggles and heartache, but the struggle and tears are the challenges of a new understanding. Things have been so out of balance that there'd been no real co-operation or fluid interaction; there had been little of the way things could be.

BL is an instigator of the change necessary to bring about a fluid, supportive way of being. There are pitfalls, there always are when you leave yourself open and vulnerable, but all those acquainted or affiliated with BL have the support and comfort of each other, so it is bearable when we do come across those who are still bent on destruction.

The destroyers don't see themselves as bad; it's just that they know no other way, so BL does not condemn them. BL is now a big organization, and we can handle some loss without being overburdened. What we are now seeing is that when we are taken advantage of, if we do not retaliate but instead give those in need a chance to participate in BL's activities in a constructive manner, then those people often become some of BL's strongest supporters.

A lot of our time is spent on education, but education and giving people a chance to participate is far cheaper than building walls to defend oneself from invasion. BL is not just trying to change material things—we are attempting to evolve the consciousness of this planet, simply by being an example of the way things can be. And it is working. Our business practices are reasonable, and people can see the advantages of co-operation. It's a new habit for sure, but it's easy enough to get used to, and it is so much more fun. Not having to be guarded or afraid of those you come across is such a relief. It frees up so much energy that people now have the time to help each other, to learn new ideas, to teach each other different ways of interacting with themselves and with their environment. It's uplifting and stimulating.

In some places, we occasionally see young women and even children walking alone, unescorted, and they are not being harassed or even judged. They are safe to explore their world without fear. This is new. In recent memory it has never been this way, and it's amazing; it's moving art and a very good thing to hear real laughter and feel honest smiles from complete strangers. From people who do not want, demand, or expect things from you; they just laugh and smile because they're happy, contented, and complete within themselves.

A few years previous, this would have been impossible, to most people's way of thinking, but for those who can get beyond that thinking, to the place of their natural way of being, this is the way it was meant to be. Most people have felt this in one way or another, at different fleeting times in their lives but sadly, for various reasons, were not able to sustain it. Yet now it seems possible. Even probable.

There are no living animals on this earth that have dedicated their energies to venture as deep into the darkness of restraining possessiveness as has man. Have we gained? Have we had enough yet? Perhaps now is as good a time as any to redirect ourselves. To acknowledge our past and our present, to begin describing to each other possibilities of something new, something grand, something worthwhile.

It will take a little extra effort to change all the old habits, but it's easier now to see that it's worth it. People are losing their empty lonesome feelings, leaving them behind and being filled instead with a sense of appreciation, joy, and accomplishment. BL's people are not giddy with naive goofiness—they are strong, respectful, and considerate, and this is influencing those we meet.

This planet has witnessed plenty of times in the past similar things that have occurred, but they were suppressed, even annihilated, by powerful organized forces. These powers were self-described as 'civilized', but some called them barbaric and ruthless. BL is a very successful business, and we've gotten this way not by competition, greed, force, or coercion, but because we are perceptive and socially co-operative.

We do appreciate you and so much look forward to interacting, sharing with you.

There is no hierarchy in our company, our organized organism. People love and respect that. Everyone has an equal say and a deep desire to see this business of enhancing all Earth life succeed—even benevolent consciousnesses not physically affiliated with Bison Leap dream energy toward our success...

For corrections, suggestions, questions, or comments...

email: johndbentley1953@icloud.com